What I Did Wrong

What I Did Wrong

A NOVEL

John Weir

AN IMPRINT OF FORDHAM UNIVERSITY PRESS 2022

This book was previously published by Viking Penguin, a member of Penguin Group (USA) Inc.

First Fordham University Press edition, 2022

Visit us online at https://www.fordhampress.com/new-york-relit/.

Library of Congress Cataloging-in-Publication Data available online at https://catalog.loc.gov.

Printed in the United States of America
24 23 22 5 4 3 2 1
Designed by Daniel Lagin

For Steve Giuliano, after all

For Ryan Black, Helen Eisenbach,
Steve Kruger, Amy Tucker,
Toni Rini, and Kimiko Hahn

And, as I promised, for Dave

Sorry it took awhile.
—Lou Reed

I screwed up. I screwed up the play and I feel terrible about that.

—Chuck Knoblauch

Thanks especially to the National Endowment for the Arts for a grant I received in 1991; my editor Rick Kot; my agent Joy Harris; Beena Kamlani; my parents Jack Weir and Barbara Owen Weir; and many other friends, especially Nancy Comley, Ken Schwartz, Jen Eriksen, Vince Parker, Peter Hochschild, Donald Stone, Glenn Burger, Jim Eaton, Talia Schaffer, Nicole Cooley, Duncan Faherty, Carrie Hintz, Harold Schechter, Steve Tanzer, Barbara Bowen, Tony O'Brien, Wayne Moreland, Naftali Rottenstreich, Tony Hoagland, Sameer Pandya, Ian Spiegelman, Giuseppe Taurino, Joe Dolce, Danielle Duffy, Esther Lin, Frank D'Amato, Lonnie Feldman, John Carillo, Marjorie Schade, Marco Navarro, Noel Sikorski, Christopher Schelling, Sally Sockwell, Randy Dunbar, John Skalicky, Stephin Merritt and his vicious snark, and my friend Jim Christon, who died before I had a chance to say good-bye.

Contents

PART ONE
GENDER TROUBLE

Is there any such thing as a man?

—Eileen Myles

Texas Is the Reason

What is the difference between accident and coincidence. An accident is when a thing happens. A coincidence is when a thing is going to happen and does.

—Gertrude Stein

But I don't want to talk about the dead guy.

It's Sunday, Memorial Day weekend, the year 2000, and I'm in the East Village, counting my pulse. My heart beats too fast. You can hear it over my breathing, like a remix where the bass line, pushed way forward, thrums *whatwhat, whatwhat*. It's the caffeine talking. I'm drinking black tea in a coffee shop, fueling up for another hundred years, and reading Saul Bellow's *Ravelstein,* about a dead guy. Everybody's got one. Mine's Zack. He's buried in Queens, behind Queens College, where I teach. Though he's been gone six years, his voice is still in my head, hectoring me, raw with complaint. Whatever, as Justin says. Why stress? Everyone is headed for a graveyard in Queens. In the meantime, I try not to hear Zack too clearly or to think about Justin, who is sleeping in my apartment. I crept out this morning without waking him, then came here for my morning caffeine fix. "Friends don't let friends go to Starbucks," says a sign on the counter, where a skinny kid pours my fourth cup of Earl Grey. He's wearing a knit cap indoors and a T-shirt that says GUIDED BY VOICES.

"That's me," I think, going back to my seat. I'm returning to *Ravelstein*, trying to turn down the volume on Zack's rasp and Justin's drone, when I look up and do a double take. Strolling into my neighborhood café is my high school best friend, Richie McShane. Richard, son of Shane. He's in a hurry, and he's headed for me.

He comes through the door with spontaneous grace. There's no tortured strategizing for Richie. Always the high school point guard, he brings the ball down the court, and you wait to see how he sets you up. The game plan is all in his head, there's no consulting the coach, and Richie never looks to the sidelines for verification or praise.

"Richie, yo," I say, posing as a regular guy. It's an occupational habit. I teach New York college kids, and I have picked up their slacker lingo: "yo," and "dude," and "chill," and the one I manage least well, "peace out." It's embarrassing to catch myself talking like a twenty-year-old, but it doesn't bother Richie. I've seen him maybe six times since high school—most recently, last Thanksgiving—and whenever we meet we fall into boyish speech patterns.

"Dude," I say again.

"Dude," he nods, as if I were expecting him. He lives an hour away by train, seven miles across Queens in downtown Flushing. What is he doing in my neighborhood? I don't ask and he doesn't tell. Instead, he gives a low wave with his outstretched hand and says, "Yo."

He's in jeans and a wife-beater T-shirt under a bowling shirt open down the front. On his feet are sandals with rubber soles. He's broad-shouldered and slim-hipped, Irish Italian, with a fighter's fluid battling stance. The diagonal strap of his mail carrier's bag cuts across his torso like a slash of black on an abstract canvas against the white of his muscle T, flattening the hair on his chest. Richie's head is regal. He's Fergus, dispossessed Celtic prince, and the back of his skull curves out and arches high, like a natural crown. His dark brown hair, short and tightly curled like Caesar's, retreats from the dome of his brow.

"Hey, old buddy," he says, coming toward me, using his dad's phrase. Richie's dad was a gambler and, when I knew him, an ex-cop, a working-class Irish guy with Humphrey Bogart's raspy voice and his slight lisp. I never met a man with more beautiful manners. He was polite as a detective luring you into a sting, and he called everyone "old buddy," including his son.

Like his dad, Richie is corrosive and neat. He holds his fist straight out and we knock knuckles as if we were still kids.

"What's going on?" he says, sitting down. He leans forward, studying my face, and reaches out with a thumb to wipe a crumb off my chin, an unconscious gesture of what Saul Bellow calls "potato love": fuzzy warmth, Mom's embrace, a reference to our common fate, humankind. All touch is a presentiment of death. That's what I said to Richie once in 1979, when I was a senior at Kenyon College in Ohio writing an Honors Thesis, "The Past Tense in Ernest Hemingway." I spent a whole year counting the verbs in *The Sun Also Rises* and separating them into groups: verbs of action, verbs of reflection.

When I wasn't busy with Hemingway, I called Richie from the dorm phone, trying to sound like an existential poet. "We're flawed, Richie," I'd say. "If we were perfect, we'd be one. I'd grab my wrist and get you." He was walking the floor of the New York Stock Exchange, and I heard the rise and fall of stocks in the crackle of his voice. "All right, Jesus," he said. "You coming home for Christmas?"

Now his thumb is on my chin, quick, automatic. He pulls back and draws his shoulder bag over his head, ducking out from under the strap like a rock star unloading an electric guitar. He sets the bag down and points at my chest. "Texas is the reason for what?" he asks.

He means the logo on my shirt: TEXAS IS THE REASON, it says in big letters, next to the Texas state symbol, a star.

"It's not mine," I say, plucking at my collar, half hoping Richie will ask, "Not yours? Then whose?" And I could tell him what happened yesterday with Justin. Richie would be the perfect guy to confide in: He's an old friend, but a distant one. We have known each other for more than twenty-five years, but still, he doesn't like to pry.

"Of course it's not yours," he says, noncommitally. I wish he were willing to be nosy, because I need to talk about Justin. Richie would probably like him, though he would have hated my dead friend Zack. I made sure they never met. I try to keep people in separate containers, like the capsules in Zack's divided pill box: Paxil, Haldol, AZT, d4T, Extra Strength Tylenol. Lately, though, their voices have been dissolving and combining in my head like mixed medications.

Dead people talk to me, and the living scold. Richie wants to know what the hell my shirt means. The dead guy gets personal. "You're over forty," I hear Zack saying. "Aren't you too old to be wearing a teenager's T-shirt?"

Justin is not a teenager. He's twenty-five. I wave my hand, like, "Back off." Richie, who believes I am talking only to him, takes the hint and starts again.

"So," he says, making nice. "You lost weight."

"Yeah," I say, both sorry and grateful that he doesn't want to know about my private life. "Yeah," I repeat. "I had to."

"You look good."

"I couldn't have gained more. There wasn't any stock left in the warehouse."

Now he's grinning. He approves of me, which makes me absurdly happy. "You look exactly the same, Richie, of course," I tell him truthfully.

"It'd be nice if I still had some hair," he says, looking around the café. "They got coffee here? Black coffee? Just the plain kind? People still serve that?"

"It's up there," I point, and he touches my arm and says, "Something?"

"No, thanks, Richie," I say, watching him go, pal of my youth. He is my most improbable friend, unlikely to know me now, maybe even less likely to have been my best friend when we were kids. I guess we have always enjoyed being unsuited to each other. We were certainly an odd pair in high school in rural northwestern New Jersey. The place was wrong for both of us. I grew up there, but Rich didn't move out to the sticks until he was almost eighteen, when his father built a retirement home way back in the woods. In the Jersey wilderness, Richie was a rare bird—a city kid, everybody thought, though he came from suburban Massapequa, or, as he said, "matzoh-pizza." He was a wisecracking nasal Long Island guy who had funny, mean names for everything. When he graduated from high school he stayed home at his dad's house and commuted to Fairleigh Dickinson University—"Fairly Ridiculous," he called it.

Our big year came when I was fifteen, a high school sophomore. Richie was two years ahead of me, a senior with a driver's license, and we rode around in his dad's car, listening to prog rock on his eight-track and getting high all over Hunterdon County, near the Delaware River. We were high on hilltops overlooking the Spruce Run Reservoir. We drove down to the south branch of the Raritan River along the Gorge Road and smoked joints on the sharp gray boulders jutting out of the current. We got high in graveyards, deserted dairy barns, and empty silos still dusty with crushed corn.

We were stoned as motherfuckers at a Jethro Tull concert in Madison Square Garden in 1974. Afterward, we went for midnight snacks at the Horn and Hardart on Eighth Avenue. We wolfed down burgers and fries, and then Richie tried to get me to leave without paying. "Dining and dashing," he called it. He had been reading Abbie Hoffman's *Steal This Book*, where Hoffman tells you how to get all kinds of supplies for free. "You finish your burger," Richie told me, "and then you slide a cockroach under your last piece of bun and start yelling."

"What cockroach are we supposed to use?"

"The one," Richie said, "that I have thoughtfully brought you from home." And he reached into his pocket and produced the bug, which was cased in a tiny baby food jar.

"Did you spike the coffee with head lice?" I ask him now, as he comes back to the table at the café. He laughs, getting the childhood reference.

"You do that *after* you finish eating," he reminds me. "Not before."

"I could never get it right."

"No, you couldn't."

He sets the coffee on the table, staring warily at the oversized mug.

"Jesus," he says, "what does it mean about Manhattan that they serve you coffee in cups the size of fish bowls? I could spawn a guppie in this."

He's smiling, happy, pumped because the Knicks won game three last night at the Garden. "Ewing they should leave on the bench more often," he says. "It's nice to see him in a suit and tie. He's their good-luck charm. Somebody has to counteract Spike Lee jumping up and down in his Sprewell jersey. That can be Patrick's job. He can be the counter-Spike. You see the game?"

I shake my head. "I was busy," I say.

"Too busy for a ball game?" Richie says. "What do you do all day?"

"Teach school. Hang out with my students."

I'm back to giving obscure hints about last night, taking a more dramatic tone, but Richie still doesn't bite. Instead, he heckles.

"Don't you have any adult friends?"

Is it Richie's question? Or is my dead friend talking again? Since the day he died, Zack has been interrogating me. Instead of dying, he got inside me, like Athena in reverse, not sprung from my brow but jumping into it, setting up house in my forebrain, giving me a headache. Until somebody splits open my skull with an axe, I've got a corpse in full battle gear taking up my ego, swinging his halberd, acting like he knows what's good for me.

His favorite theme is how I spend all my time with kids. My students, that is.

"You're their *professor*," he says, "not their classmate." "Look," he says, holding out his hands, which are covered, in death as in life, with stigmata: burn holes from a laser surgeon who was zapping his lesions. "You. Not You," the dead guy says, presenting one charred hand, then the other. "This is You," he says, "and this is Not You. Notice how they're separated? Teacher, Student. Dead, Alive. Me, Not Me. Now you try," he says. "Hold out your hands."

"No way," I tell him.

"No, I figured you didn't know any grown-ups," Richie says, emptying a packet of Sweet'n Low into his black coffee. "You like to hang with people who have to call home if they stay out past ten."

Does everyone scold me this way?

"Let's just say I'm keeping my distance from adults," I tell Richie, evasively.

"A case of arrested development," he says, pleased to be better than me. He leans over, blows on his coffee, and daintily sips, lifting the cup from the table. Then he sets it down and says, "So, yeah, I bought a car," like he's winding to the end of a long story. "It's out front."

"You bought a car? As in, 'just now'?"

"Don't make fun of me," he says, his neck getting red. "I was waiting for the bus, the Q88, I was supposed to have breakfast with a pal of mine at the Georgia Diner, you know that place?"

"I haven't—"

"You haven't crossed the East River since 1986. I know your kind."

"Richie, I'm in Queens every day. I teach in Queens."

"That makes you a native? No. You grew up with a pet horse named Clover."

"His name was Gay Sensation," I say, turning red, telling the truth.

"You see my point. You're a Jersey rich guy living in your arty New York neighborhood, teaching out in Queens, bringing culture to the savages."

I sigh, giving up. "You were telling me about the Georgia Diner," I say.

"It's a good place," he says, happy to have drawn blood. "I try to get there on Sundays, it's like a ritual. So I'm meeting a buddy from—Tommy DeSalvo, remember him? You and me and him went to a Tull concert, nineteen-seventy—Jesus. A long time ago. Anyway, I'm waiting for the bus so I can hang with Tommy, I say, 'Fuck it,' and I go buy this car. You think I'm cracked, don't you?" he says seriously, looking at me.

Is Richie cracked? Do dead men talk to him? Does he answer them? What would Richie say if I told him I was conversing with a corpse, and that I've fallen in love with a twenty-five-year-old college kid who happens to be my student? Justin. Not only does he have homework, he has *my* homework. Last night he slept in my bed, not like a boyfriend, but like a lost kid who misses his folks. I felt like his Den Mother at a Cub Scout retreat.

Justin isn't a street-smart tough guy, despite his Queens accent and black leather coat. He's a recovered high school nerd who went through a gangster phase. Throughout his childhood, he was the kid who sat in the back of the classroom and smelled funny. Girls mocked him, and boys left him out of their games. When he was twenty-two, he quit college in his junior year and started drinking.

He turned himself into a small-time drug dealer who wore black shades and dealt Ecstasy and Special K from the trunk of a black car with Florida plates. Then his mom threw him out of the house and he got into AA and went back to school to finish his B.A.

When he's not taking classes, going to twelve-step meetings, or working as a floor manager at the Home Depot on Metropolitan Avenue, he's playing drums for a Queens band called Kevin Spacey Has a Secret. They're hard-core, but "emo," which means bummed and loud. I've got a tape of them playing live at Castle Heights, but the songs are all the same. They go: "I'm sad, I'm sad, I'm sad, I'M SAD, I'M SAD, I'm sad."

Justin Innocenzio: his last name means "beyond praise" and "untouched." He calls me "Professor," which comes out truncated, so that it starts with the grossed-out "feh" and ends with hissing: "suh." It's abrading and tender, like all my students, who are cynical and naive, except in the wrong order. When you want them to love grace they're filled with disdain. Then, suddenly, when harshness would save them, they are unaccountably trusting and sweet.

Justin is the most *crushed* person I have ever met. Demolished but also air-borne, he walks the planet like a beautiful stunned space alien, folded into a human body that can't protect him from pain. He lives with a couple of high school pals in a three-room apartment in Glendale, a formerly all-German neighborhood of orange brick row houses pressed against the gloomy *grünwald* of Forest Park. Along Myrtle Avenue you can still buy salt pork, wienerschnitzel, and Gewürztraminer in brew houses like Zum Stammtisch and Hans's Gasthaus. But the place is known mostly for dead people. It's full of cemeteries. When Jack Kerouac talks about "the cemetery towns beyond Long Island City" he means Justin's neighborhood, central Queens: Glendale, Ridgewood, Middle Village, their main drags backed up to crumbling tombs. Justin's apartment is next to Belmont Steaks, a bar named yearningly for the racetrack that is nowhere nearby. Late nights, it's a karaoke bar. Justin's bedroom abuts it, facing a graveyard.

Stretched on his bed, cradled by headstones and the wafting lullabies of barflies singing pop songs, Justin writes poems and song lyrics, imitating his favorite writers: Thom York of Radiohead and Robert Lowell. For a writing pad, he uses an ancient copy of Lowell's *Notebook*. "Health . . . to your kind hands / that helped me stagger to my feet and flee," one of Lowell's poems says, and Justin has squeezed his own poem into the margin beside it. It's literally hard to read, because he wrote it while he was riding the J train past Cypress Hills Cemetery. The elevated tracks swing wide to sidestep white crypts and the chipped facades of unvisited family mausoleums, and that swoop is matched by Justin's swerving, illegible scrawl:

WORLD'S FAIR

In the dirt streets back of Shea Stadium
for seventy-five bucks
I bought a regulator for the broken window
of my secondhand car, and had it installed
by a Mexican guy who was sweating in the sun
and didn't frown at my lousy tip.
I hope he cursed me later
as I headed home on streets that are misnamed:
Union Turnpike, joining nothing
to not much.

I don't know why I find his disappointment so moving. Maybe I like him because he doesn't waste time impressing people. He has the freedom to sulk. I was so eager to please when I was his age that I could never risk being negative. I would like to turn Justin loose on my past. I want to become him and go back to my childhood in 1973 and shoot everybody with one of his hostile glares.

I met him at school last fall in a class I was assigned to observe.

It's a professional duty: teachers spy on one another and write reports. The tenured watch the untenured, the full-time watch the part-time, a hierarchy of gazing.

On a warm day early in the semester, I'm hunched down in the last row of a classroom, poised with my pen over a notebook and listening to a part-time teacher talk about *Jane Eyre*.

I don't have a copy of the book, and I'm feeling shamed and lost without one. So I turn to the kid next to me. He's tense and earnest, crouched forward, listening intently. There are thirty students in the room, most of them women ranging in age from seventeen to seventy and speaking a dozen different languages, but I'm next to the mute white guy in the corner. I lean over discreetly and point to his book, as if to say, "Can we share?"

He looks at me warily. Then he picks up his book, creases its binding so it will lie flatter, and lays it back on the desk, turned slightly to me.

The teacher directs us to a passage from Chapter Eight, in which Jane Eyre and her best girlfriend Helen Burns, stuck in an orphanage, are invited by the headmistress Miss Temple to retire to her quarters for seed cakes and Virgil. "Eyre and Burns," our teacher says, "or, air and fire. Air fans the flames and Helen burns, reading Virgil. Or they all burn in the temple, Miss Temple, who has lit the fire in her chamber and urged Helen to read Virgil aloud, while Jane gets so hot that she can feel her quote-unquote *organ of Veneration* expanding."

I'm writing "organ of Veneration" in my notebook. The serious kid next to me is following the passage with his right index finger, which is smashed, the nail brittle and cracked. He underlines the words on the page. His finger stops beneath "organ of Veneration," and, watching him, I laugh.

He is shocked; teachers aren't supposed to snicker in class. He knows I'm a teacher because I'm wearing a tie. He is wearing a T-shirt that says TEXAS IS THE REASON, which is so odd I think I can trust him. Our professor goes on about fire for over an hour, and we listen sheepishly. Then, at the midway break—it's a three-hour class—the kid closes his book and clears his throat, as if to address me. I'm waiting for him to ask a question, but he doesn't. So I ask him.

"Texas is the reason for what?" I say.

He turns red and laughs, a soft, shy laugh, three descending notes of a scale, "Hee hee hee." My students aren't usually reluctant—after all, they're New Yorkers—and his quiet bluster is engaging. He's speechless, but he's wearing a T-shirt that limns the architecture of his chest. The Texas star is rising over his heart.

Around us students are abandoning their notebooks and used Norton paperback editions of *Jane Eyre* and heading out to the hall to buy Wise potato chips and Diet Cokes from the vending machines. Three studious girls have surrounded the teacher at his desk, asking him questions about the midterm.

Soon the desks around us are empty, and there's the intimacy of being suddenly and briefly alone in a big room.

"It's a quote?" I ask him.

"No," he says.

He's aggressively quiet. Zack was not quiet. All the nervous people I know are noisy. I'm not used to this combination of tension and silence.

"It's a band," he admits, finally.

I want to ask him more questions, but people are filing back into the classroom, and it's time to start again on *Jane Eyre*. That's the end of my first conversation with Justin. After class I have to talk to the teacher, and when I go back to my desk to get my notebook, Justin's gone.

"Which is your favorite quality," Zack tells me. He says I'm drawn to men who don't exist. "If he's not there, you can make him up," Zack says, "and then you're falling in love with yourself."

He's wrong, though. I'm the one who's not there. When I'm

with Justin, I can disappear. In the spring semester, while he's taking my creative writing class, we start hanging out, riding around in his car. We're not lovers or boyhood pals. I'm not his dad. Often, I forget I'm his teacher, and he doesn't mention being my student. I'm not sure he knows I'm gay, which is a relief. With Justin, I don't have an identity. I don't even have much of a view. His car seats are slung low, literally laid-back, and we sink from sight, eye-level with the dashboard. Justin pops in a mix-tape, cranks the volume loud, and we listen to Beatles songs—John Lennon singing "Cry, Baby, Cry" in his hollow, tragic, distant voice—and to Justin's favorite hardcore bands. It's impossible to speak or even think over the noise of Unsane, or Deadguy, or Crown of Thornz.

If he's not discussing poetry, Justin doesn't like to talk or interpret, which is half his charm. Instead, we circle the repeating neighborhoods of central Queens, each block alike but somehow different. Queens is sewn with parkways and train tracks like Frankenstein's face, zigzags holding the parts in place. We speed across it, gathering fragments, assembling substance from the surface of things: public housing projects and luxury apartment towers, airline terminals, Korean Presbyterian churches, tennis stadiums, carnival relics, booster rockets jettisoned from *Gemini* crafts, and parkways swelling over bogs.

Queens has horizontal depth. It's Los Angeles with a headache, made of dense brick instead of porous adobe, "a thick document of brick," Saul Bellow calls it, meaning Sunnyside, Woodside, Jackson Heights, Elmhurst, and Corona, neighborhoods along the elevated number 7 train. "The wastes of Queens," Joan Didion says, by which I guess she means the cab ride from JFK Airport to the Upper East Side. I find it comforting. I like repetition and monotony—and Queens, like sex and modern art, is full of both. I'm not a Ramones song, I don't want to be sedated, just undefined. Justin's detachment gives me room to be nothing special. Sometimes I think I would like to be in his car forever, halfway between whatever we left behind and wherever we intend to go. It's my fatal flaw. I'm most at ease when I'm between things, neither here nor there.

Of course, I'm in love with him. Six years since Zack died, I let someone get inside of me again, past the blood-brain barrier. How did that happen? Because Justin has broad shoulders and surprisingly small hands? Is that all? He's welkin-eyed, like Billy Budd, his irises as blue as the vault of heaven. Zack's right, I don't see people, I make them up.

Well, I'm a gay man writing fiction. If I were Dennis Cooper, I'd cut him up, but tenderly. If I were Edmund White, I'd rhapsodize about his ass. If I were Genet, we'd be in prison. If I were John Rechy, talking to Justin would cost me fifty bucks. Gore Vidal would make me kill him. Mary Renault would pretend he's Greek, and we'd be headed across the Peloponnese in golden chain mail. In Proust, he's a girl; in Tennessee Williams, I'm the girl; in Colette, we're both girls. Gertrude Stein would turn him into a verb phrase. Virginia Woolf would give him a sex change. Oscar Wilde would have him sit for his portrait, and I'd paint it, and then he would never get old, which is terrible, because I'd keep aging, and if he's not going to touch me when he's twenty-five and I'm forty-one, what will happen when he's twenty-five and I'm sixty? I want him to age. I don't care about his youth. I'd like somebody in my life to age the normal way, not thirty years in seven months, but slowly, in stages, whether he wants to touch me or not.

"I want a hero," I say.

"You want to *masturbate*, is what you *want*," Zack tells me. "Why do you have to pretend you're some kind of noble aesthete every time a teenager gives you a woody?"

"Give me a break," I say.

"Give you a *break*?" Zack says. "Do you think I'm cracked?"

"No, I don't think you're cracked," I say, but this time, it's Richie who interrupts.

"Sure you do," Richie says. He's still in the room. Richie, my first Justin. We're sitting in a café near my apartment. Richie is sipping coffee and speaking through his napkin, which he holds crumpled in a ball to dry his face after each sip. He's fastidious, constantly wiping his lips as he drinks. He doesn't want anything to stick.

"You think I'm a nutcase," Richie says. "Don't lie to me."

"No," I tell him, "it's the other way around. *You* think *I'm* nuts."

Richie shrugs, as if to say, "I've got no time for your shenanigans." Then he gets to the point. "Lucky I found you today," he says. "Because I was gonna call you. I want to know if you'll do me a favor."

"Go for a spin in your new hot rod?"

"We can do that," he says. "It's part of the package. But there's more."

Richie has a cyberdate. That's what he tells me.

"You met a girl online? Don't you have a girlfriend already? Isn't the girlfriend you already have someone you've been just about to marry for almost fifteen years?"

"More or less."

"And what is it now? More, or less?"

"I don't know." He pauses for a moment and, smoothing out his napkin, says, "We're at an impasse."

"An 'impasse'? What is that? I thought you were together again."

"She's at her mom's."

"Because why? You split up?"

"No," he says. "Her mom's in Vegas. The girlfriend is house-sitting out on the Island. Wantagh. But when her mom gets back, well, the girlfriend and I are going to have a little talk. In the meantime, do you want to take a ride?"

"The girlfriend knows about the car?"

"The girlfriend doesn't know anything. Can you relax? This online girl, she sounds really hot, but, whatever, she could be hot, she could be fifty."

"She could be a guy."

"Shut up with your gutter talk."

"Oh," I say, trying to sound offended, "so in other words—"

"So in other words if she's a guy then it's a nice date for you. Because you're coming with me."

"Richie, I haven't seen you since Thanks*giving*. I mean, why would I—?"

"Because you will. Because you love me. Because we're buddies," he says, reaching around in a wide arc with his bunched fist, slow motion, and pressing his curled palm into my shoulder. "Because, what if she *is* a guy?" he says in a low tone, confidential, alarmed. Richie believes he knows the ways of the world, but he is, nonetheless, an innocent. You can hear it in his voice. His dad grew up in East New York, bordering Queens, and Richie has more than a trace of his father's street-smart Brooklyn accent. Underneath the crackle and rasp, however, is the credulity of an ingenue.

Like a lapsed Catholic in a Graham Greene novel, he is trusting as a matter of form. It's not as if he doesn't know that people are worthless scum, but he can't get over the possibility of grace. Of course, he's sure it always comes to someone else. But just in case the world is blessed, he conducts himself, like his dad, with the unexpectedly pristine manners of an off-duty outlaw in an old Warner Brothers movie.

Well, I'm still charmed by him, so I know I'm going to do whatever he wants.

Sighing, I say, "What's her name?"

Richie sips his coffee, happy, certain he has me hooked. I trust him because he doesn't need anyone. Though my faith in him has limits. The last time I saw him, for instance, at Thanksgiving, he got drunk and huffy and then showed me his dick. And not in a fun way: It was late, we were both hammered, and he did it tauntingly and threateningly in my kitchen, while I was searching for aspirin and trying to urge him to sleep on my couch.

He had shown up unannounced earlier that day with a Thanksgiving care package: five bags of groceries for my empty refrigerator. He brought bulk food: a case of Canada Dry orange seltzer, five gallons of Mott's Original 100% apple juice, Newman's Own Venetian pasta sauce in six twenty-six-ounce jars, eight boxes of Ronzoni corkscrew pasta. "Time to lay in some provisions," he said, loading everything onto the bare shelves. When Richie arrived I had nothing but two frosted-over spoonfuls of Chunky Monkey in the freezer. Within minutes, for the first time ever, the refrigerator was full.

Richie said "Woo-hoo!" like Homer Simpson, patting his belly and planning our supper, but I couldn't ask him to stay. I had a party in Brooklyn.

"I'm not welcome at your shindig?" he said. "You're ashamed of me?"

Richie plucked tensely at his T-shirt, which pictured a black-shrouded skeleton rocking a newborn son over the word MEGADETH and below it, in larger letters, YOUTHANASIA.

"Back off, Richie," I said. "You're fine. This is not about you. I'm hanging with a bunch of narcissists and college professors, if that's not redundant. You'll hate it."

"You don't got no love for me at all?" he said, getting his grammar wrong to make a point.

"Okay," I sighed. "Okay, all right, fine. Whatever. Let's go."

So we did. We wrapped a bottle of seltzer as an offering and got the F train to a quirky rambling apartment over an old Italian bakery across from a hip new sushi bar on Smith Street, in Cobble Hill. The guests were college teachers from the City University of New York. Everyone was junior faculty, including me, though I was the oldest person there.

Because of a hiring slowdown during most of the nineties there are hardly any full-time CUNY professors born since Truman bombed Japan. My senior colleagues, ardent New Critics, speak nostalgically of the intentional fallacy. The junior faculty members—we have two people under forty in my English department—quote Judith Butler on performativity and compare notes on contact zones and subject positions. At the Brooklyn bash the rooms were crawling with Berkeley-educated deconstructionists. I had to be careful what I was foregrounding.

There was boutique beer in the fridge, and we ate black olives with our fingers, spicy Moroccan carrots, and homemade tabouli. The CD player spun Beck and Nancy Sinatra, and the conversation centered on gender issues and the subaltern. Then we pulled cast-off diner chairs around the rickety kitchen table and our talk turned inevitably to tenure.

Rich, of course, was first bored, and then angry. His only salvation was a couple of gay girls who were doing a documentary on women welterweights, to whom he talked about prizefighting. But they left early, and he was subjected to an hour's grim discussion of academic presses and second readers and letters of support. "Viciousness in the kitchen," Sylvia Plath said, and that's how it felt to be in a roomful of careerists as cutthroat and humorless as any Harvard MBA.

Richie yelled all the way back to Manhattan, ostensibly because someone had spilled hummus on his T-shirt, leaving a beige smear across YOUTHANASIA; now it said YO ASIA, as if Richie were giving a shout-out to Korea.

He went for the phone as soon as we got back to my apartment.

"I have to reach the girlfriend," he said, still shouting, peeling off his stained shirt and ordering me to get him a fresh one. I was looking for aspirin. My heart ached and my chest was tight. "Why don't you spend the night here, Richie?" I said, not wanting to unearth a clean shirt in the nuclear fallout of my bedroom. "You can sleep on the couch. It's two A.M. and the train never comes. You won't be home until dawn."

Shirtless, he muttered, trying to get my cordless phone to work.

"Your fucking battery is dead," he said.

"Yeah, I know," I said, aware of my heart, which was clattering like a rusty dog food can rolling down a garbage dump. I've had these heart strains since Zack died, and I take a lot of aspirin to keep my blood from clotting in my arteries. I was in the kitchen, tracking Bayer everywhere. "I usually keep it around in those packets," I said, to no one in particular. "Those fifty-cent pack . . ."

My voice trailed off. There was nothing in the shelves above the sink, or in the cabinet next to the stove, or underneath the magazines stacked on the kitchen table. Then I went for the refrigerator. It was the only place I hadn't looked. Of course, I had forgotten the shelves were packed with Richie's groceries. I live in an old building with a sinking foundation and slanted floors, and the contents of the refrigerator slid to my feet, bottles smashing, boxes bursting open, pasta getting soaked in apple juice and Newman's Own Venetian pasta sauce.

Richie, standing on the higher ground of the doorsill between the living room and the kitchen, was still wrestling with the phone. "What kind of Luddite motherfucker goes to parties where they talk about intertextuality," he said, "but can't figure out how to keep the battery charged on his cordless phone?" Then he noticed the mess on the floor. "What do you want to put all that stuff in the refrigerator for, anyway?" he said, pointing at the pasta.

"*You* put it there," I reminded him, exasperated.

"Did not."

"Richie," I said, "shut up."

"Shut up yourself," he said. "You told those stupid eggheads we were boyfriends." He was mindlessly stabbing the phone pads with his darting fingers. I was on my knees, gathering wet pasta from split boxes. "Or you were real happy to let them believe it."

"What are you talking about?"

"Those people. They had smooth palms. I bet none of them has ever had so much as a callus."

"Will you put that down?" I said, nodding my head at the phone, which he was taking apart. He opened up the back and pulled out the battery, which dropped to the floor and mixed with my apple noodle soup.

"It's one thing to listen to their postwhatever babble. Post this, post that. 'Lemme bang your head against the wall,' I told this guy, 'and then we can finish our conversation postsurgery.' "

"You didn't say that."

"And he said, 'How long have you two been lovers?' 'Lovers,' he said. Not 'fuck buddies,' which would have been one thing. Yeah, I give it to him up the rear, I could've said. But, nooo. He wants to know how long we're *lovers.*"

"Why should you get stressed out if some guy thinks we're boyfriends?"

"Because we're not," he said. "And that's all she wrote. Except for you, it's never enough. What do you want, man? I mean, how exactly is it done? Where do your legs go? And how do I forget that it's you? I close my eyes and pretend you're Jennifer Lopez? Here," he said, grabbing his belt. He unbuckled it, unsnapped his jeans, pulled down his zipper, and, with the phone still in his hand, dropped his trousers and shorts. Now he was naked to the knees. "Deconstruct this, motherfucker," he said, with his dick out, except the phone got in the way, and as far as I know, Richie has a hard white plastic handset for a penis, with a rubber antenna. Then, tossing the phone on the couch, he tucked himself away and left my house in just his jeans and jacket. I was still on my knees with corkscrews in my fingers.

Now he wants to take me on a cyber-date—his date, of course, not ours.

"Her online name is, get this, Aphrodite," he's saying. "She spells it like a haircut, *A-f-r-o,* then *d-y,* then *t-e-a.* Afrodytea. Says she lives in Staten Island. Todt Hill. That's 'death' in German."

"So get in your hot rod, drive to Staten Island."

"But I'm meeting her in the West Village, near the water, at a place you probably know about. It's called hell. Small *h.* Some club. She picked it. Listen, buddy," he says, leaning forward, "the street it's on, it's got this Dutch name, I won't make a fool of myself trying to pronounce it."

"Gansevoort?"

"There, you see?" Richie says, leaning back, flashing a wicked Jack Nicholson grin of conspiratorial glee. "I *knew* you were the man for the job." He bangs me on the shoulder, happy. I'm the handy smart guy. "Will you come, old buddy? Come on, guy, whatta you say?"

The beautiful American word "guy." It always gets me. For one thing, a guy is never alone. What if your name were Guy? Then you'd think that all the men behind all the deli counters on Ninth Avenue were talking to you. "What'll it be, Guy?" "Mayo, Guy?" "We're outta sesame, Guy, how about onion?" Guy is friendly, whereas "man" is hostile and competitive. "I hear you, man," actually means, "Back off, dickhead, I'm in charge, here." "Dude" is useful, but thanks to Bart Simpson it's never sincere. "Buddy," "buster," and, "pal" are sturdy but tainted by camp, like dialogue from old Hollywood movies. "Boss" scares me, and "chief" sounds undemocratic and maybe politically incorrect.

I like "brother" sometimes. "Brother, you gotta be kidding," a truck driver yelled at me once on Eighth Avenue, because I was reading a book and crossing the street against the light. He twisted the word around to mean, "Die, motherfucker," but I'm a romantic, and I heard him saying, "Cling to me as we plunge together manfully into the abyss."

Still, guy is the most inclusive and universally tender, taking the back of your neck in its creased palm and saying, "I'm counting on you." It's a promise and a threat, a stroke, a supplication, and a plea. If there were an epic poem of America in muscular four-beat Old English lines, our *Beowulf*, its first word would be not *"Hwaet,"* but "Guy."

In other words, I tell Richie, "Sure." Watch him flirt with a girl? It won't be the first time. After clearing my place at the café table, I head outside to get a load of Richie's new car.

Deadguy

What did God mean, arming him so insufficiently,
Sending him into the blue part of the flame?
—Dean Young

Let's not call him the dead guy forever. His dying was so, what, harrowing? From *harwe*, to torment. Or *herwen*, to plunder. A harrow is also a farm tool with sharp teeth and a high school for rich kids and an area of London. What good are words? They lead everywhere but his death, which was indescribable, except to say that it felt distinctly deathlike. He gave a deadly and convincing performance of his own demise, my friend Zack. Isaac or Zack. Sometimes I said "Yitzy," wanting a name that was heartfelt and silly—to show that I loved him but that I was keeping my distance. The nurses called him Zachary, which drove him crazy.

His illness wasted him to a nub, and his body hung slack as a caught fish after you knife its belly and scoop out the slick handful of its insides. Except with a fish, you leave the meat. But Zack lost his flesh, too, his tissue and fat, and it would be right to gut his name, Isaac, and leave only a letter, like the bridge at the beginning of *Crime and Punishment*. I——: That's what he looked like, lying in his hospital bed, his head and feet above the covers and the flat line of his eviscerated body hardly rising higher than the mattress.

It's autumn in New York, 1994, a Monday afternoon at the end of October, and I've just been visiting Zack in the hospital. I left him in a beige room on a busy floor at St. Vincent's. Now I'm headed for Queens in the back of a cab, having my near-the-end-of-the-century moment, my sense of heading somewhere fast without the tools I need for the trip.

Of course, I'm not traveling empty-handed. I have a chocolate bar. I have a pack of cigarettes. I have a cup of tea with milk, no sugar, from Dalton's Coffee Shop on Greenwich Avenue near the hospital. I have the Smiths on tape, Morrissey keening into my headphones, "I need advice, I need advice." I'm late for class. It's my third term teaching at Queens College, and I'm unprepared, unshaven, unshowered, and unhinged.

What happens when I'm under this kind of pressure is that I merge with the collective. I start thinking not like me, but us. It's a sentimental conceit, but it's also strategic: It means I won't die alone. I think, *We're on our way.* I think, *We're hurtling out of the twentieth century without a clue as to how to survive the impact when we crash one day into 2001. Whee,* I think. *Here we go.*

Manhattan is looming up behind me like a gorgon in a 1950s science fiction movie. In my version the monster jumps out of the East River and devours the hero's best friend, whose death sets in motion the string of events that lead to the monster's demise. New York and Zack are canceling each other out. The taxi climbs the rise of highway coming out of the Midtown Tunnel, reaches level ground, then swoops back down at Calvary Cemetery, spilling me into Maspeth and Elmhurst, towns spliced together by billboards and concrete interchanges.

And I'm *The Great Gatsby* in reverse, Nick Carraway drawn irresistibly to Flushing. Looking back at Manhattan I can see the silvered tip of the Chrysler Building glinting with promise. It's behind me now, the city and its glittering towers and its hard, gold light. What it promises is that life consists primarily of losing things.

Zack is starving to death. Parasites are wearing away the undulant walls of his intestines, planing them smooth so that he can't digest any food. It's an enforced fast. He looks wasted but he doesn't act it. Instead, he's pared down to fighting weight and swinging wildly.

"You're late," he says, when I walk into his hospital room earlier this afternoon. "I could have died, and you would have missed it."

"Zack," I say, lifting my arm and showing him my watch, "it's five ten."

"I expected you at five. I guess it's not *important* for you to get here on *time*, seeing as how I'm not exactly *going* anywhere. Is that it?"

"Anyway, my watch is fast. It's more like five after."

I'm pulling a chair up to his bed, and he's scolding me and making a record of my visit on a yellow pad. Zack is a writer—he has published two novels, with a third, even now, on the way—and one of the effects of his illness is the intensification of his need to document everything he does. In addition to pads and pens he keeps a Polaroid camera on his bed. "Say cheese!" he yells, arming himself with the camera when someone walks through the door. Then he snaps away, capturing people at their worst: tired, after work, in hospital lighting, frightened of illness in general and Zack in particular.

The snapshots are tacked to the wall above his bed. I have to make an effort to ignore my picture, which shows a puffy white guy whose boyish complexion is slowly sliding off his aging skull.

"Five . . . fif . . . teen . . . pee . . . em," Zack says, still writing, sounding each syllable as if it were a pin pushed in a doll. "Or . . . there . . . a . . . bouts." He pauses, glaring at me. "Tom . . . comes . . . to . . . vi . . . sit." Then he puts down the pen. "How long can you stay?"

"I don't know, half an hour," I begin to answer, but he's already talking over me.

"I need you for an hour," he's saying.

"Okay," I say, knowing this will make me late for school.

"You stayed an hour yesterday."

"Yesterday I stayed *four* hours."

"Half an hour's not enough."

"I said *okay*, Zack. I'll stay an hour."

Sitting cross-legged on the bed, on top of his sheets, he's finally as thin as I never believed he could be, even though I've watched dozens of people over the past few years get sick and die. They watched themselves: When they saw their bodies begin to collapse, they hurried out of them. Not Zack. He's already living outside of his body, even though he doesn't think he has a soul in which to hang abstracted over himself.

He's a math nerd, a high school track star, a graduate of MIT, where, he says, "I majored in *applied* math, not *pure* math, because I don't trust abstractions!" His faith, instead, is in physics, Woody Allen, and oral sex. He believes in surface, not substance. As far as he's concerned the body is the soul. Which is why it's so painful to see him separating in two, dividing himself into fury and death.

As he gets sicker his anger rides above him like a Gothic apparition in a horror story. Thirty-seven years of rage cast out and hurled at anyone: anger about being human and mortal or, worse, about being brought up in Freeport, Long Island, "for God's sake," he says, "not to mention being short, and ugly, and smart, and Jewish, and gay, and graceless, and a lousy lay. And, by the way, infected with a terminal disease. Don't talk to me about *living* with AIDS; you're not living with it, you're just not dead from it yet."

He got furious fast. When he checked into the hospital just after Labor Day he was touchy but hopeful. He was going to stay a few days, run tests, gain weight, and go home. That was six weeks ago. Since then I've seen him change hourly as his flesh dissolves and the hysterically grim logic of hospitals overtakes him. Medieval astrologers divided a man's life into twelve phases, including birth, marriage, work, property, mother; the last and most ominous stage—or "twelfth house," as they called it—was incarceration: prisons and hospitals.

Zack's in his twelfth house. Like a freaked-out jungle warrior in a film on Vietnam, he's dressed disjunctively, part patient, part civilian, the jeans beneath the nightshirt, his backup pair of eyeglasses perched hugely on his shrinking head, which is so chiseled from weight loss that he disappears from the front. He's all profile.

His good glasses got stolen his second day here, he insists, and he had me fetch the old ones from his apartment. They're green-tinted prescription sunglasses with tortoiseshell frames, and they would look reasonable on Susan Sarandon in a bronze gown and matching eyewear receiving her Oscar for *Dead Man Walking*. On Zack, they're like a prop in a cubist portrait, slicing up the planes of his face. A movie star, a Braque canvas, a customer at Sterling Optical: The only thing he doesn't look like anymore is Zack.

A Hickman catheter is spliced into an artery below his right shoulder and poking out of his chest, and an IV needle is grafted onto his left wrist. Beside his bed there's a metal pole hung with twin plastic bags, one filled with saline solution for the IV, the other fat with a yellow biomedical soup called TPN, Total Parenteral Nutrition, which drips through a clear tube into his catheter.

Of course, the fancy soup's not working. Neither are the CAT scans, the MRIs, the bone marrow tests, the bronchoscopies, the colonoscopies, the antiretroviral drugs, pentamidine, AZT, d4T—which Zack calls "death before forty"—and, as far as I can tell, my visits.

There's a rule about being in hospitals that says, The longer you stay, the longer you stay. It's a simple, awful rule, and it reminds me of a story I read in a book about the Vietnam War: "A bunch of Marines with guns went up the hill and one came back." That's the story. It's the setup and it's also the punch line. Zack likes punch lines, though his sense of humor has always been more sophomoric than deadpan. Still, the numbed and numbing humor of hospitals both pleases and appalls him. " 'Deadpan' is 'deathbed' crossed with 'bedpan,' " he says, making vaudeville jokes like a white-faced clown in a play by Samuel Beckett, in which God is a pebble in your boot—a paralyzing irritant—or the simultaneously tedious and terrifying expectation of loss.

You want to make everything in hospitals go faster. Except when, like Zack, you're waiting to die. Then you're grateful for the quality of slowed time that is common to hospitals, car wrecks, and gambling casinos. Zack balances in hectic repose on his hospital bed. Or he's wheeled on gray gurneys to X-ray appointments. Glowing with irradiated neutrons, he glides past rooms lit by soundless blue TV screens. The corridors are resonant with rubber soles squeaking over tiled floors, the noise of nurses and attendants going up and down mauve halls in terminal white. The seamless facade of stretched sheets and bland faces is broken by the intermittent flash of naked body parts: genitalia suddenly exposed under hospital gowns, as shocking and human as the nakedness of prisoners in photographs from Nazi concentration camps.

Zack's response to his tragedy is this seeming non sequitur:

"Carrie Fisher says, *Hi*."

That's what he tells me. There aren't italics crimped enough to convey the tone of that "hi." You'd need to render it in musical notation, because it's sung like Kermit the Frog in a fit of ironic delight. Zack thinks he's being cute instead of bizarre. Or maybe he knows exactly the effect he creates.

"So, how's Carrie?" I say, deciding on a credulous but neutral tone. After all, it's possible that Zack and Carrie Fisher *are* suddenly friends. Death may not reconcile fathers and sons like in Hollywood movies, but it does create weird conjunctions, especially when one of the criss-crossing figures is Zack. He has a talent for contrast. He knows how to summon two completely unrelated notions and haul them into contact: blue jeans and nightgowns, sunglasses and hospital beds, a movie star and himself.

"She's fine. She invited me to her birthday party."

It crosses my mind suddenly that he *is* delusional. "Her what?"

"It's very soon. In Los Angeles, of course. Just after Halloween," he says, searching his bed. "Shit," he says. "Where'd I write it down?"

When Zack was admitted to the hospital he was in the middle of scheduling a reading tour for his new book, *Kiss Me, I'm a Diseased Pariah.* His writing, however, is the result, not the cause, of his compulsive record keeping. Zack's entire inner life is a series of lists. On his sole visit to a therapist, in 1983, he took notes. "Spell 'approach-avoidance,'" he said. "Is there a hyphen?"

Now he's searching through piles of stuff on his bed, looking for another list. His mattress is an increasingly cluttered desktop. Every day he sends me to his apartment to find some essential office tool and deliver it to his room: scissors, paper clips, a stapler, pens and pencils, Scotch tape, postage stamps. His yellow legal pads are dedicated to various aspects of his infirmity: drugs, visitors, phone calls, doctors' comments, medical procedures, weight loss, his bile duct. The doctor thinks the reason he's losing weight is because his bile duct is clogged, and they keep sending him off for duct tests and liver scans, to which Zack has devoted an entire pad, labeled, without a trace of irony, "Bile."

Other pads list people who sent cards or flowers; people who delivered baked goods, under the subheadings "Stale" and "Fresh"; people who FedExed care packages, "as if I were a famine victim," he says. His most dog-eared list is two pages of prepared answers in response to the telephoned question, "Zack, can I bring you anything?" "Why, yes," he'll say, holding the phone in the crook of his neck, looking frantically for the pad entitled "Guilt Offerings." "You can go to Zito's, you know where that is," he'll continue, stalling, "on Bleecker Street, north side, west of Seventh Avenue." Then, finding the list, he'll run his finger down the page, finally saying, "And you can get me a presliced loaf of pumpernickel bread with caraway seeds in a white paper bag."

Now he wants his Carrie Fisher list. "It was right *here*," he insists.

"You wrote something down on a pad," I suggest, in my hospital voice, which is unnaturally calm. I've spent a lot of time with sick friends in hospital rooms, and I have developed this strategy for coping: I listen to what people tell me, and then I repeat it back to them, as if I were doing an acting exercise. "I wrote it down," he says, and I agree, "Yes, that's right, you wrote something down." It's a tactic meant to soothe. But, of course, it drives Zack crazy. And my voice is so scrupulously drained of emotion that the absence of feeling is itself a kind of hysteria.

"For God's sake," Zack says. "Of course I wrote something down. Did anyone ever tell you that you have a keen grasp of the obvious?"

He's pushing aside books and magazines and thumbing through file folders stuffed with a lifetime's record keeping: insurance forms, story drafts, tax documents, bank statements. Lately he's been snipping headlines from the *New York Post* and mailing them to people who bug him, including hated ex-boyfriends, gay Republicans, and anyone who ever said a clumsy, well-meaning thing about AIDS. He clipped an obituary from the *New York Times*, scrawled a note in the margin—"Thanks for hoping I'm next!"—and mailed it to a friend who had sent a card that said, "God's with you in your time of need."

"Damn it," he says, still searching his bed. He's stressed, and I'm feeling more and more to blame. This is why I dread hospitals, not because they kill you, but because every time I visit a sick friend, I'm asked to manage a routine task—finding a list, or cranking up a bed, or going outside to buy a specific brand of South American coffee in a thermal cup—that will turn out to be totally beyond me. There are no odds more insurmountable than a simple request. The last time I cried was when I was looking for a slice of blackout cake all over the Upper East Side for a friend who was dying in Lenox Hill Hospital. I want to find Zack's list so that neither one of us will cry.

"Maybe it's on your night table," I suggest carefully, because it's almost as bad to help him as it is to fail him.

"Oh," he says, as if he found it first, "here it is. I left it by the phone." "So," he says, suddenly cheerful, shifting moods as abruptly as if he were wired like his bed to a mechanism that goes up and down at the push of a button, "I'm invited to a big Hollywood party. Carrie throws it every year. If you're nice, you can come."

"I feel like I walked in late to a movie. Back up. How do you know Carrie Fisher? Or maybe I mean, You *know* Carrie Fisher?"

"She called me up."

"Which, um, why?"

"She read my book."

"The new one?"

"The new one isn't out yet. You know that. You *should* know. Aren't you sleeping? She called because a friend of mine who can't visit because he's out of town asked me if there was anything he could do for me, and I said, 'Well, I've always wanted to have lunch with Carrie Fisher.' And he's a lawyer. And it turns out that he knows Carrie Fisher's lawyer. So the lawyer called the lawyer who called Carrie who called *me*. She likes to talk to dying gay men! She told me I could bring a guest to her shindig. That would be you."

It all sounds insanely plausible. "Is it RSVP?" I say stupidly, suddenly stricken with the apprehension that I'm going to be dragged on a terror trip to Los Angeles. Never mind that he's so thin he could probably float to California. And I don't know how he'd be able to travel with his IV bags and his medications and his diarrhea, which, as if to prove that nature has a sense of humor, manages to be both constant and unexpected.

Zack knows all too well that the only person crazy enough to go with him is me. We have never been lovers, though Zack says we might as well be married because "we're together all the time and we don't have sex."

It's true; he's my virtual boyfriend. Bad choice? He was always obnoxious, and I can't say what I like about him without taking on his tone, which is insistently ironic. Zack is as incapable of sincerity as other people are of rolling their tongues. I'm making up clever phrases about my dying friend, but words won't save him. Who doesn't inevitably give up on language the way you set aside the dream of true love? Yet I keep thinking I can get three nouns together in a sentence, arrange them right, and make the world turn. When Zack dies I'll be left with the words in my head, short, crisp words, Ernest Hemingway's vocabulary, which is good enough to show landscape, or to bracket a compulsion, or to wander alone in the woods. I can go fishing with Hemingway's words! I can't say why I like Zack.

"Zack," I told him once, "I love you more than anyone in my heart of hearts." And he said, "You say that to everyone. Your heart of hearts is a very crowded place."

Hemingway says if you talk about it, you lose it. Sure. But if you don't talk about it, you still lose it. Zack and I have talked and talked, as if to ward off his death. I have always known he was going to die. I have rehearsed his death, and written about it. "He died in my arms," I wrote, the last line of a novel I finished but didn't begin. I tell myself I'm saying it to keep it from happening, but the truth is, I like endings. I am not so good with the middle of things, and I admit that I long for Zack's death, maybe because my fantasy of losing him is more beautiful than anything we have done in life.

I watch him as he takes notes on his death, forming his blocky letters into bunched words across a legal pad. His hands are boyishly awkward, his fingers long with blunt, squared tips. They have not always been covered, as now, with burn holes from laser treatments for skin lesions.

"Tom . . . is . . . in . . . vi . . . ted . . . to . . . Car . . . rie's . . . do," he says. "If . . . he's . . . on . . . time." He is left-handed, and he twists his hand upside-down, scribbling plans. "I already made the airplane reservations," he tells me. "This morning."

"You bought tickets?"

"With my credit card. I can still do *some* things for myself. We're flying business class."

"To Los Angeles?"

"It's a six-hour flight," he says. "You better bring something to read, because I plan to sleep."

So he's serious. Now I'm worried. Of course he can't fly anywhere. He can hardly cross his room to get to the john. Still, it would be exactly Zack's style to die on a plane over Kansas while I sit beside him reading *Slaves of New York*.

"I got us a big suite in a nice hotel in Santa Monica," he says. "It's called Windows on the—what? Windows on the Something. I can't remember what the goddamned windows are on."

"Zack," I say, pulled unwillingly into his fantasy, "do you think you should be traveling to California?"

"I'll need someone to carry copies of my new book," he says. "That's your job. We are going to sell them at Carrie Fisher's party. All the bigwigs will be there. Tom Hanks! I'll autograph a book for him, and I'll say, 'Oh, Mr. Hanks, now that you've gotten an Oscar for playing a homosexual in *Philadelphia* who dies of a disease that he must have gotten from a toilet seat because the closest he comes to having sex with a man is to set aside his popcorn in a movie theater, maybe you'd like to read how people really get AIDS and what their parents really say and how often their parents turn out to be Joanne Woodward standing in the corner of the hospital room with an I-always-vote-for-liberals expression of maternal warmth spread across their loving faces.' Then I'll give him the book and say, 'That'll be nineteen dollars and ninety-five cents,' which, he'd better not bitch, because it's a discount."

"Zack," I say, as gently as possible, "I'm a little worried about you."

"Why?" he says, his bright grin turning manic. "Are you having your *feelings* again? Your feelings are so *useful.* You know how you can be useful? Take me to Carrie Fisher's party. 'Shutters,' that's the name of the hotel. It's called Shutters on the Beach. I need you to take my books to the plane and carry my drugs and check us into our room. I can't do that on my own. Why are you looking at me with your big sad eyes as if nothing human could offend you? I want you to be offended. Don't love me. I don't love you. *I don't love you.*"

He is still screaming when our friend Ava appears in the doorway. Hospital rooms are tailor-made for sitcom entrances, because the door is never locked. People come and go like Kramer on *Seinfeld,* not needing to knock. This aspect of abrupt appearance lends Zack's death the rhythm of comic surprise, and Ava is dressed to deliver one-liners, in a spiky new haircut, an A-line minidress, and go-go boots. As she walks into the room she holds out a brown paper bag and asks, "Who wants bagels?"

Ava writes a sex advice column for a men's music and fashion magazine called *Yo,* which has a target audience of twenty-two-year-old guys teetering on the verge of a sexual preference. Her professional name is Ava Brown, but she's also Ava Steinberg from Watchung, New Jersey, Japanese and Jewish, the daughter of a dentist and a social worker. Her mother's family lived in a detainment camp in California during World War II, and her father's parents died in Auschwitz. "I'm a survivor on both sides," she says.

Next to Richie, Ava is my oldest friend. We went to college together, in the middle of Ohio. It had been an all-boys private Lutheran school until 1972, when it began taking girls. "I feel taken, that's for sure," Ava told me, not long after we met. We spent half our time trying to figure out what we were doing there. With only fourteen hundred students, Kenyon was half the size of my public high school. Ava arrived at Kenyon from another place altogether: she had gone to Simon's Rock, a hippie boarding school in Massachusetts, where she wore peasant skirts, dropped acid, and wrote poetry. She was obsessed with Sylvia Plath. She had read *The Bell Jar* twelve times, and she carried her beaten copy of *Ariel* like a shield into classes on great thinkers of the Western tradition—all men, of course. Kenyon was staffed by ancient professors with hairy ears who looked slightly distressed to find women sitting in their classrooms. In our Shakespeare seminar the professor apologized for double entendres. "Country matters, ahem," he said, hiding his fingers in his tweed vest and saying, "My regrets to the ladies."

"I eat men like air!" Ava scrawled on a note she passed, and I giggled.

We were surrounded by men, frat boys in the dining hall, tenured pedants in our seminars, hallowed male authors in the books we read. T. S. Eliot was still the god of all texts, and we dug out his literary references, which pointed, incessantly, to an expanding list of men. Ava was furious. "Fuck all these men," she said. I sat in lectures where the teacher dismissed Walt Whitman's obvious boy love as "a chaste worship of the ideal," and Ava got punchy whenever she heard the word "Asiatic." It was the 1970s, a decade in which we were both lost in the Midwest. "I am the sole source of irony in central Ohio," Ava said.

Now we're in New York, with irony to spare, and men still the center of our lives. I think Ava must hate being an adjunct to male desire and loss, but she would probably tell me that only a man would phrase it like that. "Just because I write a sex column for guys," she says, "doesn't mean I care about anyone's penis. That's your job." She is scathing and funny, like Zack. "Anyway, you're the one who's obsessed with the center," she tells me. "Never trust a guy who whines about sexism. He means he wishes he were man enough to be in charge."

She is Zack's practical friend. I am his emotional one. We play Mommy and Daddy, roles reversed, as we tend to his death. Still, she never forgets to bring food.

"I passed Ess-a-Bagel on First Avenue on my way here," she tells us, "and all I could think of was lox schmear, which of course they were out of. So I got scallion cream cheese instead."

"My favorite," Zack says.

If I brought bagels, they'd be the wrong kind.

"And vegetable cream cheese for you, of course," she tells me, opening the bag and pulling out two bagels wrapped in wax paper.

"Ava's the über-caregiver," Zack says. "Forgive me, Moses and Golda Meir, for speaking German."

"Nothing for yourself?" I ask Ava, as she crumples the empty bag.

"I can't stay."

"Yummy," Zack says, suddenly nine, unwrapping his bagel.

"Aren't you late for school?" Ava asks me.

"Yes, but unlike you I'm not allowed to leave here when I want."

She glances at Zack, then looks at me. Softly, she says, "He's been difficult?"

"Prickly."

"Don't hate me. Later he'll be mean to me and nice to you."

"I can't wait."

I unwrap my bagel, feeling jealous of Ava, whose beauty is cast in glorious relief by hospital rooms. Not only is she the daughter of survivors, but she grew up near the Highway 78 extension that was under construction all throughout her childhood. When she says she's lived at the edge of the abyss, she means Watchung, New Jersey, where she could look straight down into the raw bed of the projected highway and the massive pilings laid for concrete overpasses. Ava's life is nostalgia for uncompleted roadwork. She longs for dynamited landscapes.

Failing that, she spends a lot of time with sick gay men. She married two of them in a row, the first one accidentally. She insists she didn't know he was gay until he got sick. He's still alive, sharing a house in Washington with a closeted Pentagon official. The second one died. For a while after that she had a girlfriend, a photographer who got famous doing a photo series on heroin chic and left Ava for a twenty-year-old riot grrrl guitarist. At the moment Ava is single, but like me she's virtually married to Zack.

"Ava is Grace Kelly under pressure," Zack says, chewing. "Are you coming for breakfast tomorrow?" he asks her. When she nods, he says, "Because I need you to take my laundry with you tonight when you leave and bring it back tomorrow morning."

"Why can't the hospital do it?"

"The hospital can't do anything."

"How do you manage to have so much laundry in a hospital?" I ask him.

"It's always important to have clean underwear," Zack says, pointing to the corner at a red net bag full of T-shirts and jockey shorts.

"Well, in any case," Ava says, suddenly all business, "the whole question of laundry is moot at the moment. We have to talk," she tells Zack, sitting at the foot of his bed. "I spoke to your doctor today."

Zack gets a look of boyish concentration, like a kid doing homework. "Did he say what I have to do in order to go home?"

Ava glances at me briefly, as if to say, Sorry I haven't cleared this with you first. "He says you can go home in two days," she tells him.

If the doctor is suddenly willing to let Zack go without finishing his dozen procedures, it can only mean one thing: He's giving up, and Zack is going to die soon. We are all silent for a while, realizing this.

Then Zack says, "Why not today?"

"The day after tomorrow is way soon enough," Ava says. "We've got home health care set up. In the meantime—"

"In the meantime, you can start packing," Zack says, looking at me with grim authority. How do I respond? I'm thinking, not, *Damn, Zack's dying*, but rather, *Damn, now I'll have to help him move back to his apartment*.

"Sure," I tell him. "In the morning."

"We can all get started in the morning," Ava says, rising from the bed. "Until then," she tells Zack, "you relax." She leans forward and kisses him on the brow. Like everyone I admire, she knows how to make an exit. That is what New York teaches: beginnings and endings; how to start a scene, and how to escape it. The intervening drama is the difficult part.

There is, between Ava and me, the comfort of familiarity, and the recent discovery that our lives have taken a shape we could not have predicted. Gathering her stuff, she turns to me, putting her hand to her ear, miming the telephone and mouthing, "We'll talk." Then she's gone.

"It must be time for your dinner, now," I say, turning back to Zack, glancing at my watch. It's five forty-five P.M. My class starts at six thirty, and the subway ride to Queens takes forty-five minutes, if I'm lucky.

"You said you'd stay an hour," Zack says.

"I lied, I'm sorry."

"All right," he says, sitting up imperially, setting aside the last of his bagel. "Then take my laundry."

In general, my response to Zack's sickness is to be invisible. I try to empty myself out and replace what's gone with him, as if we were one person. That way, I can know what he wants without asking. Intuiting his feelings, however, is not the same as honoring them. I admit that my selflessness has limits. For instance, why do his laundry now if he's going home so soon? It's a waste of time. And even if it weren't, well, should I have to drag his soiled shorts around for the rest of the day, out to Queens, back to Manhattan?

In any case, my hesitation indicts me.

"You don't want to do it, do you?" Zack says accusingly.

"That's not true," I tell him. "Of course I'll do your laundry."

"But do you want to?" His voice is hard and his face is pinched and he looks absurdly angry behind his oversized glasses.

"No one *wants* to do laundry. That's not the point. Anyway, I'll leave it with my cleaners. They even pair socks."

"Fuck you, don't. I'll ask Ava tomorrow. Don't touch it. You'll do it wrong."

"I will not do it wrong."

"Fuck you," he says again. He's shouting. "Don't fucking touch it."

An orderly is trying to get into the room with dinner for Zack and his roommate. Zack is yelling, "Fuck you, fuck you, don't help me."

I'm trying to be calm. In a low, flat voice, I'm saying, "Zack. I'll take your laundry to the cleaners. They're on First Avenue. I can't drop it off tonight. They close at six. I'll do it in the morning."

"You'll forget about it and leave it at the cleaners," Zack complains.

"I'll bring it right here."

The orderly finally manages to swerve past me with Zack's tray. Of course, there's no room for dinner on the folding table, which is piled high with junk, including my uneaten bagel. While I'm clearing things away Zack calls me a fucking asshole. Then the phone rings, and he picks up the receiver.

"*Carrie*," he says. "*Hi*."

He puts his hand over the mouthpiece. "It's Carrie Fisher," he explains excitedly, in a stage whisper loud enough for people in the hall to hear. "I'm talking to my friend," he says into the phone. "He's being very ar-gu-men-ta-tive this evening. It's because I'm going home tomorrow, and he's worried that he'll have to *walk* a few more *blocks* to see me."

His voice is scorchingly cheery, but he's gesturing frantically. He wants me to find something on his bed. I figure out he means his pad and pen and to hand them to him. With the phone held between his chin and shoulder, he makes a record of the call. "What time is it?" he mouths silently, and I hold up two hands, six fingers. "Six . . . pee . . . em," he mouths, listening to his caller while he's writing on the pad. "Car . . . rie . . . calls." Then he drops the pen. "My friend might be able to come to your birthday party," he says, as the orderly sets down his tray. Not wanting to stay to discover whether Zack is actually talking to Princess Leia on the telephone, I pick up his laundry and, showing my watch, leave without saying good-bye.

I take the stairs down to the lobby and head outside for Dalton's Coffee Shop, where I get an Earl Grey tea to go. Then I stop next door at the magazine stand for a Snickers bar and a pack of Marlboro Lights. I haven't smoked since college, and I'm hoping it'll return me to the pleasure of my first drag, when I was twelve and inhaling made me pleasantly dizzy. That would be a kind of paradise regained. If I can handle a Marlboro Light, I'll graduate to Camel straights. There's no point in doing a thing half assed, no matter how self-destructive. That's my Protestant impulse: It's better to commit a mortal sin really efficiently than to make a shambles of good intentions.

I'm a bad WASP, creating a mess. How hard is it to do somebody's laundry? I should have just said yes. Or, like Ava, no. Now I'm angry and guilty and late. I hail a cab, knowing that at this hour it's faster to take the train, but I need to be coddled. I want to sit in the back of a cab on the Long Island Expressway with my headphones up high and not care. Mahalia Jackson is singing "I Gave Up Everything to Follow Him," and I unwrap the Snickers bar and light a cigarette, hoping that the driver, who has posted No Smoking signs all over his car, won't notice. Halfway to Flushing we see the Elmhurst tanks, two massive skeletal red-and-white cisterns that are being dismantled. Not long after Zack dies they'll be gone, and I'll pass them in a taxi cab on another school day and miss Zack, feeling sentimental and ashamed, my love for him indistinguishable from industrial waste cracked and tweezered out of the skyline.

The first time I saw Flushing was from my father's new Mustang convertible, on the way to the 1964 World's Fair. The top was down, my dad was driving, and my mom was in the bucket seat beside him, wearing a scarf on her head and smoking red Pall Malls. I was in the back of the car with my brother, in shorts and a madras shirt, my skin making funny rude noises when I pulled my thighs away from the sticky hot Naugahyde upholstery. The ends of my mom's scarf flapped in the wind, and her ashes caught in my eyelashes as the Beatles came on the radio, singing "Love Me Do."

That was almost thirty years ago. Now I'm in a cab with my best friend's dirty underwear. I toss my second cigarette out the window. It hasn't brought my youth back. The strangest thing about watching people die isn't that everything changes, but that nothing does. You still get a cab to Queens, pull up to your stop, overtip the driver, and step out onto Kissena Boulevard, into the last of the daylight. It's time to return to your life now, and it always will be. There's nothing holding you in place, now, not fast cars, not chocolate, not cigarettes, but only this: anticipation. This pain that neither one of us can help. This comedy, of course.

Crossing the college campus, rushing to class with my knapsack full of student work I haven't read, I realize that I have left Zack's laundry in the cab.

Youthanasia

Anyway I wrote the book cause we're all gonna die.
—Jack Kerouac

I met Zack in the fall of 1989. I was thirty years old, and I had been living in New York for almost a decade—in Manhattan, first on the Upper West Side, near Columbia University, and then in several different cheap apartments east of Avenue A. I have a talent for moving into neighborhoods right before they are surrendered to yuppies. For most of our friendship Zack lived on the West Side of Midtown, in Hell's Kitchen, or, as he called it, "Hell's Kitchenette." He had a tiny one-room apartment as long and narrow as a bowling alley on the second floor above a liquor store, overlooking a grim strip of Ninth Avenue. In 1989, Midtown was still grungy.

Oh, that city: the Manhattan of my twenties, the city pretty much as I had known it since I was a kid driving in from New Jersey through the Lincoln Tunnel with my mother and brother and hearing the hiss of our tires against hot asphalt as we came out of the mouth of the tunnel and into the wet heat and foul smells of the West Side. It was exciting and dirty. When is excitement not dirty?

What's the point of Times Square? It's supposed to be filthy. Yet there are no more dirty places in midtown Manhattan. When Zack was alive you could still go to seedy all-night diners on Eighth Avenue and order big glazed cream puffs like the kind Neal Cassady ate in 1946 with his "beautiful sharp little chick" Luanne, the day she and Neal stepped off the Greyhound bus from Denver and started digging the New York streets.

That was when there was a Times Square sex shop lodged in the corner of every American's mind. For a long time you could still find the dives where Cassady and Jack Kerouac and their beat pals—Allen Ginsberg, William Burroughs, Herbert Huncke, the whole crew—had risky sex and angelic visions, the hustler bars and by-the-hour hotels where they met Alfred Kinsey and were interviewed for his report on the sex lives of American men, skewing Kinsey's study in favor of polymorphously perverse sex acts and moving them into the mainstream of popular discussion, making them the open secret of male desire for fifty years. That city, the place where Ginsberg put his queer shoulder to the wheel, is long gone, killed off by Disney and AIDS.

When I met Zack I was still living in mid-century Manhattan, and I was still gay. I mean, I was *only* gay, convinced that my being "a gay man" was a sufficient explanation of both my abilities and my losses. Then Zack died anyway, and I changed my mind, because it turned out nothing kept him alive: not our strident "identity politics," not all our talk in the late eighties and early nineties of "queer empowerment," which we inherited from the "gay liberation movement" of the 1970s. Those quotes are not self-conscious, but cozy. Irony is conservative, after all. It's a way of preserving the past, storing your innocence in a display case long after you realize that the hope itself might have been the inciting crisis in your string of irretrievable losses.

I spent the first part of my twenties doing volunteer work for Gay Men's Health Crisis, visiting dying thirty-year-old men, making them grilled-cheese sandwiches in their toaster ovens and talking over the last of their lives in studio apartments on the Upper West Side. Then I went to graduate school, and took a vacation from death. I was twenty-six. I thought I had learned everything I could about watching people die. Plus, I had a boyfriend, a not-so-longtime companion. I had outlasted the twin adventures of my twenties, coming out and AIDS—and I set them aside, as if they no longer stood in the way of the rest of my life.

I thought I knew what death was like. That was how my mind worked at the time: I had gotten used to wondering how everyone would die. In *The Sun Also Rises* Jake Barnes has a bad habit of picturing his friends in bed having sex. I was seeing them in hospital rooms with tubes down their throats. Everybody had a different way of succumbing to AIDS. Some died of pneumonia, with thrush on their lips. Some went blind and then crazy, with toxoplasmosis raiding their brains. There were so many obscure infections, some contracted from cats and birds, that each death could be like a lesson in animal biology. A hangnail could kill you. So could a glass of water. It made the body seem amazingly slight, possibly medieval, subject to bacteria that had been otherwise rendered harmless for hundreds of years.

All things fall apart in different ways. I figured out that people die, but I was never ready for the variations. It was splendid, I guess, in a way, to learn how, in death, everyone was unique.

Well, I had seen all kinds of death. When I was twenty-four, I ran a writers workshop for people with AIDS. That was my introduction to gay identity. The workshop went from Thanksgiving to Easter, and at the end, only I wasn't dead. I met each week with twelve PWAs. They were regular guys, as plain as the men whose faces appear, lined and alone, in close-up in Hollywood westerns. My favorite was Frank. He had a wrestler's body and a fighter's blistered hands. An ex-cop, twice my age, he was writing a book about underground drones who are sad but immune to disease.

After two weeks he hooked up with Orlando, who was twenty-three. Orlando came from a military family in Puerto Rico, and he carried himself like a decorated colonel. Yet his shiny black hair was long and shaggy and he never cut his nails. Every Monday, after visiting Bellevue Hospital, where he got twenty-four-hour injections, he walked across town to what were then the Eighth Avenue offices of Gay Men's Health Crisis. His black eyes were wet and his face was red with cold and he smiled, unwinding his scarf. It was longer than he was. We sat in the kitchen, where our group met, and wrote stuff: "A Letter to Nancy Reagan"; "A Note to God"; "A Letter to a Friend I Won't See Before I Die." I still have these letters in a closed box on a closet shelf, along with other things I got from the dead.

Frank and Orlando took off one day and got married in a Unitarian church. Their honeymoon was in Bellevue. Orlando had spinal meningitis, and when he left the hospital Frank carried him to our meeting, backpacking him all the way, carting him up the stairs and stumbling into our room. They showed off their rings, which they wore on their right hands. After class we spent two weeks' worth of GMHC's food allowance at a Cajun joint down by the water. Of course, Orlando couldn't eat the spicy food. We ended up at a diner for Orlando's favorite, cheesecake and chocolate milk.

Orlando died in Bellevue, in late March, a cold spring. Frank killed himself two weeks later. He left a message on his phone machine saying he had taken pills and was going for "a long swim." He wasn't that sick. He had just moved to a new place, and I had called to see if he wanted anything. There was his message. "I have decided not to go on," he said, a movie cliché and a disconnecting beep.

Orlando's death happened in front of me. He was in a big bright room in Bellevue, knocked out, hooked up to a machine that forced breath into his lungs every few seconds. He gasped as he was made to inhale. Then the machine went *click-click* and he breathed out. His head rocked and his body shook like stop time in a jazz riff, breath pause, breath pause. He was swaddled in white, sheets and bandages wrapped around him and ending just above his nipples like a strapless gown. Alone on a rolling bed, in a shaft of light, Orlando looked as pinned and still as the bride of Frankenstein waiting to be jolted alive.

I put my hand on his forehead and said, "I'm sorry." His mother was standing beside him. She was dressed in a wool suit under a wool coat buttoned high, like Jackie Kennedy. I don't know why she was wearing her coat indoors. I couldn't ask her, because she spoke only Spanish and I speak only English and five words of German, all of which mean, "Angry and alone in grim and devastating apprehension of nothing." We stared at each other for a long time. She was crying, and I tried talking to her with an accent, as if that would help. "Me so sorry," I said. I wonder why she didn't hit me.

He died—stopped breathing, despite the machine—while I waited at his side, my head down, embarrassed. I didn't want to watch him die in front of his mother.

The following week a new guy joined the group. Bobby. He was a trip. He looked like Marlon Brando in *The Wild One,* but he was Jewish, Bronx born, with a broken nose and pouting lips and the kind of body that you felt approaching from a hundred yards off. He was not big, but wholly inside of himself; not conceited, but present. With his long legs and his broad shoulders and his busted schnozz, he was a street-smart tough guy who happened to be queer.

He came to his first meeting with a pillow, arranged it on his chair, sat down, and immediately started reading one of his poems which seemed to be about rainfall. He'd list everything the raindrops touched or passed as they fell—cirrus clouds, custard fog, the blue dome of the Chrysler Building, kids on the Grand Concourse cupping their hands around a joint, the rain-pocked tinfoil surface of the East River, sunk cars, inner tubes, silverfish, silt, and then the core of the earth. And we'd say, "Bobby, that was beautiful, what was it about?" And he'd say, "It's about what it's like to shit with rectal tumors."

His body shrank fast. One week he was as fleet and solid as a running back, and when then I saw him on the street and he was walking with a cane, he thumped his collapsed chest and said, "I had a body once." When he couldn't come to class I went to his apartment, which was in a basement under a photographer's studio. You hauled open a pair of metal doors in the sidewalk, then stooped low and walked down a set of wooden steps, through a narrow doorway, into the cellar. His room had a cement floor, a low ceiling, and white-washed walls that swelled out here and there, and it was big enough for an unmade bed and a hard-backed chair.

He died there. The last time I saw him alive, he was wired. Dressed in boxer shorts and a terry-cloth bathrobe, he had me sit in the chair while he jumped around the room, in and out of his robe, taking phone calls, reading poetry, discussing his illness, his asshole, his vitamins, his death.

He wanted me to help him experience his own death. We shut the lights and he lay on his bed in the dark room and made me talk him through his dying. Then he turned on the lights and stood on the bed and told me about getting fucked in the ass high on methamphetamines on the downtown IRT at daybreak when he was seventeen years old. We were the same age, but the most sex I had had at seventeen was yearning for my best friend Richie. *Thank God for repression,* I thought. *Maybe Catholics are right; self-loathing saves you.* Then Bobby said his tumors hurt. They hurt all the time, not just when he was shitting. So we did an imaging exercise, which I read to him out of a book. You were supposed to localize pain. You had to find the place it came from and move there, welcome it, and say, "Yo, pain." That was Bobby's version. "Yo, pain," he said, trying not to scream. "Whassup?"

These men would be in their forties now. Well, not Frank. He'd be over sixty, and maybe he would have killed himself anyway. The rest of them were barely twenty-five. Terry came to his first workshop with an X-ray of his skull, which he handed around. He died at

Christmas on a gurney in one of the hallways of Metropolitan Hospital, which was city-run and short of beds. Jason went home to Long Island to die, which must have been weird for his parents, who didn't know he was gay, much less dying.

Dan flew to Italy in shorts and sent snapshots of himself climbing the hills of a Tuscan village, lesions all over his legs. He died on the plane coming home. Roy got so thin that he evaporated. Luis took pills. Unlike Frank, however, he planned ahead and told us about it in class. He picked a date on which to die and invited friends. I was asked to his death, but I didn't go.

Instead, I went to a memorial service for Horatio, a Christian mystic from Argentina who spoke four languages and talked nonstop about "the nature of the human condition." His eyes watered constantly from chemotherapy, and he went teary-eyed into gay bars and dance clubs carrying a folded-open copy of Søren Kierkegaard's *The Sickness Unto Death*. "The self is the self relating to itself," he quoted. He knew how to clear a dance floor with bits of Kierkegaard: "Death is a passing into life," he said, while the disco DJ spun Gloria Gaynor singing "I Will Survive." "The torment isn't death, but the inability to die."

Despair, not AIDS, is the sickness unto death. That was Horatio's message: Dying was fine. What sucked was having or being a self. Maybe he did pass from death into life. In any case, he died. So did everyone else, which is why I went alone to Mitchell's memorial service. By then, everybody was gone. Mitchell had been our prodigy. Just twenty-three, he was studying to be a doctor. KS undid him. "Kill Sodomites," he joked, but it meant Kaposi's sarcoma, a rare form of cancer. Mitchell had blue-green KS lesions on his face. Each week, he zapped himself with radiation, which was supposed to blanch and shrink the cancerous blotches, but which, instead, left him looking like a guy covered with lesions he had tried to burn off. His forehead was fried and he smeared it with pancake makeup and dusted it with powder.

His memorial service was held in Hebrew at a synagogue in the West Village, and his whole family was there. His father was a butcher, round and solid, with a Russian accent, and when he started to read from the funeral service, I was ready for words from Leviticus about stoning homosexuals dead. Even in Hebrew I would understand "you faggot." Mitchell's dad wasn't interested in scripture, however. He let go of his book, tipped his head back, clasped his hands together, and yelled. His hands were small and thick, and his suit was tight. He raised his hands to his head and thrust his chin in the air and yelled. For a long time, everybody stood there while he went on yelling, and I knew what he meant. I knew exactly what he meant. I thought I knew exactly what he meant.

Then Zack showed up, bursting into the frame like a car crash that sends the film's plot spinning in another direction. Zack was diagnosed with AIDS in 1989, and he was orchestrating his death from the minute we met. He promised to take me with him as far as I could go. Zack was my first raging angry queer—self-proclaimed—and my first professional author. As I. W. Barker he had published his first novel, *Sick Fuck,* a year before mine. "Barker" was an Americanization of "Bacharach," the "I" was short for "Isaac," and the "W," of course, was invented. "My first name is Yitzchak," he said. "My middle name is Shmuel. Am I supposed to put that on a book jacket? 'Yitzy Shmuel Bacharach?' Don't you think I want readers in North Carolina?"

"Not if your book is called *Sick Fuck,*" I said.

"Oh, well," he said, blushing, and then he laughed his barking three-syllable laugh, "Hant, hant, hant."

Zack took over the plot, and I made him the star of my life. We met shortly after I had published my own first novel, and soon after I had finally broken up with Mark White, my first love, whom Zack called "your starter boyfriend."

"No one stays with people they loved when they were twenty-three," Zack said. "Otherwise, I'd still be with Cher."

It's the winter of 1983. I'm with Mark White in a parked car on Perry Street in the West Village, facing the Hudson River and the West Side waterfront. Mark is warming the engine, and I'm beside him, choosing music for our road trip. We're headed to New England for the weekend. The trunk is packed, the dog's in back. We're dressed in coats and scarves and hats. As Mark idles his BMW I load a mix tape into the cassette deck: forties vocalists, Frank Sinatra doing "It All Depends on You." "I can be beggar, I can be king, I can be almost any old thing," Frank sings, and Mark reaches over, lowers the volume, and says, "So, were you planning on being a temp the rest of your life?"

I'm twenty-three. Mark is forty, tall and dark and as blandly handsome as Rock Hudson in *Magnificent Obsession*. He's a big overgrown boy with giant hands and a deep quiet voice pitched low to hide his midwestern accent. Smiling, standing in the middle of whatever room he's casually dominating, his thumbs in his pants pockets, he is sexy and ingratiating, equally difficult to blame or resist.

He is not just my first boyfriend, he is nearly the first person I have ever touched. We've been dating three months, and I'm beginning to discover what bugs him. Lateness. Lint. Public displays of affection. On the way to the car he wouldn't hold hands, and I'm sulking. Well, we were both carrying luggage, who had a hand free? I get that. Nevertheless, I have noticed recently that he pulls away from me when I reach for him, crossing the street. I'm all, "Hey, it's 1983. Where's your gay pride?"

I'm an idealist, not a pragmatist. Mark is a partner in an architectural firm called Surface Techniques. He was married once, and his parents think I'm a girl named Cindy. Obviously, they haven't met me. "They haven't met you, either," I tell Mark, but he laughs and says that's a private concern. "It's no one's business how I live," he says.

In fact, he lives quite nicely. He has an immaculate West Village apartment with a working fireplace and exposed brick. I've been crashing on a foam pad on the floor of my brother's place on Claremont Avenue near Grant's Tomb. I don't care about owning things. Property is theft. I told Mark that. It didn't go over big. He'd like to take a European vacation to visit Gothic cathedrals. I can hardly split gas for a ride to Vermont. On the way to his garage, hauling our bags, leading the dog on a leash, I made us take a detour to an ATM so I could withdraw my last twenty dollars. I did it with a flourish, almost with hostility, pocketing the bill and looking, I hoped, fleeced and defiant.

So when he leans close in his German car, his cold breath in my ear, and wants to know what I mean to do with my life, we both know it's not an idle question.

Frank Sinatra sings, "I could save money, or spend it."

"What's wrong with being a temp?" I ask.

"You have a college degree," Mark says.

"I was an *English* major. I can read a poem really well. Is that a useful skill?"

"You could do something with it."

"I am doing something."

"Working as a filing clerk? Come on, you're smart, you're wasting yourself."

"Not really."

"Not *really*? Tell me what you've accomplished."

Very lightly, I say, "I'm in love with *you*."

Mark leans back in his bucket seat. "Oh, sweetheart," he says, in a tone I haven't heard before: slightly campy. Suddenly he's Barbara Stanwyck, aging actress in a 1950s movie melodrama, warning her dewy screen daughter to wise up quick. It's the first time I've heard Mark sound arch, and it scares me.

Defensively, I say, "I have a plan. It's not like I don't have a plan."

I'm lying, of course. I haven't planned past the next five minutes. Naturally, I don't want Mark to know this. In order to give the impression that I *have* thought about my life, however, I say, "I want to be a New York homosexual."

I'm not being flip. I'm in earnest. And I've been reading: Delmore Schwartz, Philip Rahv, Mary McCarthy, James Baldwin, Norman Mailer, Susan Sontag, the whole gang of New York intellectuals from the Great Depression to the war in Vietnam. I want to be one of them, only openly gay. Literary, critical, published. Interviewed on television by Dick Cavett. Willing to say mean things about Lillian Hellman! I want to be professionally, even notoriously, gay. What Sontag did for camp, what Mailer did for marijuana and apocalyptic sex, what Baldwin did for "the Negro," I mean to do for the homosexual—without a trace of irony I think, "for my *people*."

Mark is laughing. So am I, joining in like I get the joke. Of course, I don't. I have been gay for eighteen months—gay in the sense of claiming it as my identity. Sitting in an expensive car with the man I love, who loves me back, and staring at the Hudson River waterfront of lower Manhattan, I am thinking, *My life has begun.* If I am just beginning to suspect that my boyfriend isn't perfect, still, it will be a long time before I fall out of love with him, and longer still before I get over New York. Even after I lose Mark, even after I figure out that being a gay man isn't a refuge from the guys who trashed me in high school, but rather, that gayness as an identity is worse than gym class, because the sissies are in charge, and if you think playground bullies are mean to fags, you should go to a gay bar—even after Zack dies, I will still want New York the way I yearn for it in 1983, staring at Manhattan through the windows of Mark's car.

The waste of whatever is already lost surrounds us. Up the West Side is the elevated highway that Robert Moses built, abandoned and rusting in the sun. Is anything more comforting than ruins? I don't miss the past, I miss the ghost of the past, industrial remains, the crumbling piers of the Port of New York. I miss how the city used to live with its garbage plainly in sight as you walked along the Hudson River, in the light of the giant neon Maxwell House Coffee cup dripping its last drop over and over into Jersey. When I first moved to the city I thought the bitter smell of coffee grounds along the West Side was a chemical response created by abrasion of river air against New York brownstone, but Mark told me it came from the Hoboken coffee plant. "Chemical air/sweeps in from New Jersey/and smells of coffee": Robert Lowell. Mark likes facts, but I prefer debris.

Until the early sixties my father rode the ferry from the Hoboken slip to the foot of Christopher Street, making his morning commute. It cost a nickel. By 1983, that ferry has been out of service for twenty years, but the pier is there, chipped and split and leaning into the harbor, covered by a steel frame shed that sprays cracked glass from its broken windows. It's a hangout for guys tumbling out of sex clubs and looking for an angry blow job in the light of dawn. Plenty of those guys will be dead soon, or they will be gay Republicans living in Houston, but there will be a further loss when the city scrubs the smell of the past from the streets, hiding any trace of the missing and the dead.

Zack said you don't stay with your first love, but I am still in New York, and I might have remained with Mark, even now—he'd be nearly sixty, probably taking Viagra—if I hadn't arrived in the city at the same time as AIDS, which is the other partner I haven't been able to leave. Mark and I had the usual problems: sex, money, our mothers. Our dads were difficult, too. Still, people get over all that. They work it out. Soon after Mark and I met, however, we started spending our quiet Saturday nights not at home but at the side of dying men in hospital beds. Mark was old enough to know the generation of men who died first. When we hung out with his friends, the evening always began with a roll call of the newly diagnosed or the latest dead. We had our first bad fight in a church pew at someone's memorial service. Most of the twenty guests who came to a surprise party for my twenty-fifth birthday were dead within two years. My brother was there, too, and he is the only man apart from Mark and me who is still alive.

Some people draw together in war—and it felt like a war, with a body count, so many dead every week—but Mark and I fell apart. Well, I was a kid. And Mark was a forty-year-old closet case with an ex-wife, aging parents, and a host of college pals and boyhood friends who had never been told he was gay. Our relationship was hermetically sealed in the West Village, within walking distance of St. Vincent's Hospital, where we socialized with our small circle of sick friends. I never met anyone's parents and there weren't many women around. That makes gay men sound clannish and self-involved, but if we were isolated, it wasn't entirely by choice. We didn't have much of a context except illness and death.

The last time I saw Mark was a snowy night in 1989. I was on my way to a gay bookstore on Hudson Street to read from my first novel, which I had just published. I ran into him on the street a few minutes before my reading. We hadn't spoken in about a month. We were "taking a break," one of many, but this time it would be for good. I was on my bicycle. Mark was walking his dog. There were white crystals on the beige shoulders of his camel-hair coat, and snow flecked his black hair. His temples were gray but somehow looked fake, as if they were spray-painted by a Hollywood makeup artist to indicate age. He was near fifty. I was almost thirty-one.

I leaned forward and kissed his cheek, which was cold.

"Hey," I said. "Don't I know you?"

I was aware that I still thought he was beautiful, which bugged me. I pressed my cheek to his face, and then, pulling away, felt his chill breath on the side of my neck. My bicycle was between us, and I noticed him leaning back ever so slightly, to avoid contact with my wet wheels.

"I'm going to a reading," I said. "Wanna come? I'm pretty sure I can get you introduced to the author."

I was still a temp, but I had written a book. It had happened in Mark's kitchen. He had set me up at his old Panasonic electric typewriter at a wooden table under a window overlooking a garden. Lots of gay couples bond over property, but I couldn't afford real estate, and instead of a house, Mark and I had my book. The whole time we were together, off and on for six years, I was writing it. Then the book was suddenly done, and it wasn't his. We were both surprised. Everything in our relationship had belonged either to him or to us. Suddenly, there was something that was mine.

There was another problem: He liked his privacy.

"Sleep with a writer, wake up in print," Zack said. It was almost the first thing he said to me, and it was a relief. Maybe he was just being flip, and I provided the subtext. In any case, I saw what he meant. He was saying what Mark would not admit, that privacy isn't a right, it's a privilege. Zack knew he was always in public. He had grown up in the floodlights, like me. Because he was Jewish, and gay, and odd, his acts and inclinations had always been on display. People were constantly pointing him out. Well, women don't have privacy, either. They find out fast that they are being watched, and Zack and I were judged as harshly as girls from the time we were kids. "Why are you a fag?" people asked. "What makes you such a fag?"

Keeping things to myself was out of the question. I was everyone's business starting at age ten. I don't know what people mean when they say they're in the closet, or when they talk about someone else being in the closet, or when they claim they have come out of the closet. What closet?

I never had any privacy. Yet I dated gay men who thought they had a private life. I am not talking about married straight guys in hiding, gay on the sly. I don't mean college guys having a fling. The men I loved in New York had relationships only with men. They knew they were gay. Still, they acted as if I wasn't there. When their parents showed up, I was gone. They lied about me at work. My high school classmates were mean, but at least they were consistent:

They always called me a fag. The men I knew in my twenties held me in their arms and pretended I didn't exist.

On the street, standing by my bicycle, Mark coughed into his bunched fist and said good-bye. Even now, with no one around, he wouldn't be seen touching me. He went down the street with his dog. I watched him go.

That was the night I met Zack. Anyone could see he was nothing like Mark. The difference that struck me, however, was this: Zack wasn't gay. He was GAY.

He came to my reading. Shifting his weight from side to side and clutching a copy of my book, he looked like a suburban housewife at the local mall, dressed in a blue down parka that was shiny and long, the hem nearly reaching his ankles and spattered with dirt from the street. Then he slipped off his coat and folded it over his arm, showing a skin-tight T-shirt that hugged the overstated muscles of his chest. He had Brad Pitt's torso, but it was perched on skinny legs and offset by a scowling face with eyebrows so arched they put everything he said in quotes. Even his smile seemed to be annotating itself. That was Zack's genius. He was ironically muscular. He got you to want him and comment on wanting him at the same time.

He told me he was a semifamous gay author. I was embarrassed that I had never heard of his book. "Of course you haven't," he said. "I'm just another fag with AIDS." I had known him two minutes. I wasn't shocked, though. I'm fatally attracted to hostility, I ought to confess. Anyway, Zack wasn't angry; he was silly. He had a voice that was both shrill and husky, like Jerry Lewis crossed with Lauren Bacall. Some of the funniest things I ever heard were Zack telling me he was that much closer to death. "I got my blood work back," he said once, about a year before he died. "My T-cell count is lower than my IQ. If I were Dan Quayle, I'd be dead now."

I wasn't surprised to learn right away that he was going to die. Gay men with AIDS almost always died in 1989—usually it took about two years. And half my friends had AIDS. So there was a 50/50 chance that anyone I met would be sick.

Of course, not everybody waddled up to you in public and predicted his own death. Zack looked like I felt: unprotected and furious. He was pushy about his self-loathing. "I'm so gay," he said, "that even the high school drama club wouldn't take me." Actually, he wasn't that gay. He was *posing* as a queen. He was exhausting, I guess, but I never got tired of him—not until he started getting really sick and his cushioning irony wasted away, leaving nothing but his cutting remarks.

He was fragmented, like me, and I took him the way you take speed to neutralize your ADD. He wasn't thin-skinned; he was without skin. Whatever bugged me, it bugged him even worse. For a long time I found his anxiety reassuring. Anyway, it was familiar. Like me, Zack had never felt safe. He was the first gay man I knew who admitted that his childhood had been as perilous as mine.

A week after my reading he invited me to lunch. He paid, of course, and I was late, which is one way of describing our friendship, and his death.

We ate at a Greek diner near his apartment. "Now, order whatever you want," he said. "We're not on a budget. I can recommend the grilled cheese." Then he laughed, "Hant, hant, hant."

The huge menu swallowed his face. I could just see his eyebrows above it. When the waiter came Zack asked him, "What's fresh?" Then he put the menu down and ordered fried eggs. "I hear they're good here," he confided, as the waiter left.

Later I found out that Zack had sex with everyone within the first fifteen minutes of friendship or not at all. In that case, I missed my chance. Not that he didn't offer. He tried to seduce me by listing his faults. "Sleep with me because you'll hate it," he seemed to be saying. Then, when he was through degrading himself, he started flattering me. He didn't just praise, he competed.

"Your book is so good, I've been jealous for weeks," he said.

"Even your jacket photo is better. I despise you for that. Will you please be my friend? I'll buy you lunch every day for a year. I don't mind paying for love. I'll even pay for your contempt. It would be a privilege," he said, giving "privilege" four syllables. "Not only that, but your book is cheaper. So it's a bargain all around. 'Don't read mine,' I've been telling my friends. 'Save yourself a buck and read his.' Thanks for robbing me of so many sales."

Then he laughed again, and the whole diner heard. "I brought you a gift," he told me, opening his knapsack and pulling out his book, which he slid across the table. Suddenly, he looked shy. The book was lying facedown next to my place mat. I never know how to receive gifts. I picked it up and turned to the dedication page, which is my favorite part of any book. "I don't see my name here," I said.

"Give it back," Zack said, "and I'll write you a note that says it's all about you."

"Are you calling me a sick fuck?"

He barked a single "hant." I handed him the book, and he opened it to the title page and fished out a pen.

"What do you want me to say?"

I was in a diner with a new friend who was giving me a signed copy of his novel. It was exciting and weird. I felt like I had reached the scene in the film biography where the young man gets his first hint of later fame.

"Doesn't it feel narcissistic to be signing your own book?" I asked.

"Of course it is." Zack said. "Why else write a book except to be able to sign it? Signing copies of your novel is how you get dates. Don't you know that, Tom? That's what novels are *for*. It's like having a really big dick. You write your book, and then you cast it out there and reel it in and see what's hooked on the end. Of *course* you need to sign copies of your book. You don't even have to include your phone number. They always find you in the phone book later on."

"What if you're not listed in the phone book?"

"What kind of gay man would you be if you weren't listed in the phone book? Do you think anybody ever keeps those numbers you scrawl for them on matchbooks?" He leaned down to his book, considering. "What should I say?"

"Sign it to some imaginary humpy stud," I said, and that's what he did. His inscription said "To an imaginary humpy stud. It's all about you. Kiss noise," he wrote, with his name and the date. Then I made him write his phone number.

Some people loathed Zack. He wore round, thick bug-eyed glasses that made his face look venomous, ready to sting. Still, his target was mostly himself. Disliking him seemed to be missing the point or, anyway, failing his test. He dared you to hate him, and when you did, he won. For a long time I chose friends on the basis of how they responded to Zack. I couldn't be bothered with people who found him annoying. I thought they were prissy; Zack said they were anti-Semitic. Maybe. I might have slept with him if I hadn't wanted to be his friend. Zack used sex to keep men at a distance, but I wanted to be close. And he could be terribly sweet.

He bought me lunch twice a week for five years. He paid my rent three times. He got in the habit of slipping a twenty-dollar bill in my pocket whenever I saw him, like my great aunt. "Tom," he said, "are we codependent? Am I enabling you? If I'm enabling you, shouldn't you be able to *do* something?"

I watched him cross the street after our first lunch. There was hardly any traffic on Ninth Avenue, but he waited for the light. "Tom," he screamed at me, when I tried to get him to walk against the red. "Don't make me do that," he said. "I don't do that." I let him go. I went south to the train and left him standing there until it was safe for him to cross. Turning back, I saw him pause. Then he headed off. He had a funny walk, with a staccato step like Edward Scissorhands, headed straight for a disaster he'll barely escape. He was thirty-three years old. "My crucifixion year!" he had told me. "Also my resurrection. I'm thinking I'll do them in the opposite order. First rise, then die." In fact, he had five years to live.

Songs for Swinging Lovers

It is better not to be different from one's fellows.

—Oscar Wilde

Nose to the ground, squat on its haunches, Richie's car is blister red, bright with sleek aluminum strips, swollen here and there in its tapering length with triumphant attachments, swiveling mirrors, trim antennae, delicate bumpers, and terraced with glass that reflects and multiplies, in its windshields and side windows, every passing jazz-juiced hipster crossing Avenue A against the gun-metal blue of the cloud-clotted sky.

"That's some fucking car," I say.

"Get in, old buddy," Richie says. "I want you to drive."

He tosses me the keys. It's an epic gesture of friendship that masks the fact that Richie doesn't actually know how to drive a stick.

"How'd you get here?"

"It's just the shifting I can't do. The downshifting. I can get it up but not down," he says, and this is such a serious admission, hinting that it might also mean the opposite, that neither one of us dares to laugh. "I can't do low speeds, that's what I'm saying. So you drive."

"Where? Hell?"

"Not yet," Richie says. "First, you're going to have to change that shirt."

Justin's shirt. I guess I shouldn't be wearing it in public, advertising my indiscretion. "I'll stop off at my place," I say, "and get a clean one."

"I don't trust your taste."

"Then we'll go to Banana Republic and buy something. You can supervise."

"Big spender."

"Look, you just bought a car because you couldn't wait for the Q88 bus."

"Calm down," Richie says. "We'll take a ride to my place. It'll be good for you, a change of scene, get you out of Manhattan for a minute. This island is just a globed minimall without washrooms. What do you do here, you have to pee? Wait, stop, don't tell me. I don't want that image in my head."

"You sure this car is legal to drive?" I say, getting in behind the wheel. "How'd you get plates the same day you bought it? On a Sunday?"

"Did you not see plates?" Richie says, easing in beside me. It's the right car for him, the right size, sleek and compact. I'm a tight fit, despite having lost weight.

"Yes," I say, folding my legs under the wheel, "I saw the plates."

"So never mind is it legal. There's plates, we're good to go."

And we do go, oohing and ahhing over the car's interior and its amenities, which Richie demonstrates: the adjustable bucket seats; the dashboard, hydra-headed with numerous gauges and gadgets; the sunroof, which he opens; the AM-FM radio; the CD player, with a detachable front panel that Richie locks in place in order to treat me to some new music. Richie's musical taste runs to the Beatles and

Sinatra, but he's spinning Fiona Apple. Afrodytea's influence, maybe. Clearly not the girlfriend's. The girlfriend likes Melissa Etheridge and the Allman Brothers.

"If this cyberdate is into Fiona Apple . . . ," I say ominously, making a U-turn in the middle of Avenue A and steering for Delancey Street and the Williamsburg Bridge.

"If she likes Fiona Apple what?"

"I don't know," I admit. "Just, I'd be careful not to call her a 'lady.' "

"Chicks dig that," Richie insists, scrunching down in his seat, hanging his arm out the window, enjoying the ride.

Scott Fitzgerald praises the Queensboro Bridge, but maybe he never took the Williamsburg, the gutted relic, star of a 1940s film noir, *The Naked City*, recently stripped of its wooden walkways and nineteenth-century way stations and left to hang by its suspenders over lower Manhattan. There's nobody else on the road. A holiday weekend! "Hunger hurts," Fiona Apple sings, but I'm stung by the sweet ache of departure, leaving Manhattan. I spend half my time in the city getting out of it. In trains and planes and fast cars, crossing rivers or tunneling beneath them, or jetting into the air, I let the city go, feeling it behind me like impacted back teeth. You have to be numbed to get things hauled out of your head, but I want the pain, the gnawing reminder that I'm going to die someday, no matter how quickly and dramatically I flee, as if running or theatrics could save me. "If it be now it is not to come," says Hamlet, which is supposed to be a relief. "If it be not to come, it's now." Yet it will come.

"Maybe Afrodytea has a friend," Richie says, dreaming of his date. "A hot babe for you. We can get you in there."

"Oh, *yeah,*" I say, playing along, feeling dishonest.

I'm not the kind of guy who calls women "babes." There's something fake about my friendship with Richie. It's a performance. Yet, for twenty-five years, I have been trying to convince Richie and myself that I'm a regular guy. Okay, I'm forty-one years old. How long can I carry around the childhood pain of being picked last for the basketball team? Other people get over it. Not me. Well, I have had adult relationships with women and men, and I've set up house a couple of times with guys I introduced to friends as "my partner." I don't mind being respectable—once in a while.

Still, in a guy's car, I regress. I am always an impostor in my buddy's car. I say "dude" and "motherfucker" and I pretend to like the droning songs that guys play over and over, songs about being flattened and enraged and frightened of girls—and equally terrified of men. Everyone has a secret repetition compulsion, and here's mine: sitting in a car with a guy who is nothing like me—who isn't, in fact, me. I can't resist the yearning I feel driving with my student Justin Innocenzio, or with Richie, his backrest ratcheted low so he can recline, his free arm wrapped around my neck guard, his knees spread as wide as his legroom allows.

I'm not talking about sex. I'm a gay guy; I know how to police my desire. Most of the time. Instead, I'm wishing I could be him—in him, not on him, of him, inside of him, not me. Men are the opposite sex. My hand brushes Richie's knee as I shift gears and we come down from the Williamsburg Bridge. "You can't lose what you ain't never had," Muddy Waters sings as Richie switches disks, and our arms rub together, briefly. And if I put my hand at the back of his head my palm would fit in the hollow and swerve of the base of his skull, as if his bones were molded for my touch, and my fingers would spread wide upward, furrowing his hair.

We're on the BQE, which skims Williamsburg and Greenpoint, level with the pedimented tops of tenement buildings. Then it cranks high to the mold-mottled Kosciuszko Bridge over Newtown Creek, skipping from Brooklyn to Queens. The BQE threads like a blanched ribbon in a funeral bouquet into the Long Island Expressway, which is bone dry in the midday sun. We've made the transition. We're out of Manhattan, into Queens, Now we're on our way to Richie's neighborhood. He has a decent setup in downtown Flushing, four rooms on the fifth floor of a brick apartment building that curves around the corner of Syringa Place, off Ash Avenue. Through his living room windows he can see a Buddhist temple.

Back in the day, though, he was living in a garden apartment in Forest Hills, working the stock exchange, and he ate, slept, and shat Wall Street. Did he have a minute free to spend his winnings on blow and blow jobs and hypersensitive stereo equipment? No way. So he quit. "Fuck junk bonds," he said, a message he left on my phone machine. Besides which, the girlfriend was agitating to get married. Shortly after I met Zack, Richie took off. He "went out west," like Biff Loman in *Death of a Salesman*, and it still isn't clear what he did there. Cattle ranching? Midnight cowboying? Oil rigging in the Gulf of Mexico? I got postcards from Tucson, Albuquerque, and New Orleans. Driving home in 1993, he had an epiphany on the highway halfway across the Florida panhandle, and when he got to New York he went straight to Brooklyn College, signed up, and finally finished his B.A. He had been eight credits short of a degree for fifteen years. Then he returned to the brokerage business. Which he's good at. He's working for a firm out on the island where the bullshit factor, compared to Manhattan, is low. He still thinks about going back to school, though, for an advanced degree.

We're off the highway now, up the exit ramp to the Horace Harding Expressway. We turn north, onto Kissena Boulevard, "which means, like, 'nice creek' or 'good wind,' in the Munsee lingo of the Matinecoc Indians," says Richie, a compulsive collector of facts and figures.

We head to downtown Flushing, past streets named for trees. Flushing was the nursery capital of the Northeast in, like, 1800, Richie says, "and there were trees here, two thousand species of trees; the girlfriend has a book about it. 'Chinese taxodium,' get that, and Japanese maple, and 'the white dwarf horse,' and chestnut, ginkgo, ilex." "Now you got two thousand species of people instead," he says, counting them off on the dashboard. "Lebanese, Chinese, Vietnamese, Colombian, Peruvian, Korean, Afghan, Dominican, Kenyan, Senegalese, Egyptian, Croatian, Sikh, Serbian, Persian, Trinidadian, Haitian, Ecuadoran, Israeli, Russian, and Jewish schmucks and guido bastards and poor dumb micks like me."

We pass Elder Avenue, then Dahlia, Cherry, and Beech, as the street slopes down to Sanford Avenue. "Turn," Richie shouts, as we reach Ash. "Turn here, motherfucker."

We go east, away from downtown Flushing. The terraced high-rise buildings along Kissena Boulevard morph into garden apartments built around airy courts. Next come attached homes of tan brick, followed by hundred-year-old clapboard houses tucked behind shrubs. Richie guides me to his apartment. There's a space right in front of his place, and I back into it while Richie criticizes my parking.

His building has an elevator, but small spaces make Richie nervous, so we take the stairs, which are wide and polished.

"If you're claustrophobic, how can you live here?" I ask him, as we enter his apartment through a narrow hallway made even more pinched by waist-high shelves lined with books: atlases; Anne Rice, which Richie doesn't blame on the girlfriend; comic books; Cormac McCarthy; and *The Last Whole Earth Catalogue*, which I can't believe he has, because I gave it to him in 1976. We used it to clean pot. It's a huge, black warped paperback, with, no doubt, crackly seeds and brittle bits of dried stem still caught in the binding and a funky smell like the backseats of hatchback cars—Ford Pintos, Chevy Vegas—from my sophomore year of high school. I grab it off the shelf and hold it to my chest like a coed on her first date as I follow Richie down the hall.

"Cool place," I say, and Richie says, "You've never been here?" and I shake my head no. It occurs to me that I've hardly seen Richie on two consecutive days since we were eighteen years old. In the meantime, everyone died. Richie's mom got bone cancer and was dead in two months. The girlfriend's dad had heart failure on the Jericho Turnpike. They found him slumped over his wheel in front of an Edwards Supermarket. Richie's uncle died, then the girlfriend's grade-school crush: drugs, alcohol, bad luck.

And I had my turn. The people I knew who didn't die in the eighties got rich in the nineties and moved to Norwalk, or Santa Fe, or Tribeca. Suddenly everybody was too rich to die, and people found Prozac and protease inhibitors and younger and cuter boyfriends and girlfriends. And because I had stopped going to the gym but had not stopped eating pizza and chocolate bars, and because I earn a teacher's pay, I was suddenly neither thin enough nor young enough nor rich enough nor dead enough for anyone my age.

"Don't get morbid," Richie says, thumping me on the back, as if he can read my thoughts. "Stroll around the grounds," he says, making a proprietary sweep with his right hand. "That room," he tells me, pointing to a closed door, "belongs to the girlfriend, and it is filled with her *stuff*," he says vaguely, with a backward wave of his hand. The girlfriend is involved in a start-up Internet business. Richie mentions a home page and a Web site and an apparently astronomical number of hits.

The kitchen is as wide as a pencil box, and we're standing at its opposite ends, facing each other. "You can't be in here side-by-side," Richie says, "which, it drives the girlfriend crazy, because she likes to cook together. And I mean *together*."

He mentions the girlfriend repeatedly, but her presence is apparitional, as if she were not gone for the day but actually dead. Her things are all around, but Richie moves among them as if they were memorial, not practical. You can feel her claim on certain items, though not the expected ones. The candles are Richie's. They're set on top of bookshelves, melted to windowsills, within igniting distance of paper and wood. The kitchen mess, however, is hers. "She won't wash up," Richie says, running water and filling a glass for me, swinging the swivel faucet in the kitchen sink way to the side, past the stacked plates and plastic *Star Wars* cups until there's room to hold a filmy water tumbler beneath the spigot.

"We get married, she tells me, someone'll buy us a whole new set of stemware. *Stem*ware. This is a reason to get married?"

We go into the living room. Low-ceilinged and doughy white, with a sighing wooden floor, it's oppressively equilateral, its squareness relieved only by two windows like breakout hatches overlooking the Buddhist temple. A fake Persian carpet with incurled edges is anchored by several blocky pieces of furniture that are pushed against the walls, as if the center of the room had just been cleared for shooting hoops—or for displaying audiovisual equipment, like an electronics showroom. Richie has a fancy stereo, a bass guitar, and a big-screen TV with a DVD player loaded with Stanley Kubrick's *Full Metal Jacket*. Across the top of the TV is a warning label run out on a laser printer: Only for Yankees and Knicks.

"Kind of risky to cheer for the Yankees in Flushing," I say, and Richie says, "Fuck the Mets and all of their minions. Except, for Edgardo Alfonzo, we will make an allowance. The girlfriend likes Edgardo." Then, with a groan of self-satisfaction—sparing Edgardo, and all—he sits in the chair next to me with a glass of Diet Coke and says, "Tell me this ain't living large." Then he lights a blunt.

"Are we getting high?" I say. "Like high school? Is it 1976?"

"You are way too tight, man," Richie says. "Smoke up," he tells me, passing the joint, "we got time to waste," and he lurches forward across the room and puts on some music. It's *Anthology* 3, the last of the Beatles' recording career, John and Paul grasping at what might still keep them together: Carl Perkins songs, fingerpicking, British music hall jokes. "You and I have memories," Paul sings, unplugged, as I smoke pot with Richie, my high school pal.

Richie was beautiful when he was seventeen. That was his best year. It was nearly my worst. We were on opposite curves, and where I was awkward, soft-bellied, and unbearded, Richie was a taut wiry guy with chest hair and broad shoulders and a face like a teenaged Clint Eastwood, with suffering, clear blue eyes. He could dribble six basketballs at once in the basement of his parents' house, not ham-handed, but on the tips of his fingers, as if dribbling were a matter of the most delicate moves, a practiced exertion of force against mass.

His face was blank with concentration as he mentally rehearsed a defensive strategy, man-to-man, box-in-one. He had played for his high school ball team in Long Island, where he was named, in a local poll, one of the ten best teenage athletes in the county. When his dad moved him out to New Jersey, though, he gave it up. He wouldn't compete. I never knew why. Maybe he was angry at his dad for cutting short his limited fame. Or maybe he liked marijuana better. Still, he had a basket bolted to his parents' garage, and after we got high in his bedroom we'd go outside, and I would sit on a tree stump and watch Richie take shots, which he always sunk. I was scared of sports, but Richie was amazing to watch, especially when I was stoned. He was as quick and bright and spinning and ecstatic as the blurred world seen from a merry-go-round.

After he graduated high school, two years ahead of me, I was left alone, without his protection, and one afternoon I got a thrashing from some kids in gym class. I left school and went straight to Richie's house. My face was smarting from contact with the locker-room door, its oak scent still sharp in my nose. Three guys in nothing but gym shorts had grabbed me by the back of my neck screaming, "Faggot," and they hit my head against the wood with a cracking sound, over and over, like they were trying to loosen the meat inside of a nut before they whacked it open and left it split and picked clean and tossed away on the floor.

"Who did it?" Richie said when he saw me, and I told him I didn't know their names, which was true. They were just three guys, part of a crowd of boys who stalked me. I'd be crossing the hall from one class to the next, and they'd grab my hair from behind, twist me around, and smack me across the face, flat-handed, leaving no mark, running away. It happened every day. What was the point of getting their names? None of us wanted to know it occurred. When I ran into one of them later, we shared a hot glance, as if we'd had sex in secret. It was better than sex, and way worse: I had watched them get angry. That was the secret we shared. I was on intimate terms with everyone's rage.

Richie kept asking, "Who did this?" He wanted to beat the shit out of the guys who hassled me. Failing that, I think he wanted to slug *me*. Then he decided what do to.

"Listen," he's saying, problem solving, "none of this would've happened if you just knew how to shoot a ball. You never had anyone take the time to teach you to shoot. All those fucking gym teachers, did they ever teach you? No, they didn't. Did your dad? Did your brother? Did I?"

"Nobody did, I guess. No one had the patience. I'm pretty bad, Richie. I can't even really hold a ball. I mean, forget throwing it. Forget *aiming* it."

"But you don't have to aim. That's the beauty," Richie says. "I don't know why I never taught you this before. There's nothing to it," he says, handing me the basketball. "Show me how you hold it," he says. "You do it with your palms flat out in front of you, don't you? Now try to shoot."

"I know I'll miss."

"And I said it's no big deal," he tells me, not at all impatient. Thank God he doesn't care about my feelings. There's not going to be any pity.

So I shoot at the basket and miss. It doesn't help that I'm dressed in hip-hugging red corduroy bell-bottoms and a shirt with a wide collar and billowy cuffs. No wonder I drive my classmates crazy. They're not beating me, they're styling me.

Richie gets the ball and gives it to me again. "Now, check this out," he says. "There are only two rules, and they're simple: Don't hold the ball, and don't aim. Can you do those two things?"

"I guess so."

"Okay," I say.

"Okay," he confirms. Then getting down to business, he says, "You're a rightie? So the left hand goes against the ball, like you'd put your hand to the side of your head. It falls away as soon as you boost the ball into the air. The other hand sort of goes under and behind the ball. But not flat against it."

He makes a crib with his palm and fingers.

"You leave a space in here," he says, sliding his free hand into his palm, scooping it out. "You don't want it flat on the ball. Now make your elbow unbend, lifting the ball and raising it up. Don't hold on, don't aim," Richie is saying, "just shoot. It'll go in."

And it does, for the first time in my life.

Of course, I miss the next one. And the next. And then the next. This is the point where anybody but Richie would go insane, grab the ball, and shatter my skull. Guys can't stand to watch me screw up. "Yeah, I kicked him in the gut until he puked blood. What was I supposed to do? The guy missed three shots." I guess I can't blame them. After all, like me, they have grown up with men, competitive dads or older brothers who can't praise, or share, or forgive. I'm their irresistible chance to be the bully. Naturally, they want to take advantage of me. I am the world's little brother.

Richie's not into that. He takes a couple of shots while I cool out, and then he throws the ball back, and I shoot some more. "I'm not gonna tell you you're a great ballplayer," he says, "but I know you can make a couple of baskets." Which sounds fair. "I wasn't planning on being Walt Frazier," I tell him, and he says, "Get some in there," and I do. I sink, like, five shots. When he figures my arm is under control, he gets me to add my legs. Then we're passing the ball back and forth, and we're both shooting. We play for an hour, and about half my shots go in.

I guess that was the happiest day of my life. I don't want kindness, exactly, or salvation, but just a way to grasp things and how to throw them away, a mental trick: Don't hold, don't aim.

"A mind can blow those clouds away," George Harrison is singing in Richie's Flushing apartment. Richie is sitting next to me, nodding his head and saying, "Twenty-six years old. Harrison. He was fucking *twenty-six* years old when the Beatles split up. Can you imagine that? You're not even thirty, and you're already no longer a Beatle?"

He shakes his head. We're side by side, two guys with less hair than we ever thought we'd have, still wishing we were Beatles.

"Justin asked me if I had seen the Beatles play Shea Stadium," I say. "I told him that was 1965. I was *six*."

"Who's Justin?"

"Somebody."

"Somebody who?"

"Somebody for whom Paul McCartney is, like, the way we thought of Frank Sinatra. You know? Our parents' music. Richie, we're old."

"Oh, motherfucker, I knew that."

"Yeah, me too." I'm not happy that I mentioned Justin, but I have been wanting to talk about him all day. To keep myself from spilling my guts I focus on Richie's arms. They're knotted, not smooth, a worker's arms. Suddenly, I'm assigning magical powers to his biceps. If I could hold them, I think, I'd be safe, and I would never want to—something. I'd never want something.

"George Harrison got a bad rap," Richie is saying, still stuck on the Beatles. "He wrote 'Something.' That's a great song. And 'Here Comes the Sun.' Also great."

"In comparison, maybe."

"No comparison. In fact. And 'Taxman.' Tell me that song sucks. And 'The Inner Light.' "

" 'The Inner Light' was never released."

"Yes it was, it was the B side of 'Get Back.' "

" 'Don't Let Me Down' was the B side of 'Get Back.' And, I mean, is your goal in life to end up the B side? Because you hear 'George Harrison,' you think B side."

"No, you don't. You think, 'B side of Paul McCartney,' which is anyone else's A side. Anyway, fuck it," Richie says. "You look like shit. Gonna change?"

"If you have a clean shirt," I say, shrugging.

"I got plenty of shirts," Richie says. "The girlfriend's big on my having shirts."

So we go to his bedroom, where Richie unloads his closetful of shirts onto his unmade bed. "The whole enormous sadness of a shirt," Jack Kerouac says. Richie has bowling shirts with stitched monograms saying "Roger" and "Buck." There are polyester shirts in metallic colors. Stüssy shirts. Comme des Garçons. There are knockabout masculine Tom Sawyer summer shirts in bright patterns from the Gap and Oxford-cloth Brooks Brothers shirts in preppie colors—lemon yellow, dove gray, pink. He's got shirts with French cuffs, shirts that are 100 percent synthetic, sporty dress shirts from Donna Karan when you need something to model on casual Friday, and the grandest in the whole collection, a red and blue and green and yellow flower-print psychedelic party shirt by Dries Van Noten. It looks like what you'd get if you could wear a tab of acid.

"Yo, Rich," I say, holding it up in the air, my voice full of mock awe. "And you wear this . . . where?"

"Don't bust my chops," Richie says, embarrassed, laughing.

"This is not a shirt. This is a relationship."

"The girlfriend gets antsy, she likes to see me in something, you know, dashing."

It's the most spectacular shirt I have ever seen—not just outrageous, but manly. Racing colors, a jockey's shirt. Eddie Arcaro would wear it to run a horse across the finish line and win the Triple Crown.

"I'm calling it 'Strawberry Fields Forever.' "

"Go easy," Richie says.

"No, seriously," I say. "I'll wear it. Can I? It's perfect," I say, not listening for his grunted assent, holding the shirt against my chest and wondering if I'm solid enough to support, and not be consumed by, this shirt.

Because how much does a man have in his life? You can't invent the wheel. That's been done. Prometheus took care of fire. And women are better at everything else: plans and provisions, legal precedents, corporate accounts. Foreplay. Women connect. Men are selfish dreamers, in the john with their Walkmans spinning Radiohead and counting all the geniuses they can't become: Homer, Plato, Jesus, Gandhi, Lester Young, Malcolm X, Frank Purdue.

It all boils down to picking a band, rooting for a team, and buying shirts. That is what the evolution of expression has left for us. And because all bands now sound the same, and a ball club is just a holding pen for overpaid superstars who can reconstitute themselves tomorrow as ten other teams, well, then, you're left with your shirt. The color, the cut. The arm piece, the back, the overseam. Was it turned in a Queens sweatshop by Koreans or Malaysians, or hand sewn by young girls doing piecework in Mexican kitchens? Do you want it to be plain and simple, unremarkable as a coordinating conjunction, a modest sartorial "and" linking necktie to belt buckle? Or is it meant to be the main clause, carrying the hefty metaphor? And how do you wear it? Buttoned to the top but without a tie, under a black blazer? Open down the front over a T-shirt? And what kind of T-shirt? Plain white Fruit of the Loom? V-neck? Muscle T?

I want to be buttoned to the hilt and naked under Richie's carnival shirt, which, Richie says, cost his whole income tax refund for 1998. "That shirt was my summer vacation," he says. "It was my grad school tuition."

"You applied to grad school?"

"Not in that shirt," Richie says. He heads for the shower. "You might wanna give some thought to washing up yourself, when I'm through," he says, sniffing. He extracts a pair of shorts and knit socks from of a pile of clean laundry swaying at the foot of the bed and disappears into the bathroom.

Where Do You See Yourself?

I think that I know something about the American masculinity which most men of my generation do not know because they have not been menaced by it in the way I have been.

—James Baldwin

Gay men are supposed to be good snoops—Guy Burgess, Whittaker Chambers, J. Edgar Hoover—because they know how to hide things, I guess, but I never met a gay guy, including myself, who was able or allowed to keep a secret. One day I was showing Zack my childhood photographs, and a shot of Richie fell out of the shoebox and exposed my former life. I don't know how I ended up with that picture. It was snapped by Richie's dad, Officer McShane, at Yankee Stadium, long before I knew Richie: June 8, 1969, Mickey Mantle Day, when they retired Mickey's number.

The photo Richie's dad got, taken from the bleachers, is mostly of Richie: an eleven-year-old kid in the foreground, a T-ball player, very young and sweet and tough and proud in his blue and gray Ozone Park Little League uniform, blurred and reaching out to

Mickey, who is tiny in the corner of the frame, motorized and speeding away.

I inherited Richie from my brother. They were pals for a while, but my brother didn't smoke pot, which pretty much ruled out their being friends. My brother wasn't easily swayed. I was more adaptive, a necessary quality for anyone who wanted to be close to Richie. It was like bonding with Sonny Corleone in *The Godfather*. He demanded loyalty, he pledged his love, he wanted to share girls and wreck things and pass out drunk in his dad's car with his head in my lap while I drove him home—illegally.

I spent most of my sophomore year with Richie. To me, he was completely alien, by which I mean he was a guy. I kept waiting for Richie to figure out I was a sissy and fuck me up. He didn't. I was afraid of him, but also, I guess, I despised him a little, because he wasn't smart enough to see that my friendship would ruin his chances at school.

If I was slightly scared of Richie, I was even more intimidated by his dad, Officer McShane. Sometimes on Sundays, when we were high and his dad was drunk, we hung in the garage, where his dad taught us how to change the oil in his Maverick. He died in a car crash when Richie was twenty-two. In the meantime, he cheered the Yankees. He was a big fan of their worst years, in the late sixties when they fell thirty games back. Richie's dad loved the romance of failure. Stained with grease, standing in his garage, he reminisced about Mantle's downfall the same way my parents talked about dead Kennedys.

Fucking Mick, he called him, celebrating on old man in his thirties who showed up at the plate still drunk from the night before, saw three balls and swung anyway. Later, Mickey cried in his teammate Joe Pepitone's arms. Pepitone held him and said, "Mick, come on, man. Hey, idol." Mick quit baseball when he was thirty-eight, and in March of 1982 Officer McShane, age fifty-one, hit a phone pole on the Wantagh Expressway, snapped his spine, crushed his spleen, and died behind the wheel, his unhurt wife beside him in the car.

Richie's dad was in love with Mickey Mantle, and Rich and I were awed by Officer McShane. Tightly wired, lean and tense, he was a little guy, a lefty, only five foot six. He always seemed to be crouched or perching or pitched at an angle, as if about to launch himself—or, more likely, you—like a pinball shot from a spring, released to fend for itself and score what it could. If he put his arm around your neck, standing behind you, a beer grasped in his palm, you felt the cold bottle damp at your chest, his fist clenched over your heart. In his other hand a cigarette burned at the side of your neck. The hair on his forearms was blond and thick and bleached out of sight, vanishing and rooted, and so was he. Smoking Kents and pulling on a Rheingold, at the end of his life, he got stuck on two lines of "Rocky Raccoon," which he whistled endlessly, the only pop song he knew that wasn't swing or Sinatra: "His rival, it seems, had broken his dreams."

They were hurt bullies, the men of my childhood, the mythical men and the actual ones, fathers and sons, showing off their strength or crying in one another's arms. Either they were coming after you for missing a fly ball or they were on the ground howling because of a stubbed toe, surrounded by worried pals and bald-pink gym coaches.

Meanwhile, I was the sissy. Pushed against a locker and punched, I didn't cry or complain. My classmates held me steady while two guys grabbed the ends of my scarf and pulled it tight until I couldn't breathe. Maybe I should blame the scarf. It was macramé. An experimental scarf! My mother knotted it from wool, and it was red and blue and green and reached to my knees. Snagging it, my classmates wrapped it twice around my neck and choked me in the hall until the bell rang and they ran to class.

The first time I took a public beating I was eleven years old. I mean, I ran for president of the sixth grade, and lost. On Election Day, I'm wearing a seersucker suit. I've also got a crew cut, and my hair, which is blond, is standing up in a cowlick in front. Later today I have to make a campaign speech. It's November 1970. I'm outside my grade school, waiting for the morning bell. Kids are wearing light fall jackets and carrying lunch pails from Saturday cartoon shows, *Underdog, Fireball* XL5. The playground is behind us, ending in a cornfield, which has been stripped and laid flat, the dry stalks turning brown. We're standing in front of the doors that lead into the hallway beside the boys' gym. I smell earth and library paste and pencil shavings, and the bubble gum–flavored toothpaste scent of my classmates. On someone's transistor radio Paul McCartney is singing, "Get back to where you once belonged."

My running mate, Llori, is nearby with her girlfriends. She lives a mile away from me at the end of my road. We held hands—once—walking home together. The guy who is running against me, Brian Sturdivant, has peach fuzz on his upper lip, and he is hanging back with his buddies, kneading his baseball mitt. Brian always cheats off my tests, and I let him copy my English homework. I'm the class brain. I was president of the fourth grade, but I'm pretty sure I won't beat Brian. Still, I smile like a good sport when I notice that he and his pals are circling me. I back away onto the hard ground to make room. They form a tight circle in a patch of grass beside the school building, and I am grinning nervously and good-naturedly, expecting to be hassled about the election.

Then Brian speaks. He pushes me with his hands, palms flat, and says, "Sally." It sounds funny, but he's not kidding. "Hey, Sally," he repeats, and then somebody joins him. I'm waiting for it to turn into a joke, but it doesn't. Llori and her girlfriends stand around the edges of the circle. The boys chant, "Sal! Lee! Sal! Lee!" Brian shoves me again, hard, and I fall against another boy, who pushes me into a different part of the circle, and pretty soon I'm bouncing from boy to boy, like we're playing bumper pool and I'm the ball.

When they get tired of calling me "Sally" somebody adds "Fay," and then my sixth-grade class is laughing and calling me Sally Fay, like we're drag queens instead of eleven-year-olds.

I'm thinking, *There goes my election*. Still, it isn't clear I don't have a chance until one kid makes the leap from "Fay" to "fag," and they drop "Sally," and now I'm being spun around a circle and called a fag by a gang of boys, while the girls watch.

If I were a medievalist instead of a sixth grader, I might know that "fay" is from the Anglo-Saxon "faege," meaning fated to die soon. A "faggot" is a bundle of sticks thrown on a pyre to burn witches, and "faggoting" is a decorator's term for a cutting design. "Queer" is from "thwerh," meaning twisted, and "thverr," to thwart. So I'm twisted, thwarted, and thwarting, fairylike but fateful, not just silly but lethal, not just deadly but fated to die, kindling for fire, powerful and burning, but also invisible, fine as delicate threads pulled tight around lace. And I am the star. Flying around the circle, surrounded and alone, I'm rejected and central, and here is the beginning of a lifelong mix-up: I can't tell the difference between attention and pain.

Who needs to pay a dominatrix? I inspire abuse. It's confusing. People can't resist me. I mean, I have plenty of friends. I'm not an outcast. Still, everyone seems to know this secret about me. It's an open secret, and they keep repeating it, over and over. When will I get it? I won't mention dodgeball. In high school, they sing it. My big rural New Jersey public high school. I'm in choir class. It's my sophomore year, 1974, and I'm fifteen. We're practicing "The Hallelujah Chorus" when our choir director, Mr. Brendan, raises his hands high and says, "Hold everything." Then he looks at me and says, "You know, you walk like a girl."

It's so unexpected that everybody laughs.

"I'm serious," he says, shushing us. He waits until we're quiet. "Everyone knows it," he says, circling his hand wide to include the whole room. "Somebody get up," he says, "and show him how he walks."

For a minute, no one moves. We're not sure he means it. Then a few guys raise their hands. Mr. Brendan picks Joey Fontana, the school nerd. Joey still wears his hair big in front and slicked back in a duck's ass. If it were six years from now, he'd be Andy Kaufman, and he'd have a sitcom. Irony hasn't happened yet to Clinton, New Jersey, however, and Joey springs to his feet and does me. He goes to the front of the choir room and strikes a pose. His arms are chest high at his sides and his wrists go limp, and then he walks forward a few paces, wildly swinging his hips.

"That's how girls do it," he says, when Mr. Brendan stops him.

"Isn't it more like this?" Mr. Brendan says. "He walks like this," he says, and then he moves big-hippily across the floor, dangling his arms.

My classmates, feeling bold, yell suggestions.

"It's more like he waddles," one of them says.

"And he holds his hands really high."

"Do his laugh," somebody says, and everyone giggles.

Mr. Brendan stops in front of me. I'm in the first row. "You're not Mae West," he tells me, putting his hands on his hips and swishing them from side to side. Then he gets me to go to the front of the room. "Come on," he says. "Walk for us."

I'm wearing a long coat. I never take it off. My blond hair is shoulder length. I'm in elephant bells and a gauzy blue shirt with big black circles printed across it. I think I'm a Carnaby Street groovy. Plus, I've got my brother's old shoes, which are too big, and they flap while my bell-bottoms rustle. I know I've been asking for trouble. In any case, I walk. I start, and Mr. Brendan says, "Tell him how he looks."

We're doing *West Side Story* for the spring musical—Mr. Brendan is directing—and I would like to play Tony, even though I'm not Polish or a tenor. So I think of this as kind of an audition.

"Maybe if you didn't let your thighs touch," somebody says.

"It's your elbows, man," someone else says.

"You shouldn't let your mom put a bowl on your head when she cuts your hair," a guy says, and we all laugh.

"Okay, shush, people," Mr. Brendan says, wrapping his arm around my shoulders, as if we were pals. We're having an intimate moment. He looks me in the face—he's handsome—and says, "I know you need this." He speaks softly but his voice is resonant and it carries, and we are sharing our heart-to-heart with everyone else. "Stand here," he says, stepping away from me, letting me go. "This is how a man does it," he tells me, and he starts walking. "Follow me," he says. "Do what I do." Then we go up the side of the tiered classroom, behind the sopranos, and back down. He walks slowly, so I can see. We go around and around the room, while my classmates shout advice.

A few days later Mr. Brendan hooks up with some other teachers and they devise a whole new course schedule meant to turn me into a man. I see the speech therapist. Apparently I lisp. I visit the school psychologist, who wants to talk about my mom. I get pulled from gym class and sent to weight training, where I have to work out with the football team.

Miss Reed is the speech therapist. She has a textbook filled with illustrations. She turns it to me and points at pictures.

"What's that?" she says.

I say, "Snake."

"Tongue behind your teeth," she says, wiggling her tongue across her parted lips and drawing it back to the roof of her mouth. I do the same. We're darting our tongues at each other. Then she points at the next picture.

"Sandwich," I say.

"Good," she says, although I can't hear the difference. "What kind of sandwich?" she says. "Isn't there meat in that sandwich?"

"I'm a vegetarian."

She frowns.

I say, "Salami."

"Good," she says. "Now," she says, pointing at another drawing.

"The snake is on the salami sandwich," I say.

The school psychologist is an undergraduate from Trenton State College. He has love beads and a beard and I think I'm his senior project. His name is Barlow, and he's into transactional therapy, which means I spend our sessions shifting between two different chairs and having a talk with myself. In one chair I'm the Good Boy. In the other I'm the Dog Boy.

Barlow has a clipboard, and he tugs at his ponytail and takes notes.

"How do you feel about your mother?" he says.

"I should answer as the Good Boy?"

He nods. "You're the Good Boy."

"My mom's okay."

He writes that down.

"What would Dog Boy say?" he asks. "Be the Dog Boy," he tells me, pointing at the other chair. My education in being a man would make a pretty good porn film. Tough guys stand over me in the weight room and say, "Push it." Older men want me as their dog. Women wiggle their tongues. I do what they say, though, because I would like to seem like a man.

I certainly don't want to be gay, because gay men wear diapers. That's what Mr. Apgar tells us in boys' health class. "Homosexuals," he says, stretching the word over many syllables, "are men who, because of the abnormal sexual sensitivity of their anus, like to put stuff in their rectum. Which is why they can't control their excrementary functions. They've got the constant runs from taking it up the booty," he says, dropping his pose, talking man-to-man. Everyone in the room is staring at me.

I'm horrified. Something in my rectum? Is he kidding? I know I walk funny. I know I'm probably a girl. It has not occurred to me, however, that I might also be a homosexual. Well, I don't have posters of Bobby Sherman in my locker. I don't like Paul Lynde.

Sure, I think about sex all the time, but it doesn't involve other people. That would be way too risky. So it's kind of a crisis when I realize, no matter how I square my hips, that I'm in love with Richie.

You might wonder how I deal with that, and the answer is: marijuana.

Thanks to Richie I spend a whole year high and drifting out of my body. I am nowhere near me. When I'm stoned, our bodies aren't involved. We merge without touching. Pot makes that happen. It's Catholic, not homosexual. We leave our earthly incarnations and our souls mingle in the fly space above our heads.

The first time Richie and I get high together, it's Thanksgiving. He comes over to my house in his dad's car. My parents live on a narrow twisting road off the County Highway. We have horses and dogs. My dad works in the city and my mom raises borzois, giant skinny hounds with long stretched-out bodies and delicate snouts. They're not threatening; they're silly. When Richie pulls into the drive, Buster, my favorite, follows me outside to look. His cold nose is against my wrist. I'm in my socks and I push open the front door and stand in the fieldstone entryway, seeing Richie.

"Go inside," I tell Buster, pushing him through the door and closing it behind me. "Don't let them drive on the lawn," I hear my mother yelling, and I walk off the porch, crossing my arms over my chest and shouting, "Richie?"

Richie's engine is loud and he can't hear me. I can hardly see him through his fogged window. Fumes spill out of his tailpipe. Intsead of going back inside for gloves and shoes, I run to the passenger door, barely touching the ground. I try not to feel the sting of cold metal as I grab the door handle. It's locked. Richie leans over and opens it while I stand on the outsides of my feet. When I swing into the seat beside him, slamming the door, he's jamming his cigarette butt into the ashtray.

"Look," I say, "I can't ask you in. We're just sitting down to eat. And my mom's having, like, a conniption."

He shrugs and says, "Check this out."

He slips an eight-track into his tape machine, turning it up loud. We're listening to John Lennon's new album, *Rock and Roll,* the one Lennon cut when he was running around Los Angeles with Harry Nilsson balling groupies and hiding from Yoko. There is John's voice, mixed way low behind fuzzy guitars, singing, "But you can't catch me."

"Can you turn that down?" I say.

He does. He looks scruffy and cute. He's got brown hair in a shag cut and bushy sideburns that are dark red, not brown. I'm a dog boy; I'm drawn to fur.

"Bad dog," Richie says, pointing to the house, where Buster has pressed his face to the window of the front door.

"That's Buster," I say, and Richie laughs. He smells like Ivory soap and Winston cigarettes, and behind his zipped parka is the flat of his chest. Looking at him I'm thinking I can never trust my body, when Richie says, "Wanna take a ride?"

"I don't have any shoes," I say, which is one of those true things that, when you say it, sounds invented. "Anyway, I'm supposed to be inside," I tell him, glancing at the front door, expecting my mother there any minute. All I see is Buster. He's at the door like a little kid told to stand lookout, except that instead of guarding you he gives you away. "It's Thanksgiving," I remind Richie.

"Pffft," Richie says. He punches the cigarette lighter and reaches in his parka for another smoke, which he holds in his lips while he waits for the lighter to pop. His parka makes a slippery sound as it rubs against itself.

"People are kind of dressed up. It's a holiday."

"No hassle," he says. He gets impatient waiting for the lighter, and he pulls it out of the dashboard just before it clicks. The metal coils glow red. Richie puffs on his cigarette three times, sparking it up and leaving a flake of tobacco burning in the coils, which fade from red to blue to gray as they cool.

"You smoke?" he says.

"Sure I do. You know that. I swipe my mom's. Listen, if we're gonna talk, do you think you can turn off the car?"

"Your mom smokes?"

"I usually grab a few of her cigarettes on my way to school."

Richie laughs, jamming the lighter back in place. He reaches into another pocket and pulls out a plastic baggie full of pot. "You smoke *weed,* is what I meant."

"Oh," I say, looking at the wrinkled plastic tube rolled around dried leaves with brittle stems and tiny seeds. "I get high, sure," I say, turning again to check the front door. Nobody's there. Even Buster is gone. "You really have to kill the engine," I say.

"It'll get cold," he says, turning the key, stopping the engine but not the tape player. The car dies down with a sound of *huffhuffhuff.* Now we're sitting quietly with John Lennon and a bag of dope. I've gotten high exactly twice before. It didn't seem like any big deal. Getting stoned with Richie is going to be different, though, and I'm not sure I want to do it in my parents' driveway on Thanksgiving.

"Really, if it were up to me, I'd ask you in," I repeat.

"Right. Your mom hates me. She thinks I'm a guido."

"Richie," I say. "You're Irish."

"Guido comes in Irish. Anyway, my mom's Italian. Don't worry," he says. "We'll sit here a couple of minutes and get high. Then when you go back to your holiday meal, you'll have a real appetite for pumpkin pie."

He's looking at me, sarcastic and hopeful. His blue eyes are shiny as armor. I shrug nervously and say, "Okay."

He takes his time, reaching into the backseat, which is littered with a pizza box, beer bottles, and a Yankees program from 1972, which he grabs. He opens it on his lap to a photograph of Bobby Murcer. Then he spills the contents of his plastic bag onto Murcer's face. "Hold this," he says, giving me his cigarette. "This is Mexican," he says, picking through leaves, "but it's mostly buds. I'm not saying it's Colombian. But it isn't homegrown. You'll get a nice buzz."

He's into the ritual of dope: sifting, separating stems and seeds, feeling the crumbly dryness of the leaves. Concentrating, he draws a thin sheet of EZ Wider out of its packet, the paper crinkly white and slightly transparent. Then he licks the gummy strip and pastes two sheets together. I watch him crease his rolling paper and fill the fold with crumbled buds. Then he rolls the joint and licks it, sealing it, puts it in his mouth and slides it out over his lips. He grabs his cigarette back and lights the joint off his butt, draws, pulls in smoke, holds his breath, and passes the stick to me.

The car is cold but warm with our breath. There's the crackling sound of burning leaves and paper. Richie and I are silent, passing the joint back and forth. "Do yuh," Lennon sings, "do yuh do yuh do yuh wanna dance?"

I notice how Richie's neck tightens when he inhales. He looks taut and sleepy, distant but so close I have to glance away. Buster is back in the window. *There's the dog,* I think, *and here's the boy,* or maybe I say it out loud. In any case, I'm laughing.

"What's so funny?" Richie asks, though he's laughing, too. Then he takes the joint away from me. We're giggling so hard we forget to keep getting high, and as the joint burns out, Richie realizes he's lost something.

"Where's my bag of dope?" he says.

I'm still laughing.

"What is so motherfucking funny?" he says, patting his coat, touching the dashboard, leaning over me to look in the glove compartment.

"I can't tell you. It's too embarrassing."

"You've got your socks on," he says.

That sets us off, and we're ten-year-olds hearing a fart joke. Richie falls across my legs howling, and I have to help push him up straight. Richie says, "I lost my shit," meaning he can't find his pot, but of course I'm thinking of Mr. Apgar and health class and diapered homosexuals.

Then I say, very clearly, "I'm the Dog Boy."

That's when my mom shows up at the front door, holding Buster by the collar, yelling my name. So I have to repeat myself. I don't want to, but the words are already formed, and in that stoned way I can't stop myself from getting involved in what already seems to have happened. I watch the words fall from my mouth.

"I am the Dog Boy."

"What the fuck?" Richie says.

"I went to the school psychologist," I say, trying not to lisp, "and he told me I was a dog boy."

My mom's still standing on the porch, yelling. What's more, she has released Buster, and he's outside, his tail thumping against the car.

"You went to a shrink?" Richie says. "Why?"

"Because I walk funny."

"That's bullshit," he says, and then he says, "Found it," producing the bag of pot. "You better go back inside," he says.

"It's true, Richie. I walk funny."

"Shut the fuck up," he says.

I'm waiting for him to add something, like, "Fuck yourself, faggot." Instead, he says, "Wait." He's searching his pockets. I'm clutching the door handle, ready to bail out in case he tries to slug me. Then he finds what he wants. "Take one of these," he says, holding out a roll of Life Savers. "Your mom's still checking us out. She hates me."

"Yeah," I admit.

"Go on," he says.

"I can't open my door," I tell him, "because the smoke'll spill in her face."

"Lemme open my side first," he says. He pushes his door open with a sound like *creek-reek-reek,* and Buster runs around and puts his big paws in Richie's lap. Richie says, "I'd pet him but I'm allergic."

"Buster," I yell, leaning over Richie and pushing at the dog's head.

"Actual dog, conceptual dog," Richie says, pointing from Buster to me. He hammers me on the arm. "You're nothing like a dog," he says. "I guess that's the point, huh? Dogboy," he says, turning it into one word. "Back to your pound."

After that, Dogboy becomes my nickname. It's better than faggot, and Richie and I are the only ones who use it. I love the scorching sound of his voice when he's razzing me and calling me Dogboy while we do drugs, listening to prog rock in his dad's car, Greg Lake singing, "Oh, what a lucky man he was." At school we get stoned between classes. Because Richie runs the light board for school plays and choir concerts, he knows about the catwalk in the rafters above the stage. There's a hatch opening onto the roof, and we throw it open and stare at the sky, watching our marijuana and tobacco smoke mingle together and curl into the air. When I go back to the world below, it feels remote. People still call me faggot, but I'm gliding, and the high school is Strawberry Fields.

At home I sit up late nights in the mudroom with Buster, smoking my mom's Benson and Hedges cigarettes and reading novels by Scott Fitzgerald, *This Side of Paradise* and *The Beautiful and Damned.* I'm in love with Scott and Richie at the same time, conceptual and actual loves. Like Scott, I have a profile; like him, I'm notorious and pretty. I stare at his photographs in a biography: Scott looks girlishly pretty at age fifteen, and tragically pretty in his army uniform, and snobbishly pretty publishing his first novel at the age of twenty-three. Like me, he has a deviant body part—not his hips, but his mouth. It's "a delicate long-lipped Irish mouth," Ernest Hemingway says. "It worried you until you got to know him, and then it worried you more."

Scott has dainty features, Hemingway says, and a prose style fey "as the pattern that was made by the dust on a butterfly's wings." Clearly he's part fairy. His "fair wavy hair" is buzzed short around his "good ears." I wonder if my ears are good. Scratching Buster's ears, which are furry and long, with cool undersides and silky tufts, I'm sorry I don't live in the twenties age of Arrow Collar ads, when men were fops and you could be pretty as Scott and cross a room without anyone but Ernest Hemingway calling you fey.

I'm dressed like Fitzgerald on a morning in June when Richie comes by my house to drive me to school. It's the day we are performing the sophomore class play for the freshmen. I'm starring, and Richie is running the lights. I have modeled my character on Scott, and I am wearing my costume: white flannel trousers and a shirt of pale rose and cobalt blue. Plus, argyle socks. Last night I dusted my white bucks with talcum powder while Buster sneezed.

Leaning over from the driver's seat Richie pushes open the passenger door, barely waiting for me to jump in before he guns the motor and takes off. With his right hand, he holds out a Granny Smith apple.

"You going to the prom?" he asks, handing me the apple. "In 1926?" My hair's cut and greased down, parted in the middle, and Richie runs his hand up the back of my head, and says, "Dogboy got shaved."

Richie's windows are open, and the wind blows through the front seat as we head down my road. The air is scented with sweet fern and undergrowth, but it can't overcome the smell of Richie's car. His dad's Maverick reeks of cigarettes and air spray from all of our efforts to mask the odor of pot. Nothing helps. The car is permanently funky, and you can get a contact high by pressing your nose against the seat backs. I wonder if Richie's dad recognizes the stench. Does he think it's dried sweat? Peat moss? If you set the Jersey woods on fire, torched the low hills of pine trees and mossy rock, the fumes would smell like Richie's car.

"Your car smells like burning Jersey," I tell him, juggling the apple. Actually, it's a pipe. Richie's gimmick: biodegradable paraphernalia, cheap and quick. You carve an L through the core, cover the apple in aluminum foil, and make a hollow for the bowl. Then you load the dope, press the mouthpiece to your lips, hold a lighter over the bowl, and suck the knowledge of good and evil through the forbidden fruit.

Richie is steering with one hand—actually, one finger—and hanging his free arm out the window, pressing his palm against the breeze as he jets down the road, turning onto County Highway 513.

"Got a surprise for us today," he says, reaching into the pocket of his T-shirt and pulling out a tiny square of hash wrapped in aluminum foil.

"I don't want to be high for the play," I tell him.

"It's not until two," he says. "No hassle. We'll both come down in time."

"I don't know," I say warily.

I don't like hash. It's a doughy high, it leaves me feeling bloated and dumb.

"Put out your palm," he says, unwrapping the hash, which he drops into my hand. "Let's light up."

"I don't think I need any drugs today. Nervous stomach."

"That's what hash was made for, man," Richie says. He lets go of the steering wheel long enough to grasp the back of my neck in a rough-palmed squeeze. "Let's get high," he says.

So I crumble the hash into the bowl of the apple and light up, ducking below the dashboard to shield myself from the wind. It never occurs to us to roll up the windows. I take just one toke, which tastes of tart apple. One hit isn't enough to get me high, and it's not enough to calm me down, either. I'm still tense as we pull up to the school building.

"Break their legs, or, you know, whatever," Richie says, letting me out. I've still got the apple, which I chuck in the garbage near the school entrance. Richie disappears, and I close my eyes and walk through the front doors.

When I open my eyes the lights come up and I'm onstage.

The play is a one-act called *Impromptu*, about four actors without scripts who are ordered by an unseen stage manager to do something "real." They spend the whole time deciding what that means. "It's not supposed to be an imitation *of* life," I get to say. "It's supposed to *be* life." My character is anguished and articulate. At one point I have to walk out onto the apron, stare at the audience, and say, "Who are you? What do you want of me?"

The other actors are three of my friends, two girls and a guy. The director is my freshman-year lab partner from biology class—we dissected inchworms together. During rehearsals we sat on the stage in hard-backed chairs and urged each other to "go inside." At one rehearsal I was alone onstage and my friends asked me hard questions about my feelings, and when I got depressed, everyone was glad.

Still, I'm nervous performing at an assembly to which the director invited not just her mother, but my mother, and our drama coach. The audience is seven hundred freshmen ages fourteen and fifteen. While I'm standing in the dark waiting for our first cue, I can hear guys in the first two rows making rude noises and snapping bubblegum.

Then the play starts, and I spot my mother against the back wall under the Exit light. She's friends with the drama teacher, and they're standing together. The director's mother is sitting in the back row near the big double doors that lead to the lobby where they keep sports trophies in glass cases. There's a pause for breath, a beat just long enough for us to hear the buzz of lights. Then we begin.

As soon as I speak my first lines, though, I'm drowned out by a kid in the front row who opens his mouth and says:

"Shut up, faggot."

The guy's words are followed by a hollowed-out pocket of silence, and then another kid says, "You fag."

Then a guy stands up. Like he's just looking for information, he says, "How did you find out you're gay?"

There's a long laugh from the auditorium. After that, everybody goes nuts.

"Queer bait," they yell. "Gay boy."

I wonder if my drama coach will stop us. Maybe Richie will shut down the lights. My friends onstage look trapped but they keep going with their lines, even though it's hard for us to hear what we're saying. The noise spreads from the first row all the way to the back, reaching my teacher and my mom. The guys in the front are now standing. The kids behind them are yelling, and the ones who aren't shouting are laughing. It's like overlapping dialogue in a Robert Altman movie, you can hear so many people at once.

Then it's time for me to cross downstage and ask them what they want of me. I'm a fool to think I could stand alone on the apron of the auditorium stage and make a plea for support. I should have seen that. Still, I've got no choice—no one's stopping the play. The adults in the back are quiet. The lights are still on. My friends in the cast are acting as if nothing is wrong.

So I walk out onto the apron, and say, "Who are you? What do you want of me?"

There follows a silence different from the one at the beginning of the play. We've crossed the line from art into life and for a second everybody in the room is savoring the transition. A real moment is taking place in somebody's actual life in the guise of a performance about people searching for real moments in their actual lives. The levels of irony are too complex, and years from now I'll still be deconstructing them. At the moment, though, my main concern is my body, or rather, getting out of it. I want escape, to be outside myself. I don't mean by getting high on sex or drugs or God. It's not transcendence I want but expedience, like when you're about to be in a car crash and the smart thing is not to be there when it happens.

So I get myself out of range, until I'm swinging from the arc lights in the space above my head at the moment of impact. Looking down I can see myself mounted on the stage, arms wide, neck bared, face lit. *Any moment now,* I'm thinking, *Richie will throw the dimmer switch and blacken the house, rescuing me.* But he lets me dangle.

I'm thinking, *There's my gay body*. It's my first postmodern moment. My classmates aren't just hectoring me, they're turning me post-structuralist, theoretical—French! I'm a "body" caught in a "contact zone," the "site" where seven hundred fourteen- and fifteen-year-olds discover their power. I'm the symbol of their strength, a skinny, doughy white boy, sixteen years old, dressed for a high school play, wearing greasepaint and powder, eye shadow, eyeliner, lip liner, and rouge, straining and hot under the stage lights, bent forward, trying to please. And they're yelling, "We want you to die, faggot."

I'm thinking, *Aren't they tacky?* Instead of fighting back, I'm critiquing them. Maybe that's what gay means: "Critic." My body is a text. I read it in the aqueous light of public display.

I watch my gay body float.

But it isn't my body. I mean, it isn't *only* my body, it's also Zack's body, exposed and naked in the bathroom light, skimming the surface of the bathwater like a spindly-legged water bug, eighteen years from now, two weeks from death.

I ring his doorbell and Marie, his home health care attendant, lets me in. She leads me to his bedroom, where Zack is on his bed in diapers and oversized eyeglasses. Otherwise, he's naked, except for a strip of gauze taped over the Hickman catheter spliced into an artery in his chest. It hardly matters that I lost his underwear in a taxi cab. He hasn't worn anything but diapers in his home since he came back from the hospital two weeks ago. Suddenly, I'm grateful for his diarrhea. Without it, I'd have to tell Zack that his underclothes are spinning through New York in the backseat of a yellow cab.

His olive skin is now blanched and hangs on his skeleton like a sheet tossed over a corpse. I'm immobilized by his skull. He can see my terror, and he feels framed by it. I had always thought we were the same person. I had figured we would die together, that I could roll him up next to my heart and he would leave his body and stay with me, stay *as* me.

But I was wrong. Inside/outside: It's hard to maintain the

conceit of merging with someone you love when his head is a fright-movie prop. He opens his mouth to speak and I want to scream. I'm afraid there will be nothing past his teeth, no soft palate, hard palate, cartilage, and membrane. Just air and Zack's rage.

And his voice, which is eerily linked to a mind still scathingly intact.

He says, "I cut my hair."

It's true, though to call it a haircut is to display a romantic readiness for hope. His bed is strewn with his hair. The electric clippers, still vibrating, are on the bedside table. Zack is grinning defiantly.

"Did Marie help you with this?" I ask.

"I *did* it my*self*," he says, with hysterical glee. "How do I look?"

"Like you just swam the English Channel," I want to say, which is a line from *All About Eve*. Even my private emotional life is staged for laughs. Why am I always Bette Davis in a crisis? "I'd love to kiss you, but you just cut your hair," I'm thinking, paraphrasing her line from *Cabin in the Cotton,* a movie I saw with Zack at the Film Forum. That was when he was farting uncontrollably, a two-month phase. I was never sure it wasn't on purpose. A day after it finally stopped, he got diarrhea.

"What do you think about my haircut?" he asks again.

"Zack," I say, trying to be sincere, "I wish I could figure out what I'm feeling."

"What?" he says. "You want to know what you're *feeling*? Again?"

"I know it's corny."

"*Have* your *feelings*? Are you out of your mind? What the hell would you want to do that for? There has been some small progress since we were apes! *Have your feelings*, for God's sake."

"Oprah recommends them," I say, in a small voice.

"I *cut* my *hair*," he says again. "I want to know how it looks."

"It looks fine. Maybe a little uneven."

"You are such a fucking liar. Uneven? A *little* uneven?"

"Do you want the truth?"

"I'm asking for the answer."

"All right," I say, sighing. "You look like hell."

Now he is really pleased.

"It does look bad, doesn't it? I knew I could trust you for *something*. I did the best I could. You'll have to finish. Tidy me up."

"Zack, I don't know anything about cutting hair."

"You don't know anything about saving my life, either, but that doesn't stop you from sitting by the side of my bed day after day with that pathetic look of deep and oceanic human concern on your face, does it?"

"Okay, fine," I say, surrendering.

"I'm going to *die* because you can't end the AIDS crisis. The *least* you can do is cut my hair."

"I said okay, Zack. I'll do it."

"Bring the clippers," he says, and then he screams for Marie, who helps him into the bathroom while I follow with the equipment.

Zack's bathroom is a disco palace. It's the main attraction of his new apartment, a one-bedroom in Chelsea, which he bought a year ago, shortly before he started getting sick. The john is vast and commodious, split-level and entirely tiled, with a sunken tub, a sauna, recessed lights, music piped through invisible speakers, makeup mirrors swiveling from flexible arms, an art deco sink with heavy porcelain toggles marked *HEISS* and *KALT*, and a silently flushing commode as streamlined as an aeronautic module designed for weightless life on the moon.

Zack flips up the lid of the toilet, un-Velcros his diapers, drops them on the floor, sits down, and takes a dump. He never stops talking, spurting watery shit and draining the last of his worked-over gym body through old plumbing into the nineteenth-century septic system aqueducts that empty past slave graveyards and the Dutch and Iroquois underground of the ancient Isle of Manahatta, into the thick silt bed of New York Bay.

"Plug in the clippers," he says, pointing to a socket. "The bottom outlet."

"Does it matter?"

"I said the bottom one, goddammit."

"Okay."

"Okay," Zack mimics, rolling out toilet paper and wiping himself. Then he hands me a wad of tissue and says, "Wipe the bowl. You see the toilet paper. Wipe the outside of the bowl. Please."

He weighs ninety-five pounds. I can't imagine what I'll be demanding when I'm like him. I wipe the bowl and take the tissue and the diaper to the living room, where I toss them into the bin for medical waste. When I get back to the bathroom Zack's got the top of the toilet seat down, and he's sitting on it, with his legs crossed.

"I want a shag cut like Jane Fonda in *Klute,*" he tells me.

"Sure," I say. There's not much I can do except shave the rest of what's left of his hair, AIDS hair gone lifeless and pin straight. I stand in front of Zack, holding the electric clippers, with the wire hanging like a noose under his neck. "I'll do what I can."

I put my palm flat on his head. I feel his bone. The front of his head is sheared clean, but there are tufts of hair in back. With the clippers in my right hand I razor off his hair. I don't want to hurt him, pinch skin, pull tight. He has hiked his genitals in order to cross his legs, and when I look down I see the bones of his legs, his right foot swinging, the sag of flesh from his thighs, the sack of his balls, his penis, the pubic hair as limp as the hair on his head, his belly sunk, skin stretched over a void, rib cage, his nipples clipped to his chest like buttons sewn onto a coat, the gauze bandage guarding the catheter near his right armpit, his long arms of nothing but bone, his sinewy neck, his shoulder plates in back and spinal nubs that poke through skin. My friend.

"I'm finished," I tell him, when I have shaved the last strand of hair, and he looks up and says, "Run me a bath."

While the tub is filling he checks his head in one of his mirrors.

"I look like Telly Savalas crossed with a Holocaust Jew," he says.

I'm testing the water, putting my hand in to my wrist. When the bath is full Zack stands up and walks slowly to the tub, and I help him in.

"I can't get my catheter wet," he says, touching his gauze.

Then he slides into the tub.

He weighs less than the water.

He's floating, limbs and all spread out. It's like a Robert Longo painting where men in business suits are splayed and off center, arms and legs akimbo. But Zack's not dressed, he's stripped to the bone, no hair on his head, penis floating, elbows, heels, knees, wherever the bones join is where the most water is displaced, and there are lucent circles swelling around the joints and balls of his ankles and the outflung wings of his hips. He closes his eyes. The gauze pad gets wet and drifts loose, and I want to press it back in place, but I don't.

Instead, I watch his gay body float.

Already Gone

His wanting will be haunted by a dread of being what he wants, so that his wanting will also always be a kind of dread.

—Judith Butler

Then I went to Queens College and fell in love with my students. I teach creative writing, and I walk into my classroom, searching for types. Good thing I'm surrounded by New Yorkers—there are enough characters in one of my classes to fill a Dickens novel. Still, they don't believe they're special. My job is to make them self-conscious. I want to challenge their longing for an unbroken world and peel them away from their parents. Most of them still live at home, and they sit in my room, squeezing into gum-tufted blue plastic desk chairs, hating their dads, and waiting to be convinced they exist. My students feel jilted by the world, which is to say, in particular, by their dads. Queens is the land of missing fathers. I guess that doesn't make it unique. Like me, like Zack, like all the women I know, and, it turns out, like most of the men, my students have never met a man—a buddy or big brother or gym coach or boss—who didn't eventually make them feel like a worthless piece of shit. In that way, homosexuals are just like everyone else. America is a place where everybody has a bad relationship with a man.

I'm trying to be the first nice American man. It's a tricky job, because I'm the gay professor. I'm in Queens, in the middle of the most ethnically diverse county in America, and my students tell me I am the only homosexual they have ever met. Sure, everybody has a gay uncle, but he leaves his lover home when he shows up for weddings and funerals. My students have all had a gay grade school teacher or a girls' gym coach, or they have been taught by priests and lectured by nuns, or they have seen *Cats*, or served in the military, or held hands with Pluto at Disney World—they have had contact with representatives from all the gay professions, in other words: education, entertainment, religion, and the Marines. Yet I am their first homosexual.

Some of them are homosexuals themselves, part-time, or on occasion. A few of the guys in my classes have gotten high on Ecstasy and kissed one another on the mouth at raves and dance clubs on Long Island, or they have jerked off with their straight pals in parked cars and graveyards, drunk on beer, still clutching their forties. Lots of the women have staged a lesbian kiss to turn on their boyfriends, or they have messed around secretly with their best girlfriends in somebody's bedroom at a house party in Woodhaven. Religious Jews, Mets fans, and married guys go to a porno movie theater in East Elmhurst, near LaGuardia Airport, where they hook up with men who have stepped away from a family dinner. And my students all know about Larry's Lane in Forest Park, where dudes hang out on Saturday nights, cruising each other.

Of course, some people are "obviously" gay, and my students have all mocked the high school kid who minces or lisps or wears her hair really short or likes field hockey too much. Some have gone into the West Village and roughed up a bunch of fags. Gore Vidal says that "homosexual" is an adjective, not a noun, and that it describes an act rather than naming a person, but it seems to me that "homosexual" is in fact a verb: It is in the way you stand or sit, or wave your arms around, something your body does, a motion you make. My students stay away from people who seem too "homosexual," and they assume everyone else is straight.

If I have too much information about their sex lives, it's because I teach creative writing, and twenty-two-year-olds take creative writing courses in order to write about two things: suicide and sex. I'm the guru of repressed desire. I am also a dude magnet. Straight guys can't resist me. Who knows better than a former high school faggot how scary it is to be a man? I've been trashed by straight guys and snubbed by men in gay bars, and I know the need to vanish from the room even as you appear to be filling it.

So I hold court for wounded straight guys. Dressed half homo, half hip-hop, in Kangol hats and droopy pants, with trimmed goatees and multiple earrings, they strut their Afro-Ameri-queer culture. Some of them are as skittish as small animals at the road's edge hurrying into the underbrush. They wait for me on the bench outside my office, reading poetry. Allen Ginsberg is a favorite—fuming Ginsberg, not cocksucker Ginsberg; "America, I've given you all and now I'm nothing," not, "Neal Cassady was my animal." Another hero is Vladimir Mayakovsky. "I shall rage on raw meat," my students read, probably missing the lines that suit them better: "I shall grow irreproachably tender:/not a man, but a cloud in trousers!"

They know they can't be tender and stay men. So they're brutally absent, or else ironically present, attitudes I understand, and practice.

Like me, they are in love with failure. It isn't black-and-white small screen 1950s TV failure, like something Paddy Chayevsky wrote for *Playhouse 90*. Ours, instead, is hectic, high-speed catastrophe and loss, comprised of many moods and driven by late-night monologues and quick runs in borrowed cars to the country or the city or the beach. Bringing home a wad of cash on Sunday night from restaurant jobs in Manhasset, my students blow it by Tuesday at a casino in A.C. "Ruin me, ruin me, ruin me," is what they shout despairingly into the night, not, "Fight AIDS, not Islam."

They're outsiders, not pariahs. Their irony is different from mine. The defining crisis for them is their disbelief in other people, while mine is disbelief in myself. Straight guys are conspiracy theorists, wrecked by the knowledge that they can't control the world. Yet I learned early on that I can't control, well, me. I yearn for guys. I am what I want. Straight people aren't asked to justify their yearning. They don't have to boil themselves down to an impulse or an act. Unlike me, they think: I am *because* I want.

Of course, I have to be cool when I get pulled aside once or twice a semester by a guy who clears his throat, drops his voice, and says, "Professor, are you gay?"

My student Kenny is a mute pal, the original silent buddy. He's Irish and Jewish and his knit cap never comes off. I rarely see the top of his head or hear him use a transitive verb. He starts every sentence with "I" and fades to "whatever." "I, sorry, sorry, man, whatever . . ."

He's in a Queens band, Merchants of Chaos. He wrote their big hit, "Whitestoned," which was in heavy rotation in the Buzz Bin on MTV. The band split up right before they signed with a major label, though, and Kenny went back to school. I found out about his recording career because he gave me a copy of his CD instead of homework. It's called *Cross Island*, and it opens with Kenny's song "Bad Clams in Oyster Bay": "Hurl motherfucker, hurl motherfucker/Bad clams in Oyster Bay, bad clams in Oyster Bay."

When Kenny offers me a ride home one night after class, it turns out that "home" means not my home, but his. He takes me to Whitestone to meet his mom. Kenny's car is a sea green Honda Civic, sturdy as a Coke can. My door won't close, and I have to hold it shut against my shoulder so it doesn't spring open and launch me into the cyclone fencing and roadside shrubs. Kenny pops in a cassette, but even when he shoves a matchbook under the tape to keep it on track, the music slurs.

"What are we listening to, Anthrax?" I ask, trying to sound hip.

"Samuel Barber's *Adagio for Strings*."

Air blows through rust holes, stinging our hands and faces. It's February. The lights strung on the Whitestone Bridge glow cold and white, and we swing off the expressway, twisting through concrete curlicues. Suddenly, I feel safe. I'm weightless in the gear-shift change of direction from one ramp to another, undefined on highway entrances and exits.

Kenny lives with his mom in a small white single-family two-story house with a yard and a basement and a fence with a gate. In the kitchen, a tall skinny white guy with a red beard is sawing wood. Standing in sawdust, he's shirtless in blue overalls, the waistband of his boxer shorts riding high on his hips.

"That's my brother Fergus," Kenny says. Once inside his house Kenny is suddenly able to construct whole sentences. Fergus nods and we go to the basement, where Kenny's mom is sitting at a round table in front of a tub sink. She's wearing big square glasses and reading an astrology magazine. I'm closer to her age than to Kenny's, and, after Kenny introduces us, we smile at each other, embarrassed, until Kenny says, "You'd like my professor. He knows everyone's sign."

"Kenny's a Gemini," I say.

Mom says, "I know."

"Geminis have a glittery surface," I say, trying to sound both psychic and professorial, "but then there's this precipitous drop to a scary subtext."

"Mom knew that," Kenny says, steering me to a room in the corner of the basement, where I meet his other brother, Terry, who designs tattoos. Sitting at a drafting table in a tiny cinderblock room with no windows, he is trying to work up an octopus, a squid, and a white whale. He stands to shake my hand, shyly but elaborately polite. Before I get a chance to ask questions—"How do you etch a white whale on pale flesh?"—Kenny grabs my arm again and leads me back upstairs. "Where's Dad?" I ask, and Kenny says, "Dead," and I say, "Oh, sorry," and he says, "That's my word."

His room is on the top floor, under the eaves. The ceiling slants to paneled walls. Kenny has a bed, a window, a closet, and a metal stand for his electric keyboard.

"Gotta play you something," he says, pushing laundry off the bed and making room for us to sit. He pulls his Casio close and says, "I wrote this last night. It's called 'Valence Electron,' which, it's a reference to my personality, or, in other words, I don't think I have one. Sorry, man, sorry."

The music sounds like Debussy crossed with Rancid. "Maybe you'll like this better," Kenny says, and he plays Chopin's *15th Prelude in D flat major*, the "Raindrop" prelude. He sits with his wrists high and straight and his fingers curled, playing carefully, even delicately. I'm sorry when he's done, but he shrugs and laughs. He's living in an artists' colony and he doesn't know it. Tattoos downstairs, woodwork in the kitchen, preludes in the attic. And Mom stargazing in the basement.

"Kenny," I ask him, "why do you act"—I pause, hearing my tone, trying to put it in his words—"why do you act all, you know, like you don't mean shit? When in fact you're like this groovy bohemian?"

"Oh, man," he laughs. Then he drops his voice and lets go of his sentence structure and I know what's coming.

"Professor," he says. "I mean, sorry, man. It's just, I sort of assumed. You know? Like, it's none of my whatever. But I figured you were, you know. Aren't you?"

"You mean you figured I was gay."

"Oh, sorry. Sorry, man. Sorry."

"So, yeah. I am."

"Oh, man, I figured. And I gotta say. You know, because, like, whatever. Be gay. You know? But I mean in other words I'm saying, like: I'm not. I'm sorry, man."

"You're sorry you're straight?"

"I'm sorry I can't help you out."

"Can't help me *out*? Kenny, I'm your *teacher*."

"Oh, yeah, well. That wouldn't stop me. I mean, if I were a teacher, and I had all these cute chicks, you know—"

"Inviting you home?"

"Sorry, man. Sorry."

He shrugs and laughs and drives me to the train. He's low-key, he doesn't care what I want. His classmate Rick Carp, a cop, is more exacting. In class, he writes vicious, funny poems about the Mets, rhyming "Todd Hundley" with "mango chutney." At an end-of-semester party in my apartment, however, he's in correctional mode, stern and interrogating. Grasping a Red Dog and smoking a cigar, he flags me down. "Dude," Rick says, "I gotta ask you something." He takes a swig of beer. Then he lowers his voice and says, "Dude, are you a homosexual?"

Straining to hit the right note of self-acceptance crossed with complete nonchalance, I say, "Well, yes, Rick. I am."

And Rick says, "I *did* not know that." He takes another hit of beer. "Then halfway through the term," he continues, swallowing, "you said something about going on a date, and the pronoun you used was suspicious. It was 'he.' And I suspected that. So I poke the guy sitting in front of me. Rivas. Cool guy. I say, 'Rivas, is he a fag?' And he says, 'Duh.' And, man, I gotta tell you, I was stunned. Because, in high school? I was the worst fucking homophobe? Dude, and I mean we used to hassle fags in the Village. And one of those fags could've been you. So I'm over it, man." He downs the last of his beer. "You got me over my homophobia, because you inspire me."

I've had a couple of beers myself. Feeling reckless and relieved, I put my arm around his shoulders and say, "Thanks, buddy."

"Easy, dude," Rick says, pulling away. "I said I was over my homophobia, but I'm not that over it."

Nobody is. That's what I tell my student Ben, driving him home one night down Cross Bay Boulevard toward Jamaica Bay. Ben is my genius, a brilliant, skinny twenty-year-old with a big impressive beard and a skullcap, dressed in sweatpants and homemade tie-dyed T-shirts with hand-printed slogans like JESUS IS COMING, LOOK BUSY.

Ben is *ausgedreht*, all wound up. Headed for his parents' house in a religious Jewish neighborhood in Far Rockaway, near Kennedy Airport, we're discussing his favorite topics: eighties teen girl pop stars and *Little Women*. It's late June. The car windows are open, and Ben holds down his yarmulke like a blonde protecting her hairdo in a fast car in the fifties.

He is trying to convince me that I should like Debbie Gibson. "*Deborah*, not *Debbie*," he is saying. " 'Debbie' was never her idea. It was the record company's name."

Then, in his high, sweet, cantillating voice, he sings Gibson's "Foolish Beat," off her first album, *Out of the Blue*: "I could never love again the way I love you, oh."

"Ben," I say, "are you sure you're not gay? Debbie Gibson, *Little Women*?"

"There is no eighties pop without Deborah Gibson. It's a cultural fact. And *Little Women*," he says, getting excited, "is not *gay*, any more than Eleanor Roosevelt is *gay*. How are you going to apply a late-twentieth-century understanding of a constructed social-sexual category to a book written in the late 1800s for the pleasure and edification of an emerging group of young middle-class American women looking for a place in the postwar Reconstruction economy?"

Then we come to a tollbooth. We're at Broad Channel, halfway across Jamaica Bay. When we reach Ben's house on the Rockaway peninsula he makes me wait while he runs inside to get a Deborah Gibson CD he wants me to borrow.

It's late afternoon. A plane swoops for a landing at JFK. In all the neat square houses that line Ben's block women in long dresses and head scarves are coming out onto their porches to chat in the ochre light. They talk and shoo flies, minding their children, idly but definitely keeping an eye on the street. Dudes blasting hip-hop swing around the corner, the deep bass of their car stereo thrumming. The dudes watch the local women watch me watching the dudes watch them. It's an orgy of gazing, with no one at the center. We're all marginal, Jewish women, Queens guys, gay professors.

And Zack says, "Oh, Tom, of course your students say you don't *seem* gay, because a) how is that a compliment? and b) has it ever occurred to you that they know who's giving them *grades*? 'Oh, Professor, I never would have guessed, you're just so butch, can I please have an A?' Of *course* you're flattered, like Jews taking compliments from Nazis. 'You're nothing like a rat,' Goebbels says, and you go red and say, 'Oh, *you*.' But guess what? You're still a Jew. Because that's what being a Jew means. It has to do with: Nazis decide. 'Oh, I'm not gay; that identity is so con*strict*ing.' Wait until you're in the cattle car with your 'postgay' pals. Then you'll know from constraints."

It's November 1999. Zack has been dead five years, and I'm in my office at Queens College, where I basically live. For a few weeks after Zack died I tried to spend time in Manhattan. I sat up late at night, listening to the beep of the garbage truck as it backed to the curb outside my apartment at five in the morning and making mix tapes eulogizing Zack. "God, please don't let me not die," I was thinking. If you're in pain, why can't you die? I had never talked to God before, or asked myself or anyone questions that sounded so much like dialogue in a Russian novel.

So I gave up on Manhattan, and started spending most of my time in Queens, teaching class or sitting in my office, floating high above my desk and staring down at stacks of student writing. Sometimes I reached down, grabbed a story, and covered it with remarks.

On a five-page story I would write eight pages of single-spaced typewritten comments. My students were turning into writers, and I was up in the air hanging over myself, watching my body move through the world.

I'm still floating on this damp November day, nearly the anniversary of Zack's death, when I notice a familiar kid standing in my door. There's no telling how long he has been there. Of course, I remember him. He's the guy in the TEXAS IS THE REASON T-shirt, Justin, the student with whom, a few weeks earlier, I shared *Jane Eyre.* He stares at me a minute, not speaking. Either he's mute or he's being polite, an outside chance. Then he points to my wall and says, "Cool map."

My office is papered with a map of Long Island pieced out of gas station road maps and showing Walt Whitman's Paumanok, Newtown Creek to Orient Point.

"You do that yourself?" he says.

"No," I say, "I hired a design team."

If only I were James Baldwin, whose irony has a wrenching subtext. Baldwin penetrates, however, where I pinch, and my sarcasm makes people feel giddy rather than awed. Justin laughs and takes a step into the room, and I notice he's limping.

"Are you hurt?" I say.

He shrugs. "Messed up my knee playing ball," he says.

"Um, bad?" I say, forced, because of his reluctance, to downshift to his speed.

"Not really," he says.

"Yeah," I say, not quite knowing how to engage him. Consequently, I'm fictionalizing his pain. It's an occupational habit: Instead of writing my novel about Zack, I make up stories about my students. I'm looking at Justin and thinking, *Bum legs and American literature: Ahab leaning on whalebone.* Henry James's dad with a wooden leg. Jake Barnes losing his third leg in the lousy war. "The sun also rises like your dick if you had one," Hem jokingly wrote to Fitzgerald. Hobbled ex–track star Brick mourning his Skipper in

Cat On a Hot Tin Roof. I'm picturing Jack Kerouac on crutches in the fall of 1940, the "fleet-footed backfield ace" sidelined in New Jersey when he broke his leg and ended his sports career in a game of college football.

Spinning references in my head, I have turned Justin into a literary trope, when I finally realize that of course he needs to sit down.

"Come in, come in," I say, feeling ashamed and suddenly maternal.

"Yeah?" he says, mistrustful of help.

"Yes, please, for God's sake," I say, waving him into the room. He's hesitating, so I get up from my chair and come around my desk toward him, breaking the line that separates teacher from student. Like a matador playing close to the bull, I'm crossing into his turf in order to clear a solid place for him to sit. It's a challenge. My chairs, piled high with student work, are unstable. Wobbly as stage props for a sight gag, they roll and tip, with adjustable seats that abruptly sink to the floor and armrests that dribble foam stuffing from exposed metal grips. I'm thinking ruefully that a lame guy in a trick chair is a metaphor for government support of public education when Justin suddenly comes forward and sits, getting his sore leg out straight and angled to the floor. He's anchored, and the chair holds.

Determined to show my concern, I point at his leg, saying, "You're not wrecked for life, are you?" Which immediately sounds like I'm asking if he's impotent. But he's not stressed. "I seen your door open," he says, apologetically.

"Yeah, sure," I say.

"I mean, unless you're busy or something."

"No, fine," I tell him.

Talking to Justin is like easing into water and feeling acutely the change in heat and density and resistance as you substitute fluid for air. There's no reaching him unless you're willing to be immersed in his realm. His integrity is in what he doesn't reveal, and his silence is a test. He's used to being dissed in Manhattan as bridge-and-tunnel trash. So he'll act dumb and hope you don't guess it's a routine. He gets off on your not knowing what an idiot you are.

I try not to act too smug. "So you fucked up your leg," I say.

He looks at me like this is new, a college professor who says "fuck."

"It's really no big deal," he says. "Twisted something playing ball. Whatever."

"You're an athlete?"

"I'm nothing special," he says.

He looks around the room, checking my books. I'm stashed in a yellow room. "Dirty is yellow," Gertrude Stein says; my office walls are smudged and grimy. Blurred sunlight seeps through a glass brick window, and the office is noisy with the hum of conduits and cables and aluminum pipes nested overhead and dully reverberating. The recessed fluorescent ceiling lights brush a mortuary sheen on sanguine flesh washed gray in the thrumming glow.

It's a grim closet filled with maps and books: "passing" novels by Nella Larsen and Walter White. All the Harlem Renaissance bisexuals: Wallace Thurman, Countee Cullen, Claude McKay, Langston Hughes, Alain Locke. Hemingway and Fitzgerald side by side, *Men Without Women* next to *All the Sad Young Men*. Virginia Woolf sharing a room of her own. Melville ever in flight, in *Typee* ("Six months at sea!"), in *Omoo* ("We made our escape!"), and in *Mardi* ("We are off!"). James Baldwin in Paris. John Cheever showing his penis to strange men in the public john at Grand Central before heading home to his suburban lawn and his smoking barbecue and his wife's warm breasts. Jack Kerouac and Neal Cassady searching for a loving father in the dark woods or the gloomy night. Gertrude Stein, Gertrude Stein, Gertrude Stein.

My books are a tax write-off and, someone suggested, a uterine wall. They're also an art installation, transforming my office into an oak-paneled reading room. As if you could look out the room's small, square, distorting window and see not the graveled surface of the building's tar paper roof but Gothic arches and heavenly spires and the Princeton dusk; as if you heard, in the distance, not the drone of ventilation pipes but youthful voices risen in song, boisterous freshmen in a white-clad phalanx linking arms and strolling up University Place singing, "Going back, going back from all this earthly ball/Going back to Nassau Hall." I'm nostalgic for privilege and the Ivy League. So are my students, who treat Queens College as a convenience store, a heady 7-Eleven where they get their degrees the same way they order Diet Cokes and a *USA Today*. My office is meant to cut against their sense of education as utility.

"You see?" Justin says, moving his arm to indicate the room.

"See what?"

"I want to be surrounded by literature," he says. "Like you."

He's in earnest. My students know how to be sincere, to reveal their faith in absolutes, in God and Jesus and Steve McQueen, in "traditional" family roles for men and women, in literature. Of course, I believe in literature, too. That's my modernist flaw. I still trust in beauty and art and the existence of a self, however freaked out and fragmented. Some of my postmodernist colleagues would say my longing for wholeness is totalitarian schmaltz. But I'm an East Coast liberal born just a few years before Kennedy died, and I can't help my yearning to connect with something larger than myself.

What I mean is, my students are just as stupid with yearning as I am, but they're not afraid to show it. All beauty exists by deprivation, John Ashbery says, and my students, denied a sense of their own magnificence, are exquisitely real. I can feel myself rushing forward to meet them, as if I had a soul that you could merge with, or I could lose.

So when Justin asks if I want to read a poem he wrote, I say, "Sure."

He reaches across my desk, handing me a folded sheet. I spread it out on my blotter. Most student poems consist of rhymed clichés centered down the page: "I'm blue/When you're untrue." So I'm surprised by Justin's poem. It's called "The Art of Losing's *Really* Hard to Master."

"Hey," I say, "you like Elizabeth Bishop?" He looks at me blankly. "Elizabeth Bishop," I repeat. "Poet? Died in Boston? Alcoholic and gay? I'm not saying that's cause-effect. You're quoting her in your title."

"That's a quote?" he says, maybe playing dumb, maybe not. "It's something I heard my teacher say. I thought he made it up." Then he looks at me like, "Are you gonna read my poem?"

So I do. It's this:

THE ART OF LOSING'S *REALLY* HARD TO MASTER

I'm a Yankees fan. I'm not a Mets fan.
I got enough loss in my life,

I don't need
to see my team lose. So what, they're corporate
motherfuckers, poker-faced, Republican?
They win stuff.
I'm not into bondage, either, or S/M—
don't have to hire a dominatrix to feel like I'm
nothing.

I know I'm nothing.
Kerouac says: "Accept loss forever."
I do.

You see how, in that case,
it'd be redundant to be a Mets fan.

"My brother's a big Mets fan," he tells me, as if apologizing.

"It's a sonnet," I say.

"Yeah, I know," he says.

"Anyway, fourteen lines."

"It's not like I'm saying I'm Shakespeare."

"You're funnier than Shakespeare," I tell him, which he ignores, kind of pleased. "No, really," I say. "Shakespeare would've gotten all heavy-handed about the Mets, called Edgardo Alfonso 'thee.' Would that work?"

Now he's laughing. "Come on, man," he says. "Tell me if it sucks."

"I like it."

"For real," he says.

"I mean, are all your poems party jokes?"

"You're saying it sucks."

"I'm saying I bet you write about other things besides baseball."

"Not so far," he says, pulling at the front of his shirt.

Then he tells me he wants to be a poet, and that he is thinking about applying next fall to graduate school, to get into a creative writing program. He has come to my office, he says, because he heard I could help, which is true. I'm the People's Professor. Students at Harvard and Princeton and Yale have parents or friends or advisers who worry them through the quirks and requirements of their grad school applications, especially the personal statement, which is its own uniquely punishing literary form. My students have me.

Many of them are the first people in their families to graduate college. High school, in a few cases. Their parents want them to get decent jobs. Who the hell goes to school to study creative writing? Well, I did. They should do what they want. If one of my students can land a scholarship to a graduate program in Houston, or Minnesota, or Phoenix, with tuition paid by the university and a stipend to cover the rent, that's two years living away from home for the first time, free of charge. Of course, it's murder to convince them of this. Though Queens has a parkway that will take you straight out of town, its neighborhoods are ringed by oatmeal moats, and the thick pasty substance traps anyone who tries to flee. So what if I'm a missionary? My students give up before they grasp what they truly want, and I don't like to see them go empty-handed.

So Justin is right, I can help.

The following semester he takes my class and turns out to be a great student. He knows how to steal. He's a scavenger, lifting tropes and techniques from poems he likes and dragging them into his work. His poems evolve: His first drafts are imitations of whatever poet he's reading, Sherman Alexie, or Gary Soto, or Sharon Olds. In the second draft he breaks apart his careful mimicry, and something else starts to emerge. By the third or fourth draft the poet he originally aped is present as a kind of beneficent force, guiding Justin's hand. I'm not saying the final version is genius. He still hasn't learned how he sounds, or what it means to have a sound. Still, he doesn't quit.

He comes by my office three days a week throughout the spring term, bringing his poems. Or he swings past the school in his car, waiting for me in front of the pizza parlor, his engine running. When I walk up he's at the wheel, ready to roll. We have a funny way of talking about his work. The rule seems to be: Pretend we don't know what we're doing. He denies he can write; I insist I can't teach. It's an orgy of self-effacement, taking place in his car.

"What's goin' on?" he says, bundled in his knit cap, down parka, cargo pants, and Velcroed sneakers. There's music on his CD player, usually Radiohead, and a poem in his coat. Once I'm settled in his car, he pulls the poem, folded in four, out of his pocket. Cold as his coat, it's perilously sheer, the black ink faintly impressed on thin white paper by a dot matrix printer.

For a while, we are hooked on *OK Computer*. "I'm amazed I survived," Thom Yorke sings as I unfold Justin's poem, smoothing it on my thigh while Justin drums the wheel. "I don't know nothing about poetry," I tell him, in my hokey yo-dude voice. Why am I always posing as a regular guy? Justin doesn't seem to be thinking about me, though, which is his best quality.

He says, as always, "Just tell me if it sucks."

"It's good," I say after studying it a couple of minutes. I tell him what I like about it, and he says, "Don't lie," and he keeps at me until I find something wrong. Then of course he attacks me. "Can't you see what I'm doing?" he says. "Well, *duh,*" I say. We argue until I surrender. Which bugs him even more. "No, man, don't give up," he says. "You're right, I'm sure you're right." I repeat my criticism, and he shrugs. "Okay," he says, quietly. He always argues, and then he brings back a better draft next time.

After poetry, we head out for a bite. We hit the Hilltop Carriage House Diner on Union Turnpike, where he has an egg-white omelet and I order grilled cheese and fries. Then we go to Queens Boulevard for the F train, my stop. I feel awkward leaving, but Justin knows how to unhook. "Later," he says, already on his way.

Sometimes he calls me at home late at night to read me some poems. "What's goin' on?" he says, and I say, "Nothing, what's up?" and he says, "Nothing," and there's a pause, and he asks, in his soft voice, "Do you want to hear a poem?" Then he reads someone else's work, James Wright's "Autumn Comes to Martins Ferry, Ohio"—"all the proud fathers are ashamed to go home"—or C. K. Williams's "From My Window," where the narrator watches a paraplegic Vietnam vet roll down the street in his wheelchair followed by a buddy, maybe his lover, the two of them drunk and tumbling into the gutter, Williams's long lines also lurching hectically forward, like Justin's voice, the soft tense sound of his voice carefully repeating something awful, paralyzed men falling over each other.

Hanging out with my students, I forget I'm not twenty-five. What happened to my adult life in Manhattan? I let it go. Justin says, "Come over my house," and we sit around his room, reading poetry, which is far more intimate than sex. No one I know is as unself-consciously in love with poetry as Justin. Reading poems with him I have permission to gush about John Keats. "That's so awesome," he says, reading "Ode on a Grecian Urn," and I'm thinking, "It really is." One of his roommates walks in, stares at us crouched over a book, and says, "You can't eat poetry." Meaning, I guess, "Get a life." I don't mind the snub.

I like Justin's room. It's tiny, dark, and brown, furnished with things he bought cheap at the Queens Center Mall: a beach chair, a mattress, his iMac. A window over Myrtle Avenue lets in the sidewalk noise and the drone of the 55 bus. Across the street is the cemetery where Houdini is buried. Anyway, that's what Justin claims. "Motherfucker got out of everything but Queens," he says.

I'm a hermit crab, safe in other people's shells. In fact, I belong in an apartment on the Lower East Side filled with Elvis icons and furniture that refers ironically to seventies TV and the design scheme for *The Brady Bunch*. Yet I would rather be out of place in Justin's room, getting sappy about Keats. Above his bed are two framed prints. One shows Goran Ivanisevic, the Croatian tennis player, shirtless and kissing a trophy. The other is Salvador Dalí's *Christ of St. John of the Cross*, which looks down Christ's broad shoulders and the back of his head, as Christ drifts over the fallen world, which has storm clouds in the blue sky and a big lake where two fishermen are holding a boat. These are Justin's role models and his household gods. Round-shouldered like the drooping Christ, scratching his chest, Justin is the hero of his crowded room.

"How can you sleep under that?" I ask, pointing at the hanging Christ.

"That's me," Justin says, pointing at one of the fishermen, who has his back turned to the vision of Christ. "You're all, 'Dude, look, Jesus is coming!' But he's too busy with his stupid boat. He's missing the chance of his life."

Does he think of me as his chance? Am I treating him as if he were mine? Sometimes he puts out no vibe, at all. Zack was so certain about everything. Justin doesn't make up his mind, although he can be intractable. He has a harsh, quiet voice, which is both rasping and apologetic, self-abasing but aimed at me. Zack would call him passive-aggressive, which is true, but in the wrong order: He's aggressively low-key. His voice is beautiful because of what's missing: his r's. He says "pock" instead of "park." Not a Boston accent, it's crystalline rather than metallic, glass, not ore, "caw" for "car," it's made of sand skimmed from the surface of the earth, not dug up, no hollow behind it, just grit. His voice is your skin coming home from the shore, that abrasion. And now I have called him my skin.

Justin is finally ineffable, and so is Zack, though I used to believe with sentimental assurance that I would be able to "capture"—weird word—the essence of Zack. I started writing about him long before he died, rehearsing my account of his death. But his actual dying was so painful it ruined my plot, and I had nothing believable to report. So much for my immortalizing the beloved. I figured if I wrote about him honestly enough, even scathingly enough, I could preserve him. His infected body would be replaced by the body of the book. He'd be alive now, he'd be this, you'd be turning him in your palm.

The difference between Justin and Zack is that Justin still has a body, still *is* a body. When I met Justin I knew right away that no matter how I grafted my soul onto his body, this silent, hesitant guy would never be me.

His favorite Radiohead song is "How to Disappear Completely." I want to tell him "I know how to do that." Disappearance. I know how to watch it and how to achieve it. What I can't do is merge, attach, combine. I'm not him, so I have made this book about him.

Well, not just him. Can I admit that my students saved my life? As much as I yearned to save theirs? I was awed by them from the day I stepped into class. Did I find them exotic? I guess. They were working-class kids from Queens, and I was an art fag from lower Manhattan. We were each other's queer. Some of them looked like the thugs who hassled me in high school. They didn't trash me, though. They looked up to me. That was shocking, at first. *Why aren't you beating me up?* I kept thinking. Well, I was their teacher. They wanted my approval. Could they tell how much I wanted theirs? I stood in front of them and said, "You're interesting." I wasn't lying. I was a guy whose friend had died, and nothing I had learned in thirty-five years had prepared me for that. I wanted to know how other people lived, and how they survived.

In class I talked about how to write a sentence. I fussed over word choice. I tracked the balance of sentences inside paragraphs, their relative lengths, and I wondered where to put the word that carried the most emotional weight. That's the kind of material you can teach and discuss. What I can't express is how grateful I felt for their everyday lives. Zack died enraged, a form of narcissism. There is nothing as selfish and luxurious as pain, because it's all about you. Zack's death was terrible and special. Watching it, I felt terribly special, too. Afterward, though, I was tired of being important. I didn't want the glamour and egotism of pain. My students taught me to get over myself. I'm not calling it therapy. I can't stand easy self-expression or daytime TV, but I was moved by their stating the plain facts of their ordinary day. I wanted them to know mine.

PART TWO
OPEN SECRETS

It is the nature of some performances that they leave the reader feeling rather helpless.

—I. A. Richards

Sick Fuck

My body does not have the same ideas I do.
—Roland Barthes

"You alive in there?" Richie says, rapping on my forehead with the bunched knuckles of his right palm. "Shower's free," he says.

We're still in Flushing, getting ready for our Memorial Day Weekend cyberdate. John Lennon is singing, "I need a fix," and I'm searching my pockets for aspirin. Richie is standing before me showered and shaved, aromatic as a groomed dog after a flea bath. His fur is damped and dried, and the hair on his head is shiny with gel. Cologne evaporates from his skin like antiseptic from a puncture wound, and his body is wrapped in black: black T-shirt, black suit, silk with synthetics, cuffed trousers, ventless jacket, round-toed lace-up black patent leather shoes, thick-soled and spongy with rubber. Snaky black socks. Black silk briefs, for all I know. A gold watch, the face strapped as if in secret to the underside of his left wrist, where the flesh is tender with veins. A gold friendship ring is on the third finger of his right hand. He looks like a film agent in West Hollywood on his way to sign a mall rat to a development deal.

"All those groovy shirts and you're wearing that?" I say, pointing at his T-shirt.

"Hey," he says. "I saw George Clooney in this getup."

"Well, anyway," I say, patting my trousers. Frowning, distracted, I say, "You look good."

"You don't," he says. "What are you doing? Frisking yourself?"

"I need some aspirin."

"You've got a headache?"

"A heartache."

I'm not being metaphorical. Literally, my heart hurts. It isn't knifing pain, just pressure, as if somebody tied forget-me-not strings around the veins in my chest, squeezing my arteries shut. If I'm not disconcerted by clenching, I'm dizzy. Or my heart beats too fast. Or it doesn't seem to be beating at all, and I feel dead at the center, but not in a romantic way. I'm not a glamorous husk hollowed out by drink and resignation in a lyric play by Tennessee Williams. My problem is more routine: I figure I'm dying any day now, prosaically, alone, with dirty dishes piled high and one mangled porno magazine jammed in the cabinet under the sink. *Black Inches*. That'll make me look slick.

I bought it at a newsstand outside the Queens Center Mall. Ashamed to get porn in my own neighborhood, I thought I'd sink below the radar in Queens. But the guy in the kiosk kept calling me "boss" and making me repeat myself. He'd touch a magazine and say, "This one, boss?" and I'd say, "No, *Black Inches,*" and he'd point to another and say, loudly, "*This* one, boss?" and I had to say, "No, not that one. *Black Inches*."

People were walking past, some of them maybe my students. I don't know why I didn't settle for *Torso* or *Stud*, his choices. Except that I'm pricked by an acquired but helpless fidelity to a long-lost Anglican code: A gentleman persists in his folly, even if it makes him look absurd. Shame as self-discipline. A kind of demented pride in your own bad taste. I learned that from an Alec Guinness movie. If I'm determined to buy a splatter rag that objectifies black guys, I get what I deserve, public dread, middle-aged shame, my desire a sidewalk spectacle. I'm a pasty-faced Manhattanite in Queens, a college professor, slinking past Stern's Department Store and clutching a volume of poetry and the February number of *Black Inches*.

"My mind's not right," I think, quoting Robert Lowell. I'm not a person; I'm an anthology.

"Hey, buddy," Richie says. "You smell bad. Gonna wash?"

He shoots me a look as if to say, I don't know where you went, but as far as I can tell, we're still on the planet. Unlike me, Richie knows his life is happening in three dimensions. It's his privilege to feel both the pain and concentrated joy packed into matter. I think of him shooting balls in 1976, how gravity favored him, how the earth seemed to hold him a second longer and then release him inches higher than anyone else. I think of his body, light but concussive. You can bang against him. He knows material ecstasy, joy in his substance and his soul. I don't want a soul. I want the body to be the soul. *If flesh is spirit,* I think, *then you've only got one thing to lose when you die.*

"I've got no aspirin here," Richie says, watching me. "I've got Advil."

"Advil won't work. It doesn't keep your blood from clotting."

"Your blood's clotting?"

"No, of course it's not clotting. I mean, it clots just fine when it's supposed to. I'm a nutcase, Richie. I'm convinced I'm dying of heart disease. People take two aspirin a day and a glass of red wine to keep their blood—"

"Yeah, sure," he says.

"It's gotta be aspirin, I mean."

"I get it," he says. After all, he has his own unreasonable fears: heights and small spaces. His anxieties keep him out of elevators, wedding vows, and single beds. Right now, he thinks the answer for me is a shower. He's a man of action. He gathers together fresh soap, still unwrapped, an unused stick of roll-on Old Spice deodorant, a blue disposable razor, Edge shaving cream, a face cloth, a loofah, nail clippers—an entire toilet kit, which he spreads out on the bed.

"You want aspirin, you gotta hurry up and wash, we'll reach the 7-Eleven quicker. Shampoo, the girlfriend's got every brand in circulation, plus she collects hotel samples, around the rim of the tub; the goddam things get knocked over easy, step lightly, take your pick. Because in any event . . ."

I'm collecting the shower supplies and heading for the bathroom.

"In any event," he repeats, "I figure that we have about twenty minutes to lam outta here, which, I know I sound like Jimmy Cagney."

"You do sound like Cagney."

"Thanks," Richie says, and I yell back, but I'm in the bathroom with the shower running, and the pin-prick hot water jet stream cancels our voices.

So does the noise of the plane arching low over the hood of Richie's fast car thirty minutes later. It's near dusk, and we're dressed to the nines. Richie's in his tycoon suit and I'm wearing his colorful psychedelic shirt. The red and the black: From a distance, I'm flaming and he's embers. The sun is hauling ass like a Mets fan out of a losing game in the bottom of the eighth, and the plane swoops near enough to drag its livid gut across our cheeks.

"Why do they fly so low?" I ask Richie, knowing he can't hear me. "It's like we're being followed," I mouth, pointing at my lips, and he shrugs. As before, he's riding and I'm driving, and we're both silenced, watching through the open sunroof as the plane passes over. I feel monitored by air transport. I'm shrinking from choppers and 747s like Ray Liotta on a drug run, tailed by the FBI in the last segment of *Goodfellas*.

"We're in a flight path to LaGuardia," Richie explains, after the jet boom swells and contracts, and our eardrums, tensile as snares, stop vibrating. "Can you chill? You're making me jumpy."

He's flicking lint from his jacket and checking his razor burn in the rearview mirror. His Rat Pack vanity. That makes me Shirley MacLaine, the chick who never gets with any of the guys. Though sometimes, when the men are drunk enough, they toss an arm around her and say, "If only you were a hot babe with a forty-eight-inch ass. If only you had big titties."

"If only you weren't such a pussy," Richie says, goading me.

"I don't have any problem being a pussy," I tell him. "You wanna insult me, work harder."

"Buddy, I don't want to insult you," Richie says. Of course, he means the opposite. Like me, he's compulsively snide, but his sarcasm is menacing, not campy. He believes he was meant to live in paradise but flung into hell. Whereas I'm the vicious invert: Hell's my home. And if we wander together over the burning marl and stinging shores of flaming lakes, the tender architecture of our paws baked black, it's not because we're equally damned. One of us—Richie, that is—got ruined by accident. And he might still get back to the world of light and beautiful oblivion, thoughtless but illuminated, blessed with unself-awareness.

We would both like to be stupid again. In the meantime, someone has to take the rap for giving us the bad news about just how far we are from the Lord. Richie, straight boy, thinks the heavenly world could open for him like a jeweler's safe if somebody gave him the code. I don't want to be inside. I'm the pariah, from the Tamil word for "untouchable." It also means "festival drum": designed for a beating.

"Turn, motherfucker, turn, turn," Richie shouts.

I want to head straight down the Expressway to the Midtown Tunnel, but Rich can't stand to be underground. Plus, we're early for his date, so we take the longest possible route, south through the center of Queens, bound for Jamaica Bay.

"It's Queens, motherfucker!" Richie says. Utopia. Queens was once somebody's country club. It was someone's eighteenth-century religious haven. It was a real estate hunch, the Hamptons of the 1830s. Herman Melville vacationed in Flushing. In 1910, it was

Hollywood. Charlie Chaplin shot films in Astoria, and Buster Keaton married Constance Talmadge in a mansion at the north shore of Bayside. In the 1930s, in Sunnyside, developers built spacious housing for the workers of the world. The numbered street names are like an experiment in composition by John Cage, difference in sameness—Fifty-eighth Avenue, Fifty-eighth Road, Fifty-eighth Court, Fifty-eighth Lane, and Fifty-eighth Drive.

Haunted by the ghosts of gold coasts and golf courses, Thoroughbred racetracks, potato farms, breweries, tinsmithies, and nude bathing beaches, Queens is glorious and plain. Its grandest street, Queens Boulevard, wide as Berlin's *Unter den Linden*, rises to meet, not the Brandenburg Gate, but Kinko's Copy Shop and the blunt rectangle of the beige Con Edison building. In Kew Gardens, at the center of things, the borough is policed by a bully: "Civic Virtue," a Beaux Arts sculpture of a German cop from 1902, a naked sword-swinging warrior hoisted by sea beasts above an empty fountain and standing on the heads of two women representing "Corruption" and "Vice."

It's the borough of cruel boys and jazz babies. Bix Beiderbecke, jazz suicide, drank himself to death in Sunnyside clutching his horn. Between road trips Louis Armstrong lived in Corona. Billie Holiday was nineteen years old, cleaning houses for rich white folks in Long Island, when she sang her first gigs at the Gray Dawn, a club in downtown Jamaica. "No road is lonely," Holiday sings. "If you will only." Richie's car jets through Queens against a shifting landscape: the curved shiny Flushing Library. "Lose all your blues." Green parks, brick housing projects, parkways, Tudor facades, white gates, minimalls, flatlands, Jamaica Bay. "Laughing at life."

Headed for Howard Beach, we pass Jack Kerouac's house in Ozone Park. These days it's the Lindenwood Volunteer Ambulance Corp. In 1949, though, Jack lived here with his mom after his dad died. Sitting at the kitchen table he broke open nasal inhalers for the drug-soaked cotton strip, pure speed, which he crumbled into balls and dropped in his coffee. Tweaking, chain smoking, and eating his mom's food, he wrote an early draft of *On the Road* while his pal Neal Cassady stood over him yelling, "Yes! That's right! Wow! Man! Phew! Everything you do is great!"

"Then came springtime, the time of great traveling," Kerouac says, and Rich and I are on the road, headed to Manhattan, giving Howard Beach the finger. "Motherfuckers," Richie says, the world's most American word. Like Kerouac, Richie once lived in Ozone Park, "ozone" meaning both "pure air" and "poisonous agent used to *deodorize* air," effect and cause, evil and good, a contradiction in terms like most Queens neighborhoods named for what they later lost: Fresh Meadows and Woodhaven and Rosedale. "Ozone" is also *ozein,* Greek for "smell," and I count the scents in Richie's car: saltwater, cold rubber, benzine, wood smoke, dry leaves, airborne PCBs, rust, lead, black coffee, and Richie, who smells as clean as hand soap with a subtext of tense dude, bitterroot, prickly dread.

"Yes, zoom!" Kerouac says, and we're on the Belt Parkway. A belt is a fist in the arm, a shot of booze, a part of your car. We cross the border into Brooklyn, where the ground is flat and sandy near Starrett City and the highway changes names from Shore Parkway to Leif Ericson Drive. The Verazanno Narrows Bridge glides into place like a zipper joining oiled waves, and Manhattan is behind it. "There it is," Richie says, "there it mother*fucking* is."

Manhattan has all the iridescence of the beginning of the world. That's Scott Fitzgerald. "How funny you are today New York/like Ginger Rogers in *Swingtime*": Frank O'Hara. Riding the Gowanus Expressway, a straight shot out of Bay Ridge, then a jog left through Red Hook, we jet toward the East River. From Brooklyn, over the Brooklyn Bridge on this fine evening, we cross Melville's island of the Manhattoes to the West Village. Miraculously, there's a parking spot on Gansevoort Street right in front of the bar.

We stroll inside, and Richie, still posing as a movie gangster, tells me, "Case the joint; I gotta piss." As he runs to the john I stand alone in the vast room, which is dim and empty. I'm searching for someone who could be Afrodytea, when I notice a woman sitting alone at the bar. I walk close to get a better look.

And it's Ava Steinberg, from out of the past. My oldest friend, next to Richie. I have hardly seen her since Zack died. Instead, our phone machines communicate. We leave each other messages, arranging dates that we know ahead of time neither one of us can make. How did people manage commitment anxiety before the answering machine? I like to miss things: phone calls, deadlines, friends. Ava and I have been out of touch. Maybe it's my fault. I got busy at work, a suburban dad's excuse. Was I ducking her because I didn't want to be reminded of Zack?

Zack is gone, and therefore permanent. His absence is more real than anything I can still touch, and his death wiped out not my past, but my present. I haven't moved beyond the last three months of his life. If that's true, then I hardly need to see Ava in order to be with her. Her image is burned on my retina, caught in the flashbulb freeze-frame of her snapshot, which Zack hung above his hospital bed next to the photo of me.

Before Zack's death most of my friendship with Ava took place in a bar, so it isn't odd to find her here, nursing a drink. In college she was a bartender at the V.I., the Village Inn, which was famous for its cheese soup, and where we drank pitchers of Stroh's 3.2 beer, the original Bud Light, legal for eighteen-year-olds. Ava had long black hair then, and she wore tube tops and blue jeans, exposing more midriff than Britney Spears. She was as slender as a boy, but she had what she called "my aunt Sophie's Jewish shtetl tits." Top-heavy, tottering on cork-soled platform heels, she was Bette Midler crossed with Keanu Reeves. She should have been a chanteuse or an action star. Instead, she was, like me, an English major. When she was done with work, and the bar was shutting down, we sat at an empty table drinking leftover wine and reading Sylvia Plath and Robert Lowell.

"I should wear tiger pants, I should have an affair," Ava quoted.

"I'm tired," I said. "Everyone is tired of my turmoil."

Then we laughed, delighted at our own pretentiousness. When Zack was sick she would sometimes turn to me in his hospital room and rattle off a snarky line of Plath. "Meanwhile, there's a stink of fat and baby crap," she'd say, which was vicious, and necessary. We needed some relief from Zack's rage and his wasting flesh.

Of course, she was with Zack the day he died, and I was not— another reason I have been avoiding her. She watched him die. All right, I'm jealous. My terrible sin: I thought Zack's death was about me, and I resented him for sharing it with Ava instead. I know how selfish and sepulchral that sounds. Still, I wanted that final intimacy, to help him leave. I have always suspected Zack of punishing me for coveting his last breath. Can people decide when to die? I know they can. I have seen a dozen men do it.

Now Ava spots me in the downtown bar, and she barely shows surprise. Is she Afrodytea, Richie's date? I don't ask. Our eyes meet, and there are no preliminaries. To say "hello" would seem bathetic. Instead, when I walk up to her, she puts her hand on my face, brushing an eyelash from my cheek. "Make a wish," she says, holding the lash on her fingertip. She waits a second, then she blows it in the air. "What did you wish for?"

"You," I say, kind of meaning it.

"You're such a liar," she says.

She's sitting on a bar stool near the door, twisting her slender Audrey Hepburn neck to see what's playing above her on the TV screen. Her pale arms are naked to the shoulder, bent at the elbows and balancing her face, her hands together palm to palm beside her cheek, the first two fingers of her right hand stretching out to hold a cigarette. Its smoke turns colors as it moves through overlapping shafts of bar light and TV light and rings her black hair like a corona.

I wonder what she's doing in an empty bar on a Sunday night. Maybe I've walked into a Hal Hartley movie, where Soho types are stranded in lonely rooms looking for guns or lovers or shelter from the law. "Don't move," I tell her, sitting beside her, whispering into her small white seashell ear. The juke box plays "Wonderwall," Liam Gallagher singing, "I don't believe that anybody feels the way I do about you now."

"You lost weight," she tells me. "You look good."

Which is just what Richie told me this morning. They're perfect for each other, I should have introduced them years ago.

"So you're Afrodytea?" I ask her.

"No one's ever said it out loud," she laughs, "but now that you mention it, yes, I answer to that name."

If she *is* Afrodytea, does she think I'm Richie? "Were you expecting me?" I ask.

"I'm expecting *some*one," she says. "Is it you?"

She's drinking seltzer with lime through a straw. Not Scotch, to calm her blind-date jitters? She isn't jumpy, though. And she hardly needs the Internet to get laid. If she figures I'm Richie, well, would I be surfing chat rooms for girl sex? Maybe she's here on business.

"Is this research?" I ask. "Are you writing a column on cybersex?"

"Oh," she says. "You've been reading *Yo* magazine? They changed the name of my column. It was called 'Ask Ava,' and now it's 'Inside Ava Brown,' which makes me feel like a porn star, not really in a fun way."

"I'm too old for sex advice," I say.

"Me, too. The other day, my editor told me I had to cut a reference to *Annie Hall*. 'Our readers don't know what that is,' he told me. I'm not sure he knew, either."

"Yeah, no cultural memory further back than Stone Temple Pilots."

"Even that's occult," she says. She takes a long sip of club soda, then mashes the lime with her straw. When she turns her head back to face me, her gaze is a camera lens panning from my knees to my nose, adding fifteen pounds. I'm awaiting her judgment. "You look cute," she says. "Fancy shirt," she says.

"It's not mine."

"Well, it's working. You can get away with it."

"I guess that's a compliment. Anyway, you look amazing," I tell her honestly.

"Thank you," she says simply, exhibiting one of her charms: She knows how to accept praise.

"If I were as gorgeous as you, I'd have to punish myself," I say.

"Spinning class."

"It would take a lot of spinning for me to look good in my underwear," I say, touching the strap of her dress, which is really a slip, blue silk, and she's wearing toe-thong leather sandals, her legs bare. She is gray-eyed like Athena, and her face is serious and delicate, chiseled and soft. She has just enough gray in her black hair to let you know not to fuck with her.

She's complicated but linear. In your mind she moves quickly through scenes spliced together by jazzy jump cuts: Ava waking at noon and remembering her Sunday night cyberdate. Ava soaking two hours in a tub in her echoing white-tiled bathroom on the Upper West Side, and then, in her bathrobe, writing notes for her next magazine piece. She dresses, choosing a lacy bra, daubing perfume on her collarbones.

Wearing her blue slip, she takes a cab downtown, eating a carton of yogurt and reading a paperback book, *Deviant*, a true crime novel by Harold Schechter, in which women are killed and skinned and worn like overcoats by their attacker. Then she's greeting me, while I shyly and impulsively run my fingers through her cropped hair, feeling it soft and flattening and then rising between my fingers.

Hemingway wouldn't know what to do with her. Neither would Henry James or Scott Fitzgerald. She's not a dewy virgin or a perfect white bride, neither Daisy Miller nor Daisy Buchanan. She's not a loving mother-nurse who gives oral sex and talks baby talk, like Catherine Barkley in *A Farewell to Arms*. There's no biography of her that stands for girlhood in America. There are no silk ruffles on her pale blue dress. She doesn't have a voice like money or an animal's nickname and an impulse to call her lover "darling" so many times that you want to divorce her.

You'll never get her essence. She'd say she's half-Japanese, which accounts for my need to treat her as inscrutable. She'd tell you about the playground rhyme she learned when she was ten, sung to the tune of "Whistle While You Work":

Whistle while you work,
Hitler is a jerk.
Mussolini was a meanie,
But the Japs are worse.

She'd say that even the men who flirt with her on the street get it wrong, calling out, "Hey, Suzie Wong, come walk on my back," when "Wong" is Chinese and she's not. "I'm an island, baby," she tells them, "and I wouldn't make it across the water for you." She calls herself a product of occupied Japan, "like an ashtray," she says, "or a table lamp. And then again, I'm half a Jew, which means my allies want to cremate me."

Zack said she took self-loathing to a whole new level. "You're like a Jewish joke," he told her. "Did you hear the one about the self-hating Jew who slept with the Gestapo? Ava was born!"

"My mom's Japanese, not German," she reminded him. "They weren't burning Jews in Tokyo. Anyway, my mom's from Hawaii."

Zack and Ava had this fight once a week. It was a competition: Which of them was the bigger suffering Jew? Zack claimed Ava wasn't Jewish at all, because Judaism comes from Mom, "just like homosexuality," Zack said. "What's the difference between a gay man and a Jew? They both cross their legs at the knee. They both like musical theater. They are both secretly Republican."

It's true that homosexuality seemed Jewish when I was thirty, and Zack and Ava and I belonged to ACT UP, a street-fighting political group, the AIDS Coalition to Unleash Power. We were queer radicals!

Which sounds biochemical, possibly atomic. It strikes me, in retrospect, that we were still recovering from the Holocaust, because so many of my friends at the time had grown up with survivors. Zack's dad had spent the war hiding in a village in France. Ava's three aunts died in Nagasaki. We were children of the *brennende Kinder*, some of us, and gay liberation often felt like the last act of World War II.

We were self-named dykes and fags, lying down in the street, blocking traffic, handcuffed together through lead pipes in the January cold, stretched out on the pavement in front of Jersey pharmaceutical companies, agitating for an AIDS cure, and chanting, "AIDS Won't Wait." Police officers, standing by, eyed us, drinking coffee from paper cups. The cops were the kind of guys who would later be my students, and I can imagine the jokes they must have been making through their walkie-talkies.

We pointed at them and shouted, "Arrest the real criminal!" Then we warned, "We'll never be silent again!"

We went to ACT UP meetings every Monday night, where seven hundred of the cutest gay guys and chicest lesbians in lower Manhattan sat together in auditorium chairs yelling, "*Act up, fight back, fight AIDS.*" Every few weeks somebody, usually a white guy in his late thirties, pushed to the limits of his rage, stood in front of the room and screamed at us, "*Where is your anger?*" And then we planned another "action" or "zap," playfully at first, and then more desperately, as more people died: dressing as church ladies and handing out condoms; going to sports bars on Monday nights and kissing each other at first downs; spreading across the floor of Grand Central Station at rush hour to keep commuters from their trains; storming through a neighborhood in Staten Island where a gay kid was killed; trying to fling the body of a dead man over an iron fence onto the White House lawn; dressed as demons from hell and picketing a church. "What do you want from us?" a worshipper asked, and a drag queen in a tattered housedress and work boots yelled, "We're coming for your children, and what we can't fuck, we'll eat!"

Those were our days of rage. The anger was liberating—at first. Finally, the balance of power had shifted, and playground sissies, tomboys, and fairies had control. We were reliving high school, and this time getting it right. Anger is a useful political strategy, but as a lifestyle, it has its drawbacks. As more and more people died, it became clear that no one knew how to deal with loss, and when we should have been mourning, we were still screaming, "Arrest the real criminal!" During Zack's last year on the planet, while Ava and I watched him die, all we did was yell at one another. And sometimes have sex.

We're in Amsterdam in June 1994. Zack has diarrhea and five months to live. He, Ava, and I have taken this trip as a kind of family vacation, time away from our activist chores, a last chance to bond. Since we landed in Holland, however, Zack has been shitting every hour. Dutch food is all about dairy, which Zack can't digest. To me, Holland means bathrooms and cheese. And rain. For a week, it rains all day. To escape it we take a train to Haarlem to visit an ACT UP friend who moved to the Netherlands with his Dutch boyfriend. Of course, he's in the hospital. We know dying people all over the globe. The next day we visit Gouda, where we are surrounded by cheese.

In the Rijksmuseum we see Jan Vermeer's *The Milk Maid.* The mere sight of dairy makes Zack shit, a tribute to Vermeer's realism. Ava and I sit on a bench in the museum lobby, waiting for him to come out of the bathroom. When he shows up twenty minutes later, he looks tired and old, and I notice that his jeans, normally tight, are sliding off his hips. It's the first time it occurs to me that he *is* sick, instead of getting sick, and I feel acid back up in my throat.

For days, we go to the bathroom. In the Anne Frank House and the Van Gogh Museum. In the brown cafés. Some of the toilets are porcelain and new. Some flush from overhead, and you reach up to a wood handle on a metal chain. Some are piss holes in the tile floor, and you have to squat and aim. We look for bathrooms in the red-light district, where pimps offer us girls. Ava is in her gender-fuck androgynous drag: rolled-up blue jeans, combat boots, a torn white T-shirt, a black leather jacket, a crew cut, and a turned-around New York Yankees baseball cap. "What's the matter, men," the street barker hollers after us as we walk along the Achterburgwal, "you don't like girls?" "Of course we don't like girls," Zack yells. "We're fags."

On our last night in town, in front of our gay guesthouse where Zack has spent a lot of time in the john, we are fighting. A street lamp hangs its noose of light over the Herengracht. We have just been to a half-price movie theater to see an American film with Dutch subtitles, Daniel Day Lewis in *The Last of the Mohicans*.

"Clearly," Ava tells Zack, "your critical faculty is immobilized by the sight of Daniel Day Lewis's nipples. I guess you didn't notice that the movie trashes Asians."

"Mohawk Indians are not Asian," Zack says. "They're from Albany."

Nobody laughs. It's early, and Ava wants to go out. Zack has to shit and pack, because we're leaving first thing in the morning. All night, there will be the sound of his footsteps on the stairs to the bathroom one flight up, silence, the toilet flushing, more footsteps. "I can't face that anymore," Ava whispers to me, and she takes my hand and tells Zack, "You can sleep. Tom and I are going out."

Zack says, "Fine."

He goes into the guesthouse, and Ava squeezes my palm and pulls me away.

"We shouldn't argue," I say. "It's bad for his immune system."

"He's bad for mine," Ava says, hurrying me through dark streets past bicycle traffic. "Let's get some hash brownies," she says.

"Hash makes my heart beat really fast."

"Well," she says, "it slows mine, which is what I need right now."

We go to several brown cafés. At each one Ava tries to score while I wait outside, feeling like a character in *Go Ask Alice*, where depressed teens search for numbing drugs. "Eureka," Ava says, swinging through a heavy door into the street, coming out of the third or fourth café. She's holding a square of something wrapped in tinfoil. "I think it's banana bread," she says, unwrapping it. Beneath the foil is paper towel. Then the baked good. She breaks off a piece and pops it into her mouth.

"Chewy," she says.

"I hope it isn't cut with speed," I say.

We down the hash clump, eating silently. Maybe all we wanted was quiet, not to be bickering with Zack, not to be constantly talking about other things in order to ignore the focus of our trip, Zack's shitting, which is as relentless as pornography: Every ten pages the action stops in order to render in graphic detail a messy bodily function.

"I'm high," I say suddenly, not happy about it.

Ava waves her hand and nods agreement.

"This is like speed," I say, holding my heart. Then I try to be playful. "Suddenly everything looks three-dimensional," I say.

"Two new dimensions for you," Ava says.

"What now?" I say.

Ava takes my hand again and says, "Meaningless sex."

She knows a gay bar on the Spuistraat—research, she says, for a possible magazine column, "Ava Does Holland." She's leading, and I'm following, content to let her drive. It's a flashback to high school, to getting stoned with Richie. What if I had touched him in 1977? What if I had kissed him? Maybe we'd have fallen in love, and we'd be living together now in a pink stucco house in Orlando, Florida. I'd have a job as a chorus boy at Pleasure Island, and Richie would be a dolphin wrangler at Sea World. And at night, in our air-conditioned bungalow, we'd watch rental films in our boxer shorts, comparing tattoos . . .

"Hey, *fruitjes*."

There's a voice behind me. Not Ava's voice. It's faraway and close up, both at once. Ava's got my hand, and we're on the Spuistraat, which is empty.

I hear the voice again:

"*Fruitjes.*"

Ava and I are being followed. Young men in creased pants and polo shirts—a preppie mob of Euro thugs—are tracking us and calling us *fruitjes*.

I think, *Fruit-*yuhs, *it sounds like a breakfast cereal.* I think, *Scrubbed boys in duck pants? If I'm gonna be fag bashed in Amsterdam, can't it at least be tough Teutons calling me a fucking faggot?*

My hand slips out of Ava's, and though she's next to me, she's suddenly nowhere nearby. Instead, I'm alongside a guy who is asking me, "Are you a *fruitje*?"

So he's bilingual. Pale and skinny, with a beaked nose and fuzz on his face, he's younger than my students and he's carrying a stick, which looks like a two-by-four. *That's interesting,* I'm thinking. *He's armed.* The stick is slung across his shoulders, with his elbows looped over the ends and his wrists dangling. He's a droog. Suddenly, I'm in a scene from A *Clockwork Orange*.

I'm warning Ava telepathically, but of course, she can't hear me; she's stoned, not psychic. Instead of tuning into my brain waves, she takes off down the street. The guy swings his stick around my ankles, aiming but not hitting, and asking again, "Are you a *fruitje*?"

It's a familiar question, one I've heard most of my life. Actually it's two questions, or rather, two threats. "Tell me why you're a faggot, or I'll kill you." That's one. "If you talk to me, faggot, I'll kill you." That's the other. What choice do I have? I keep walking, which is what I've always done. They follow, of course. I hear their stick whooshing near my legs and over my head. "Never show them your fear," my mother said, when I was ten. She was talking about angry dogs, but the lesson applies. I get shoved but not hurt. As quickly as they appeared, they are gone.

My footsteps echo down the Spuistraat. I'm alone, listening to the echo. Suddenly, Mickey Spillane–like, a pale arm appears, reaching to pull me from the visible action into the even scarier unknown.

Of course, it's Ava's arm.

"Coast clear?" she asks. She's crouched in a doorway, breathing hard, high on speedy hash and thrilled by her flight from risk.

"Thanks for watching my back," I say.

"Why didn't you run?"

"You're not supposed to run. Running is bad," I say. "You're just supposed to stand there and let them sniff you."

"It sounds like sex."

"Sex is fun."

"They thought I was a boy," she says. In other words, it *was* fun.

I say, "They thought I was a boy, too."

"You are a boy."

"Yeah, in what context?"

"In this one," she says.

And then, for the second time in our friendship, she kisses me.

All the girls of my childhood were bold. I grew up in the sticks, and we got into the kind of trouble you read about in Erskine Caldwell novels. The boys I knew were loud and crude and talked a big game, but the girls didn't brag, only kept quiet and wrecked things—usually themselves. They jumped from barn roofs, or swam naked at midnight in the Spruce Run Reservoir, or snuck into bars with fake IDs and got drunk with pot-bellied dairy farmers and local cops. I went horseback riding with wild girls in the Jersey woods, galloping along railroad tracks, teaching colts to stand still for passing trains. I never thought boys were courageous. They screamed "fag" and ran away. The girls I liked wore hot pants and dared you to fuck with them.

Ava was like that in 1976, when I met her in college. She was my first gay love. She was not the opposite sex, not to me. We were both girls, and our friendship was Sapphic. We lay on the Salvation Army couch in her dorm room, while she played with my hair. She was the butch, I was the femme. During my sophomore year she dyed my hair three times: first orange, then black, then blue. "This is like having a Ken doll with genitals," she said, while Joan Jett and the Runaways sang "Cherry Bomb" on her phonograph.

We were in love with the same guy. His name was Chip, a preppie white boy from Philadelphia. He edited the school's literary journal, in which Robert Lowell had published his undergraduate poems in 1939. Ava lived on Chip's hall, in a special dormitory at the top of a neo-Gothic building where four rooms were set aside for the college elite: the student council president, the yearbook editor, and the editors of the student newspaper and the literary journal. Chip and I played basketball in the hallway while Ava watched. That is, Chip played, and I pretended I could. It was another version of shooting hoops with Richie. What I really wanted was to fall asleep in his arms, with my head against his hairy chest.

Of course, he was dating a rich girl from Squirrel Hill, in Pittsburgh. One night, Ava and I stole a six-pack out of the Village Inn and sat in her room, getting drunk. Then we smoked a joint, and shared our love for Chip. Ava liked him, she said, because he was wounded. I guess she got her romantic faith in wounded men from Sylvia Plath—certainly not from Chip, who was quite hardy, tall and broad-shouldered and oblivious, a former high school soccer star. Ava said he looked like Ted Hughes, Plath's heath-handsome husband, another agonized poet, another "Daddy."

After a while, Ava and I got quiet, and she put Joni Mitchell on her stereo. It was *Blue*: "Will you take me as I am, hung up on another another man?" Discussing Chip with Ava was the closest I had ever come to admitting I was gay, and I put my head on her lap, feeling giddy and abashed, and said, "Hold me. I'm wounded, too."

Then she kissed me—and, to my shame and relief, immediately passed out. She fell on me with her long hair in my face, and we slept there, and lied about it in the morning, like two guys who tell each other, "Christ, was I drunk last night."

That was the first time we kissed. I never thought it would happen again, but here is Ava, kissing me in the open, in a doorway, taking my face in her hands, my cheek between her palms, trying to get me involved.

"You must be high," I tell her.

"Don't underestimate your irresistible charm," she says.

"I don't think I can do this," I say.

"Are you telling me 'no' means no?"

"Are you raping me?"

"Is that what you want?"

"Ava, you're weirding me out."

"Lighten up, can you?"

She leans forward, her mouth against mine. I pull back.

"I won't be your gay fetish. I won't be the one gay man you've ever kissed."

She laughs. "You're way too late for that. Come on," she says. "Doesn't hash make you horny?"

"Hash and fag bashing and Zack's shit?"

"Oh," she says, acting campy. "Now you're talking."

"Don't be so creepy. Are you pretending you're a guy?"

"No, I'm pretending you are."

I'm a sucker for a one-liner. What the hell? Playing my part, I bend down to her delicate face, and I kiss her. It's sort of fun. My students ask me, "What do gay men do?" And I say, "What do *you* do?" "No, but I mean, what do you *do*?" they repeat. "Well," I tell them, "I guess I kiss."

So I do what gay guys do. I kiss her. Her breath tastes very slightly of warm milk. My eyes are closed. I put my hand around the back of her head, pulling her face to mine. She's not shy, which is nice. I'm kissing for show, but she is kissing for real, and I get nervous.

She's a Taurus, I'm thinking, *dead earnest about her desire.* Not that she isn't playful. She's willing to pose, to dress as a boy or a girl. Once she decides you're the one, however, she gets sincere. She kisses the way I want to be kissed, trying to connect. That's rare enough. I've kissed gay guys who posed like they were in a porn film, keeping their tongues in sight, as if for the camera. Ava isn't performing now. So I hold her more tightly, my arms around her back, pressing against her, and, to my surprise, it turns me on. *It's the hash talking,* I think, or maybe it's her Yankees cap. I love accessories. In any case, I've got a hard-on, and I can't hide it.

She draws back, and there's the thrill of separation. I feel her pull away, and suddenly I want her back. I reach out like an infant, my fingers curled into fists, and she laughs and says, "Let's try something." Then she undoes my pants.

I say, "Please don't look at my belly." I say, "What if those bashers come back?"

"They'll be searching for fags," she says.

"So this is camouflage?"

She says, "Shut up."

Anyway, my dick's out. I'm thinking, *I hope she doesn't put it in her mouth.*

Girls should never have to do that. No one should. It's impossible to laugh with a dick in your mouth, which is really what's wrong with gay men. If anything calls for laughter, it's sucking dick. Vaginas get a bad rap, but what can you say in praise of dicks? They are unbearably foolish. Testicles! Explain them. Why is the word for toughness always "balls"? Dogs walk with their nuts exposed, and don't they look foolish?

Mine are out, like a dog's. Ava cups them. "Cups": The word is so tender, and so is her gesture, her hand upturned, held out, palm curled, as if offering friendship and protection. "I think I'm in love," I say.

"Don't be such a girl," she says.

She undoes her jeans and shows her boxer shorts. She's dressed like Madonna. That's hilarious and sexy. The shorts are cobalt blue and the waistband is frayed. I can see elastic through the fabric.

"Let's fuck like they do in the movies," she says. "Like no one really does. You know, really fast, lots of thrusting. Okay?" she says, very sweetly.

I nod. She pulls her boxers down, and considering that she has to do gymnastics to reach me, and I have to bend my knees, we manage, not too awkwardly, to get her on me and me in her and the two of us holding each other. I'm laughing.

"Hey, *fruitjes*," I shout, and Ava says, "Ssh." She says, "Don't wreck the moment." It's difficult to know what's left to destroy, though, because I'm squatting and she's straddling my knees, and I keep falling out of her.

"I thought it was supposed to be seamless with heterosexuals," I say.

"Are you calling this heterosexual?"

"Well, according to some definition."

"Not when we're both fruits," she says. Then she bites me on the lip and says, "How do you ever get laid? You never stop talking. I thought boys didn't talk. Try and pretend you're a boy."

"Okay," I agree. In other words, I better stay hard.

"Say it," she orders, holding my dick. "Say, 'I'm a boy.' "

"I'm a boy."

"Convince me," she says.

"I'm a boy," I repeat, and the evidence, I guess, is my dick, which is still hard, sort of to my surprise.

So we do this ten-minute herky-jerky thing together. She's got her arms braced against either side of the doorway, and I'm trying to keep my balance and watch over her shoulder, both at once. I have my eye out for fag bashers and passers-by, when Ava, sensing my distraction, says, "Now tell me you're a girl."

I do what I'm told. I say, "I'm a girl."

I lose my balance and fall. I'm lying on my back in the doorway.

"Stay still," she says, and she gets on top of me and says, "*I'm* a girl," and I say, "Sure you are," and she says, "You are, too," and then she makes me say that over and over.

"I'm a girl."

"Sell it," she says.

"I'm such a girl."

"You're a Dutch girl."

"*Ja ja*," I say.

"Okay," she says, and she takes my hands and puts them up her shirt, on her breasts, and says, "Sweet girl." I'm looking up at her and touching her lovely breasts, her, what, soft? Round? But they're not soft and round, they're too complex for that. I'm trying to figure out how to hold them. To cup them, as she cupped my balls. Going straight for her nipples would be corny. There have to be digressions in storytelling and making love, and I'm turning breast cupping into a narrative, when Ava, who has been playing with herself, suddenly says, "I'm going to come."

"I thought girls took forever," I say, laughing, out of breath.

She says, "Shut. Up."

If she were a guy I'd hold her tight and say, like, "Yeah, buddy, that's right, buddy," which is what, for want of a better idea, I do. I hold her breasts and say, "Buddy," like we're Boy Scouts, and she leans down and kisses me. She catches me mid-Buddy. "You come, too," she says, arching back. I have never come inside a woman before. I'm worried I can't. "Shut your eyes," Ava says, "and dream of Dennis Quaid," and she stays with me until we're both through.

"Thanks, Dennis," I say.

"It was nothing."

"Gosh," I say. "My heart's really pounding."

Ava reaches into the breast pocket of her leather jacket and pulls out the sheet of paper towel that was wrapped around our hash. She wipes herself, she wipes me. The best part of sex: cleaning up.

She tosses the paper towel, pulls up her shorts and her jeans, and sits on the door stoop. I tuck away my dick and join her, and we sit side by side.

"I don't feel like I really know anyone until we've had sex," she says.

"Do you know me now? After seventeen years?"

"Some people have their 'sex personality.' You're not fucking them, you're fucking a column they read in *Penthouse* when they were twelve."

"What am I like?"

"You," she tells me, "don't change, at all."

"Is that good?"

"It's familiar. I guess you really never do stop talking."

"I could have told you that." Then I say, irrelevantly, "My students don't like women at all."

"Most people don't," she says, in a funny tone, not acid but wistful, even sweet.

"You wouldn't believe the stuff they write," I say. "Not just the guys."

"I have an idea," she says.

"A straight man is someone who wants to spend all his time with men. That's what I learned from my students."

Ava says, "I'm really high. I just realized it."

I say, "I guess that makes me straight."

"Well, you're a tiger," she says, punching me in the arm.

"My heart won't stop pounding."

"That's a bad thing?"

"I wonder if Zack's awake."

Which, of course, he is.

"I'm in the *bathroom*," he's screaming, ten minutes later, when we're back in the hotel, "I'll be down in a *minute*," he shouts, and Ava and I turn, and look up, and wait for him to come down.

They Live by Night

It takes time to make queer people.

—Gertrude Stein

Then Richie comes out of the bathroom, headed for his blind date, looking like John Garfield in a forties detective flick. Men in the 1940s, all their upholstery: girly undergarments, socks, sock garters, tailored shirts with the tails tucked, high-waisted trousers under the broad-shouldered jackets of their double-breasted suits, black-and-white wing tip shoes, and the accessories, cuff links, suspenders, neckties, tiepins, hats obscuring hairlines. You could never tell what their bodies were like under all that fabric. But you knew their flesh had to be pampered and important.

Richie swaggers up to Ava, figuring she must be his girl, Afrodytea. If he had a hat, he'd be tipping it. Instead, he is carrying a rose. When did he have time to get a flower? A dewy red rosebud. He hands it to her, wrapping his free hand territorially around the back of her chair.

Two beautiful people who have both taken down their pants in front of me are within grazing distance of my fingertips.

"For the lady," Richie says, giving Ava the flower.

I'd like to see her face, but Richie is between us.

"Whose little boy are you?" Ava says, accepting his floral tribute.

"I'm not taken," Richie says.

"Anyway, not for the night," I say, trying to crash his high.

"Not taken for the rest of my life," Richie says, doing the guy thing of being incredibly courtly and sweet to a possible love. There's swing in his stance. You feel he would bounce you onto the floor and turn you through a dance number, Count Basie's "One O'Clock Jump," followed by Doris Day, as bruised as she ever was, singing "The Very Thought of You," with torrid obbligato trumpet licks by Harry James.

"Obbligato": in the background, though not to be left out.

I try to wedge myself between them, saying, "You've met?"

"Not in the flesh," Ava says. If she *is* Afrodytea, no doubt she's trying to gauge the relative merits of two possible coincidences: Either *I'm* the guy she met on the Internet, or I'm friends with the guy she met on the Internet, and he has brought me along on their date.

"Let's get this over with," I say. "Are the two of you going to stick to phony cybernames? Or shall I introduce you by your real ones?"

Before I can wreck the bliss of our ignorance, however, we're distracted by a sudden clatter. From various doors around the bar rock band roadies noisily emerge. They lurch into the room, hauling equipment, rolling amps, swinging mike stands. Apparently, we have shown up just in time for Thrash Night, a musical poetry slam, where a dozen hardcore bands will compete to Reign in Hell. We are set to be their audience. Techies carry cable and search for outlets, moving as grimly and mechanically as drones assimilated by the Borg. Some of them even have Borg implants: pierced chins, tongue studs.

They're cherubim of hell. The barroom, carved from a meatpacking warehouse, is a concrete dungeon. Its cement floor and walls are slicked with glossy scurf. Bar tops and tables are polished ore. Red drapes hang in doorways, and red picture frames hold photographs of bat caves and mine shafts. The lights are low.

Through the visible darkness the bartender looks alarmingly like Chuck Knoblauch, baseball's fumbler, my favorite New York Yankee. Chucky Garlic: *Knoblauch* is "garlic" in German. Knoblauch is a second baseman who was moved to the outfield because he started throwing like a girl. Firing the ball, he watches it go, as if waving farewell: "Good-bye, ball." And he swings like no one else. Bat high, face scrunched, he sucks in his cheeks like a supermodel. His number is 11, identical figures standing side by side: two gay men? Plus, isn't he in love with shortstop Derek Jeter? After big wins he flings himself in Derek's arms, hugging him like a lover or a son.

His doppelgänger is a downtown bartender. Chuck Garlic, serving drinks in hell. I ask him for a seltzer with lime. Rich gets a bourbon neat. Ava, sitting on her bar stool, demigod on a golden seat, lets Rich buy her a Scotch.

Richie tastes his drink, winces, pleased, and finally answers my question.

"I've got a perfectly good real name," he says. "It's Samson, 'cause I got no more hair. Wish I could say a girl took it off. Anyway, I didn't lose none of my power."

Richie gets his grammar wrong to tease girls. I resist the urge to correct him. Instead, I say, "Your online name is Samson?"

"Who said online?" Richie asks. "It's my middle name."

"Your middle name is Andrew. Richard *Andrew* McShane."

"Oh, you're *Richie,*" Ava says.

Now it's Richie's turn to look perplexed. "I never said my name," he mutters. "You've heard of me before this?"

"Of course," Ava tells him. "You're famous. *RAM.*"

That freaks him out, and he shifts quickly from prowling to suspicious. I can tell he's worried that Ava knows his girlfriend. "I never said my real name," he repeats. "Not yet. And I've got no reputation except in Vegas, and that was 1980 . . ."

"Richie," I say, shocked at how much I enjoy watching him squirm, "let me tell you a secret." I'm ready to spill the truth about Ava and me, but before I say another word, the tech crew runs a sound check, and we're silenced by the Zombies doing "Time of the Season." The volume goes way up, then down, levels out. "What's your name? Who's your daddy?" the Zombies sing, as the street door bursts open and a pretty girl makes an entrance.

Light breaks across the floor, and she walks into the triangular glow, looking waif-thin but ready to fight, balanced on spongy black platform shoes. Tiny and fierce, she has long dark brown hair and a scarf crossed over her head like Anouk Aimée in Federico Fellini's *La Dolce Vita*. She is wearing her Gucci sunglasses indoors. Her stretchy black bell-bottoms seem brushed on with nail polish, and her pink top is decorated in gold glitter with the words "Wet Pain."

She holds her cell phone, carrying other needed objects in a small black leather backpack. Her arms are bare, and her neck is tender and fine, with blue veins. She hurries ahead, looking around.

Seeing us at the bar, she pauses to consider her options. Then, making a decision, she comes up to me, maybe because I'm sitting closest to the door.

"Shit, shit, *shit*," she tells me. There are no customary greetings, and she talks to me like a wild niece I've known for twenty years. "I'm always late," she says, not apologizing. "I *hate* that," she says. "I'm not a bimbo. I thought I knew the neighborhood. Listen, I can find Cleveland from here. I'm Tammy. Of course, you know me as—" She stops abruptly and says, "You're the Internet guy, right? Justin? Anyway, that's the name you used. Are you Justin?"

Well, and what is the answer to that? Am I? I can feel Richie's panic. He wants me to take this girl off his hands so he can hit on Ava. "Please let my buddy cover for me," he's pleading. Or maybe he's wondering, "If she's Afrodytea, who is this other chick?" And

Ava is no doubt surprised to learn I've been scoping babes on the Web. *What did I do to him in Holland?* she's worrying. I pause a minute before answering Tammy, happily letting my friends dangle.

Then I figure, what the hell. She's hot. "Yup," I say. "I'm Justin."

"Justin Thyme?" she says.

Doing a slow burn, I turn to Richie. " 'Justin Thyme?' " I say.

"Great name," Richie says, blushing a confession. Now that he sees he can trust me he is focusing on a more urgent concern: Does Ava know his girlfriend? Is she a private detective the girlfriend hired to trail him?

I turn back to Tammy, who is checking me out. She is not ashamed to let me see her doing it. "All right, then," she says, making up her mind. "I'm glad you're twice my age. Though you told me you were twenty-four. Whatever. At least you're not twelve. Can you do me a favor and order me a drink that's at least two different colors?" She's searching for cash in her miniknapsack. "Here," she says, pushing a wadded ten-dollar bill into my palm. "I don't want anything blue," she says. Then she flips open her cell phone. "Do you mind?" she says, dialing the cell, walking away. "I'll be a minute. I promised a friend I'd call and let him know you're not Norman Bates."

I watch her cross the room to a bank of amplifiers. She turns her back and makes the call. Then Ava's cell vibrates thrummingly on the bar top. Ava shrugs, smiles, and moves down the bar.

Richie takes this chance to grab my arm and pull me aside. As we talk, roadies swing past us with audio gadgets.

"Two guys, two girls, we're set," Richie says.

"Yeah, according to whom?"

"You know her?" he says, pointing through his chest to indicate Ava.

"I might. More importantly, Mr. Justin *Thyme*, do you know *her*?" I nod my head toward Tammy.

"Whatever," he says.

"You hooked up with a little girl?"

"She's legal."

"Cockfighting is legal in Texas."

"Don't be vulgar," Richie says. "How do you know her?"

"Which one?" I say.

"Heads up, heads up, coming through," yells a tech guy with a beer gut and a red beard, nearly stabbing us with mike stands.

Richie doesn't flinch. He stretches his arms, shoots his cuffs. "Oh, I got a feeling this could be *good*. I need to know, is that lady at the bar familiar with the girlfriend?"

"Maybe they were dorm mates in college," I say, shrugging.

"Hey, man," Richie says. "You and me, we're on a roll. Buddy? Don't jinx it. You probably know her from somewhere, is what I'm saying."

"Listen, if you like her, I'll leave. You can score, and I'll go home."

"No, no, no," he says, hand on my shoulder. "I need your help. This could be huge. Did you see the tension, man? You could've stretched a bungee cord, plucked it, seen the vibrations between us, that's how we were connecting. Please. Oh, please, Jesus," he says, putting his hands together in prayer. "The little one's Afrodytea, then," he says, changing tone, taking time to get the facts.

"Well, are you Justin Thyme?"

We're laughing.

"It's my porn name," he says.

"Okay, there's too much stuff you haven't told me."

"No, man, haven't you ever heard that? If you were a porn star, you'd take the name of the street where you grew up, and the name of your first pet."

"You had a pet named Thyme when you were ten years old?"

And then he says, very bashfully, with a sweet resonant hum in his voice, like Louis Armstrong bending to a falling note, "My kitty cat."

"Christ, Richie."

"From a litter: Parsley, Sage, Rosemary. And Thyme. My mom named them. It was the sixties, come on. Thyme was mine. Cool cat. He had gigantic ears. Humped all the neighborhood cats. Man, I loved him. All black with yellow eyes. I treated him like a dog, scratched his belly, at night he'd bring his catch to my bed. Dead mice. I thought he had a fight he couldn't win, but it turned out my mom put him down. She was allergic."

"Okay, Richie," I tell him. "Tell me what I'm going to have to do."

"Dogboy," Richie says, grinning.

"Can you say that louder?"

"You're my dogboy," he says, his fist on my shoulder, though he's not watching me. He's checking out Ava, who's still on her cell, while Tammy, among cables and amps, clutches her phone in the bar light. "First I need info," Richie says. "Who is she?"

"Well, you've heard me mention Ava."

"Oh, man," Richie says. "That's the chick who does the sex stuff?"

"She's been on TV. Don't you watch Conan O'Brien?"

"The girlfriend hates him. Jesus, the girlfriend. You don't think they know each other, do you, the girlfriend and her? She heard of me because you told her?"

"Sure, I've mentioned your name. Richie. You're my oldest friend."

"Oh, this is sweet," he says. "Scratch the girlfriend connection. You didn't tell her why we came?"

"Listen, Ava's not stupid."

"Fine, whatever, and Miss Moonboots over there thinks you're me. So here's what we gotta do," he says, as if offering a treat. "We gotta pretend," he says, and of course I know what he wants. I'm going to be Tammy's date. "I didn't tell her anything about myself that you don't already know," he says. "Okay, I lied and said I was a Leo. She seemed to care. She said she never met an Aries she liked. How do I deal with that? Our birthday's August first."

"Ours?"

"Mine," he says. "I mean, yours."

"And what are you going to tell Ava?"

"Don't sweat that, man, it's my business. Far as she knows we came here for drinks. We're buddies."

"Okay, except Ava knows I'm gay."

"Sure, we all know that. I'm sure Moonboots knows it, too. So what? You're always saying how you hate those *categories,* right?" He makes Dr. Evil air quotes around "categories." "So here's your chance to prove they don't exist. Come on, you talk the talk, you say, 'Richie, blah blah blah, we're basically all bisexual,' you *taunt* me until I agree. So when a pretty young girl shows up looking for her date, suddenly you decide that maybe there *is* such a thing as being only straight, only gay? No no, my friend. You gotta live by your ideals."

"What if I told you to take some guy on a date?"

"Is he buying?"

"Richie."

"If he looks like Johnny Depp, I might consider it."

"You would *not.* I mean, she's *hot,*" I say, lowering my voice, glancing quickly over my shoulder at Tammy. "She met you on the *computer*. She's looking for sex. How am I supposed to handle that?"

"You never had sex with a girl?"

"Well, yeah. No. Kind of. Not exactly. What do you mean by 'sex'? Or 'girl'?"

"Christ, you complicate everything," Richie says. "Let's make it easy. Let's say desire *is* a choice, like you're always telling me, and get you in there. If you don't want to be in there, well, fine, buy her a couple drinks, take her number, and don't call. Don't you know the definition of a date? Buying drinks for someone you don't intend to call. Look, she's off the phone, here she comes, she's got no hips, like a boy, you like that, don't you?"

Before I can respond, he's gone to Ava.

Now I'm standing with Tammy.

"Are people ever mean to you?" she asks.

She has removed her sunglasses and pulled her scarf from her brow and draped it over her shoulders. She's got hair horns, twin bunches of hair pulled tight and sticking up like antennae at either side of her head.

"Oh," I say, startled. "What are you asking me?"

"Never mind," she says. "You told me you were into sports. You said you were a high school jock. You don't look much like a high school jock."

"I'm sure I said a lot of stuff."

"Well, I was totally honest," she says. "I always am. You better know that right now. Because if you can't take it—"

"My name's not Justin Thyme."

"Fine," she says. "Don't tell me your real name. I'll make one up. Blank Man."

She's insulting me. Now I'm interested. "What's your real name?" I say.

"Just what I told you. Tammy."

Her eyes are brown and her voice is as gingery and warm as Billie Holiday singing a line from "I Must Have That Man": "My heart is broken, it won't ever mend."

"I should believe you?" I say. "Because you told, um, me, on the Internet—"

"Yeah," she says, cutting me off, "Afrodytea. Silly name, huh? I wanted you to think I was, I don't know, anyone but me. I don't like myself."

"Well," I say, "self-loathing doesn't stop you from talking a lot."

She laughs. "I'm trusting you for some reason."

"After thirty-five seconds?"

"You said some sweet things on the Internet. Like how you cried at *Frequency* with Dennis Quaid." She looks around the room. "Did you get me that drink?" Tying her scarf in a knot at her throat, she says, "I'm Tammy Dyer, which is Norwegian, I guess, though I haven't lived with my dad since I was ten. My mom's from-Italy Italian. I was born in Hewlett Harbor, Long Island. My parents met on a boat in Hewlett Bay. You didn't get my drink, did you?" She grabs my hand, where I am still holding her ten-dollar bill. "I'll do it," she says. "I always do. People aren't ever mean to you?"

Mean? Richie's pretending he's single and I'm bisexual. I'm pretending I'm Richie pretending he's Justin. What is Tammy pretending?

We stand at the bar next to Ava and Richie, and Tammy orders a colorful drink—triple sec, Chartreuse, and Kool-Aid. It looks like Jello 1-2-3. While she's waiting for her potion to be mixed, she tells me she's a seamstress.

"I'm a *novelty* seamstress, actually," she says. She builds masks at Rubie's Costumes in Queens, under the elevated tracks of the J train. "I told you about it on the Web," she says. "You don't remember? Were you multitasking?"

Chuck Garlic delivers her drink. "Tastes like Sweetarts," she says, happy.

Ava, who has been keeping an eye on us while she fends off Richie, leans toward us and says, "What a pretty drink. What's it called?"

Richie wants to be included. "Must be fruity," he says. "Is it named for a fruit?"

I'm worried he means me. But Tammy, toasting me, says, "I'm calling it an Instant Message, in honor of how we met."

Now the lie is official: Word's out that I found Tammy on the Internet. Richie flings his fist in the air, giving me a mock "thumbs up." Ava grins at me like, *I thought your specialty was drunk straight boys having a blackout.*

"To us," Tammy says, knocking drinks with my seltzer. We grin and gulp. "You've got nice friends," she tells me. "They are your friends, aren't they?"

"Introductions, we never did introductions," Richie says. Having learned Ava's name, he presents Ava to Tammy. "I'm Richie," he adds. "I guess you all know this clown already," he says, poking me.

"That's Blank Man," Tammy says, and everyone laughs.

"What's in your drink?" Ava asks Tammy. She's in journalistic mode, ready to go with anyone's self-delusions as long as it makes a good story.

"Taste it," Tammy says, and Ava takes a delicate sip.

"Yummy," she says. "Lavoris."

"Aren't you the sex lady?" Tammy asks her. "I think I saw you on TV."

"Hey," I say. "A fan."

"I love your work," Tammy says. Then she bangs her hand on the bar. "Damn," she says. "I almost forgot. I brought props. Masks. I stole them from work."

She slings her knapsack on the bar top and digs inside. "I was telling Blank Man, I make costumes for a living. It's a day job, really. Anyway, before I left work, I snuck into the Halloween stash, and . . ."—she pulls a package out of her bag—"here we are." She lays the bundle on the bar, unties string, and folds back tissue paper, uncovering four items: two furry latex wolf mitts, a rubber Frankenstein face, and a pair of red devil horns sewn to a red velvet band.

"Oh," Ava says, genuinely thrilled. "This is the best party *ever*."

"No doubt we'll read about it in next month's sex column in *Yo*," I say.

"You won't mind if I say you're all bisexual, will you?" Ava asks.

"Nah, darling," Richie says, hypocritically. "That's how God made us."

I want to slug him.

"Oh, don't quote *me*," Tammy says. Apparently, she is the only person in the room, including Ava, who ever reads *Yo*.

"Paws," Richie says, grabbing the mitts and sliding his palms inside of them as if trying on a pair of boxing gloves. Their rubbery claws are long and pointed. "Ain't I the shit?" he says.

"Can I try the ears?" Ava says.

Tammy holds out the horns very graciously and solicitously, and Ava clips them to her head. The girls are bonding over accessories.

"What do you think?" Ava says.

"They are so totally you."

"You're not just saying that?"

"Those two women think they are a pair of queens," Richie says. He is very happy. "You try," he says, giving me one of his gloves. It's hot and slimy inside. We knock hairy knuckles.

"Blank Man gets in touch with his inner wolf," Tammy says.

"And his outer wolf," I say, looking at Richie.

Tammy rolls the Frankenstein mask over her head. She turns to Chuck Knoblauch and groans. Chucky roars back. The mask devours her head and neck and falls straight to her shoulders, which are as narrow as a family-size pill bottle.

"That reminds me," I say. "Do you have any aspirin? Richie was gonna buy me some, but . . ." I close my wolf fist over my human palm in an attitude of prayer.

She doesn't hear me. Instead, she is fixated on Chucky Garlic. Quickly, impulsively, she rolls off her mask and holds it, offeringly, over his head. He grunts assent. Very sweetly, he bows down, his neck bent, his brow laid in her hands, accepting his new self. She accidentally pinches his ear, smoothing the rubber, but he doesn't wince. We all watch as he receives his face.

"Oh, you look lovely," Ava says, delighted.

"Dude, it is an improvement," Richie says.

"It's so less scary than you were before," Tammy agrees.

Ava puts the devil horns on Tammy's head, crowning the creator.

"Satan," I beg Tammy. "You got aspirin? I need drugs."

Finally, Tammy is glad she came. "Satan is not always pleased to gratify the human beast," she tells me, "but for chemicals that rot the lining of your stomach we can make an allowance."

Who guessed "Satan" was the secret word? I glance at Richie like I found her G-spot, and he's all, "Dude!" And I'm all, "Is what I'm saying!" Even Frankenstein chimes in with manly praise. Now I know why straight guys do double dates: so they can watch each other get hard over girls.

"One should either *be* a heterosexual, or *wear* a heterosexual," I'm thinking, misquoting Oscar Wilde, watching everybody's crossover from human to satanic, or animalistic, or divine. As long as I'm deposing, I want to kiss them all. Okay, Richie would be first in line. Despite my polymorphous wishes, I'm anchored to a single urge. I do wish desire were a choice. I want to place my paws in Tammy's hands and feel that I yearn for her. Maybe I need a prosthesis.

"Can I try that?" I ask Chucky, and he nods, peeling off his face and sliding it over my head. He is careful, nearly kind. I remember being fitted for shoes when I was ten, when salespeople still bent down to tie your laces. Chuck is as tenderly solicitous as a long-ago shoestore clerk. He puts his flat palms at either side of my head, adjusting my mask. "You're set, man," he says.

Now I'm part werewolf, part Frankenstein.

"Kiss me," I say, turning to Tammy, who smacks me, not hard. She's laughing. Then she strokes my high flat shiny brow. "You *are* repellent," she says, getting into it.

Richie has his arm around Ava's shoulders, and his mouth is close to her ear. I lumber over, separating them. "Kiss me," I tell Ava. She busses my nose.

"You," Richie says, knocking his bunched fist against my arm. He's on his second bourbon, loosey-goosey, acting out. "Why don't you say what you really want?" he tells me.

"I want my bride," I say.

"I know what you want. Watch this," he tells Ava.

Leaning toward me, he puts his hand around the back of my neck, pulls my head forward, and kisses my rubbery lips.

I have seen Richie kissing women in this fashion, the intimate gesture—partly proprietary, partly affectionate, perhaps vaguely threatening—of putting his hand around the back of their necks and tipping their heads to his lips, as if to get at what's inside of them. It's thrilling to watch. It makes them feel wanted and controlled, and they don't know whether to surrender or run.

In my case, however, he does it not to give me something, but to take it away.

"There!" he says, releasing me. "See?" he says. "You're not King Pimp."

Then Ava figures that she's had enough.

"Well," she says, finishing her Scotch, "this has been fun and I have to go."

The bar is filling with out-of-towners. Chuck Garlic, unmasked, is serving them drinks. Our happy group is breaking up; everyone feels it. Ava is meeting a guy. Not one of us, but a real guy, someone she's been seeing. He was the voice at the end of her recent cell phone call. Named Adam. "He's a cultural critic," Ava says, "for *Rolling Stone*." She was planning to meet him here for drinks, but he decided instead to head to Astor Place to interview skate punks for a lifestyle piece on runaway rave kids.

If I were Richie, I'd give up. But he's smarter than me. He figures, if your rival knocks at the door, ask him in.

"If it's punks he wants," Richie tells Ava, "bring him here. Isn't this a punky place? Twenty minutes, this'll be wall-to-wall white kids from Westchester with spikes in their noses and their old man's credit cards."

"He's got a point," I say, but Ava just shrugs.

"I'll call him," Richie says. "Gimme your phone," and to my surprise, she does.

"Now I really need that aspirin," I tell Tammy, peeling off my mask

"All I've got is Midol," Tammy tells me. "And zinc."

Richie, holding Ava's cell phone, has Adam on the line. I don't hear his conversation, though, because Tammy grabs my arm and leads me down the bar to a TV monitor that lights the bar top blue. In the TV's glow she searches in her knapsack and finds a giant bottle of cheap aspirin.

The tech crew has finished setting up the bandstand. Chuck Garlic pours beer for Jersey dudes and the women who love them. Looking bored, he is keeping an eye on the TV monitor, watching the first episode of *Survivor.* "Vote off the fat guy," he says.

With my index finger I push two of Tammy's aspirin far back on my tongue.

"Testing your gag reflex?" Tammy says.

I take my finger out of my mouth and wash down the aspirin with warm seltzer, my ice all melted. "You're awfully fresh," I say, after I swallow.

"*You're* checking out the bartender."

"You're a smart-ass from Staten Island."

"Who said I was from Staten Island?"

"Well, you did. You implied," I say, trying to remember what Richie told me she told him, "that you were sort of imprisoned. In Staten Island. Todt Hill. And he's—we're—*I'm* supposed to rescue you. Basically. Didn't you say that?"

"Listen," she says, "you're not my father."

"You don't live in Staten Island?"

"I live in Port Mobil on the banks of the Arthur Kill. My backyard is the clay pits. You're gay, aren't you?"

"I'm—"

"That's right, do that. Your shocked and bumbling routine. It's cute. You think you're going to convince anyone you're not gay in that shirt?"

"It's Richie's," I say, protesting, running my palm over my chest.

"It looks like Jessica Rabbit threw up on your stomach," she says. Then she dives again into her knapsack. "You need candy," she says.

"I'm sure you said you were from Staten Island."

"I live in Willowbrook, the loony bin, which is now a college campus. Doesn't that make you want to apply there?"

Then she finds two Jolly Ranchers, which I happen to love. Suddenly we're both quiet and happy, unwrapping our candy.

"You really are pretty, you know," I tell her, meaning it, and for once she smiles.

Who would I be if I wanted her? A middle-aged white guy with no money and an average dick. In other words, heterosexuality wouldn't change me. I'd still be twice her age and three times her weight.

Tammy pulls the drawstrings of her knapsack tight and says, "I'll tell you my secret, since everyone here seems to have one. Don't think I haven't guessed you're not the man I met online. Whatever. I didn't come here expecting Mr. Wonderful. In fact, I'm here to see a friend. He's playing tonight with his band. That's why I picked this place to hook up. I decided I'd give my blind date about twenty minutes, and then I could watch my friend's band. He's on last, I think, but he should be walking in here any minute now. What I'm saying is, Would you keep an eye out for him while I'm in the john? You can't miss him. He looks like you twenty years ago. Cute in a bland way. I like guys who are nothing special. And the two of you have the same name," she says, shouldering her backpack and flitting away.

I sit there, wondering if I've been dumped. If so, it's a first: blown off by someone else's blind date. Now I know why I'm not bisexual. It doubles your chances of being rejected.

I wish I smoked. Instead, I flag Chuck and order a real drink. I leave it to him what kind. He gives me gin and a manly pat, as if to say, "Buddy, I've been there."

The barroom is noisy with customers. Suddenly, I'm surrounded by average white kids, who crowd the space separating me from Ava and Richie. I can't see my friends, but I can hear Richie on Ava's phone, giving Ava's boyfriiend Adam a sales pitch. "Come on down," Richie is saying, like Bob Barker on steroids. When Rich is in a mood to sell you something, he is almost irresistible. He puts on such a magnificent performance as a trustworthy guy.

And who am I? Somebody waiting for a guy whose name is the same as mine. Tom, for God's sake. The only Tom I ever liked was a man I dated for a few months in 1986. He looked like Gene Hackman in *The Conversation*, sexy and solid, sturdily handsome, Irish Italian, my favorite combination, impressive in a suit and tie. I thought he was swell. Naturally, I said something stupid about him in a magazine article, and he split. Sleep with a writer, wake up in print, Zack's quote. Why can't I get along with gay men? Whereas if you're a mute straight man half my age, brother, I'm yours. I'm thinking how badly I want to *be* an invisible straight man when a guy with my name appears in the bar, carrying part of a drum kit and wearing what I recognize as Richie's Megadeth T-shirt. He sets down his stuff, looks around, spots me, and says yo.

And it's Justin. Not the online "Justin," not Richie or me posing as somebody else, but the real one—Justin Innocenzio, Tammy's friend, it turns out. Are they dating? Justin and Tammy? That would be weird. Last I knew, he was sleeping with me.

How to Disappear Completely

Never tell anyone anything ever.

—Ernest Hemingway

Not even two days earlier, Saturday, Memorial Day weekend, Justin rings my apartment buzzer. I'm barely awake, though it's noon. I have been sleeping on the living room couch. Groggy, I press the intercom. The answering voice says, "Yo." A startled, hopeful, apologetic "yo." Grumbling, I buzz him up, which is a first: He has never been inside my apartment. The elevator will haul him here in a couple of minutes, and I have two choices: to get dressed, or tidy up. I'm in a T-shirt and boxers. If I were twenty-three, I'd think I *was* dressed. So fine, I'll pretend I'm Matt Damon styled for a magazine shoot. I grab my sheet and pillows off the couch and throw them in the bedroom, hiding evidence of my disorder, closing the flimsy slatted double French doors that lead to the bedroom and hoping Justin doesn't ask for a tour. I have time to pick three books off the floor and straighten the cushions on the couch before I hear his knock at the door.

He comes in with his bike and his messenger pack and a book of poetry by Louise Glück, *The Wild Iris*. He's hoisting the bike on his left shoulder and wearing the pack high across his back. By way of hello, without unloading any of his gear, he hands me the book and asks me to read the title poem.

"It's awesome," he says.

How can I think about poetry when I'm barely awake? But Justin is intent. I don't want to disappoint him, though I can hardly see him, my eyes are so blurry with sleep. In cargo pants cut off at the knees and his TEXAS IS THE REASON T-shirt, he's an olive blur reeking of Downy.

I take the book. Justin gets his glasses out of their black case, carefully puts them on, and we both read. The poem opens with a couplet:

> *At the end of my suffering*
> *there was a door.*

"Isn't that awesome?" Justin says.

"Yeah, sure," I say, and then we stand together, not speaking, for a solid minute. Justin is still hoisting his bike. I could invite him to sit, and he might ask for something to drink, a glass of water, a Coke. Instead, we crowd together by the door, attending to literature. Justin is as quiet as a Louise Glück poem. I don't mind. After years of talk, I am willing to give silence a try.

"Okay," I say, when I'm done reading, and he says, "Yeah." That might be the cue to enter the room like adults, set down the bike, get dressed, begin. But Justin reaches over, turns the page, and says, "Read that."

It's the book's second poem, "Matins." Here's how it ends:

> *We merely knew it wasn't human nature to love*
> *only what returns love.*

I'm wondering, Is Justin giving me a hint? A diagnosis? A prediction? But poetry is not about me, after all. Justin just says, "She's amazing."

"Yeah," I tell him, learning to be appropriately awed. I remember a story I heard about Robert Lowell teaching poetry at Harvard. Lowell would read a famous poem out loud, and when he was done, he'd say, "Isn't that great?" And that was the lesson.

"She's great," I say, emulating Lowell. Then I say, "Don't you want to put down your bike?"

"It's not heavy," he tells me. Which doesn't seem to address my concern. He's right, though, it's a trick bike for teen stunts, a silver GT Pro Performer as tall as your thighs, with a front wheel that spins 360.

"Did you *bike* here?" I ask him, still parental. "On that?"

"I came on the train kinda early this morning," he says. "I been riding around your neighborhood, waiting for you to wake up. I know you sleep late. So I got us some lunch. I went to this place, I know a kid who works there, he packed some stuff, free of charge. It's health food, but so what? Anyway, that's what you eat. It's what you *should* be eating. What's goin' on?"

The image of him biking all morning exhausts me.

"I can't face you until I mainline some caffeine," I say, and he holds out a bag from the corner deli: tea with milk, no sugar. Milk is protein. That's allowed. "You think of everything," I say.

Then he mentions an apparently long-planned trip to Woodlawn Cemetery in the Bronx to see Herman Melville's grave. Melville is Justin's latest obsession. He's into *Bartleby the Scrivener,* maybe because Bartleby is a protoslacker. "I would prefer not to," Bartleby tells his haranguing boss. It's the same stunned tone in which Justin says, "Whatever." Though Justin does have preferences: He loves *Moby Dick*. He's brought a small blue plastic whale that he means to put on Herman's headstone. He bought it at Star

Magic on lower Broadway. It has a see-through belly filled with viscous fluid, and when you turn it, the liquid sloshes and bubbles, showing a tiny Jonah floating in its gut. "Moby-Dink," he calls it.

"Hurry up," he says, pushing the tea at me.

Justin has a rock band drummer's contradictory gift for hiding in the background and controlling everything. And like one of Melville's noble savages, he's got an awesome tattoo. It's on his back, inked from the swell of his buttocks to the nape of his neck. He has shown it to me twice, but I can't describe it. In fact, I refuse even to look at it, because his casually intimate gesture of peeling back his T-shirt to display it is nearly pornographic, as if the thought had never occurred to him that there might be something sexy about a guy lifting his shirt to show you his shoulders.

I haven't touched Justin. Okay, the odd knock on his upper arm with my bunched fist. He's straight, and the thing is, I think he thinks *I'm* straight. In fact, we've never discussed it. Unlike all the other guys at Queens College who want to hang in my office or drink with me in bars or take me home to their moms, Justin hasn't asked if I'm gay. He's the first friend I've had in my adult life—maybe my whole life—to whom I haven't named myself. He hasn't asked, I haven't told. Hanging with him, sometimes *I* think I'm straight.

So we're both surprised when I find myself putting my hand, very lightly and briefly, on the side of his face.

"You're sweating," I say, to cover myself, rubbing my fingers together as I pull my hand away from his head. Of course, he doesn't respond, which is why I trust him.

Then he says, "Aren't we visiting Melville?"

"Melville," I say, feeling slightly absurd. "Visiting Melville. Of course we are. It's noon, I'm not awake, you've got a stunt bike, it's a holiday weekend. Why not? Will the cemetery even be open?"

"We're riding our bicycles there," he says.

"To the *Bronx*?"

"Come on, it'll be fun," he says simply. "It's not too hot outside."

"Don't you want to stay here and, like, shoot heroin, or something?"

He's still got the bike on his shoulder, a feat of strength and endurance that I find oppressive. His muscular agility intimidates me. To get him to put the bicycle down, I say okay. Then I tell him I need time to get my shit together.

"I'm not even alive, yet," I say, "much less awake."

"Cool," he says.

He unloads his bike and scans my CD collection while I shower and dress. When I come out of the bathroom, scrubbed and nearly good to go, he's in the living room, bent down, reading liner notes and listening to Mahalia Jackson. "I bowed on my knees and cried holy," Mahalia is singing, and Justin himself is kneeling, stationary, balanced on his toes, his knees bent, his back curved, his eyebrows arched in concentration while he studies the CD and listens to Jackson's astonishing voice.

He is beautiful as if for no reason, perfect and detached. The American century is over, and our side scored the victory, and now Justin, its beneficiary, doesn't especially seem to want it. I don't know what he wants. He's mechanical, not physical. Like most of my students, he treats his body like a machine. If something hurts, he gets a body part tattooed or pierced, and the apparatus of self is supposed to respond to the implant or engraving. I would like to know if he feels anything.

So for the second time this morning, I touch him.

I lean down next to him, put my arm lightly across his shoulders, and try to say something noncommittal and manly, assuming there's a difference. I settle on, "Yo, Justin," and he reacts to the sound like a creature in a psychology experiment. He is motivated by tiny electrical shocks, not ethical questions, not contact, not love.

"Drink your tea," he says, standing up.

"Isn't it cold?"

"Reheated," he says, nodding toward the kitchen, where he had dumped the tea in a saucepan and let it simmer on the stove. "It'll taste of ore," he apologizes, as I pour it back into the blue paper cup.

"I clapped my hands and cried holy," Mahalia repeats, with a slight variation, and I guzzle my tea, and we go. We roll our bicycles out to the street, where we make last-minute adjustments. Justin checks his brakes, he checks my brakes. I correct our grammar. Teacher and poet: We're playing at being constantly wrong with a priceless set of vocabularies. Justin says he's a poet of boredom; that's his great subject.

"It's all I know," he says, opening his knapsack, hauling out tofu cheese and giving us each a hunk.

"You think you're boring?"

"Pretty much."

"I don't think you're boring. Come on. You eat tofu cheese."

He laughs and we scarf down the faux dairy. Then we're off, starting under the statue of Lenin on top of Red Square, a luxury high-rise built on East Houston Street in the eighties, when there were still activists in the neighborhood shouting, "Die, yuppie scum." Who would have thought I'd be nostalgic for eighties yuppies? At least they were visible foes. All they wanted, it turned out, was Connecticut. Software millionaires are harder to identify and resist. They're online, in the wiring, behind walls, like rodents.

Without a class war to watch, Lenin isn't ironic, he's merely iconic, safely a symbol. He salutes benignly as we bicycle north on First Avenue, past the shushed and huffy enclave of Stuyvesant Town, under smoke rings blown at the noon sky by the East Fourteenth Street Con Edison plant. We pass Bellevue Hospital, where I watched my friend Orlando die, almost twenty years ago. Then there's Midtown Tunnel traffic at East Thirty-fourth Street and the slow climb to United Nations Plaza. We level out at Fifty-ninth Street under the Queensboro Bridge, a giant prop from a Woody Allen film.

Justin, untiring, cycles west on East Sixtieth Street, and we turn into Central Park at the East Drive, trying not to hit too many German tourists. Unlike Justin, I'm a road hazard. I have bike path rage. Justin moves in a straight line, uphill, downhill, like a smooth stone launched from a slingshot. I'm careening after him, yelling, "Dude, wait up." He's Richie and we're eleven. Finally, I get him to stop for a shot of carrot juice.

"Don't we have time to see the sights?" I ask, and he says, "No way." He frowns, mock serious. "We gotta reach our destination," he tells me, as if quoting from a film script. Justin has a repertoire of voices—gun-crazed action-adventure superhero; brutal army sergeant; George C. Scott as the manic annihilator Jack D. Ripper in Kubrick's *Dr. Strangelove*—and he can glide into his poses like Tom Cruise with a high-tech sound-strip glued to his voice box in order to impersonate the enemy in *Mission Impossible* 2. He will go on saying, "Oh, yeah" like John Shaft forever.

"Do you even know the route to Woodlawn Cemetery?" I ask him.

"Oh, yeah," he says.

"Do I get to know?"

"Baby, we go north."

He smiles and passes me the plastic container of carrot juice. We kill the bottle. Our cells replenished by betacarotene, we jet uptown. Harlem's streets are flat and empty, and we cut through a valley of brownstones and churches as the sun goes behind clouds hung like chiffon garments filling a walk-in closet. On 125th Street, a man with a megaphone shouts, "Nobody comes to the father but through me."

So we pass through the closeted sun in search of the father.

It takes a long time to find him.

Our escape from Manhattan is across the Harlem River at University Heights Bridge, which is covered with graffiti dating to the summer of the Son of Sam. "Shouting out to the B-X," Justin says, as we bike up Fordham Road to Webster Avenue. At Gun Hill Road, we stop at McDonald's, because what great American journey does not begin or end with McDonald's?

Of course, Justin won't let us go in. Instead, we buy bananas for twenty-five cents at a deli grocer. "Magnesium, cures headaches," Justin says. I want to go home. I've never felt so worn out. We've been biking for three hours, long enough to sing the score of *Jesus Christ Superstar* twice. Woodlawn is just up the hill, Justin tells me. I get another banana. Then we climb our last rise.

We're practically in Yonkers, mounting Manhattan schist. At the corner of Webster Avenue and East 233rd Street is the entry to Woodlawn Cemetery.

Respectfully, we walk our bikes through the gate.

Justin gets out an old cemetery map. It has torn seams and coffee stains across photographs of monuments and crypts. "It's my dad's," he tells me, and the way he says the word "dad," you can feel it up the back of your neck, a whole history of rivalry and loss in three letters, the *d*'s pushed together, crowding the *a,* which sounds pinched and hurting and only just let go.

He shows me the back of the map, which lists the names of all the important deceased laid within the cemetery grounds. "Military Men" says the first category, including Union soldiers and a couple of Confederates. Woodlawn opened in 1863, just in time to bury Civil War dead.

Justin folds the map and tucks it into his bag, and I follow him up the hill into Woodlawn, a romantic delusion: a nineteenth-century rural resting place, four hundred acres of corpses washed eternally by big weeping trees. Three hundred thousand husks of bodies, some of them skeletal, some bone chips and ash, some clumped in urns, and some rotting in tombs, gentled under earth or sheltered in crypts neatly arrayed across green lawns.

I say, "Everything's awfully white."

And he says, "The whiteness of the whale," in his Jack D. Ripper voice.

He's an able navigator, and we get to Melville quickly: Central Avenue to a tomb marked Robinson, left on Catalpa Avenue, headed uphill. On the right is a big blank gray tombstone marked Edgar. Then Stoddard, Clark, Mott, and Stitt, WASP names. But Miles Davis is here, and so are Duke Ellington, W. C. Handy, and Countee Cullen.

A pebbled asphalt walkway on the right is marked with two square ankle-high stones, engraved S and *M*, for Stitt and Mott. But maybe also for Stanwix and Malcolm, Herman Melville's sons, both dead before their father. Herman had four children, and only the girls outlived him. Bessie, the household virgin, suffered from "muscular rheumatism"—a euphemism?—which was treated by shaving her head. Franny married and survived everyone, the last of the Herman Melvilles. She had four daughters, no sons.

Stanny, unmarried, died of leukemia in California. He was thirty-five years old, tended at death by someone a biographer later called "a male companion." Mackie, Herman's first son, and the first of his family to die—he did not even outlive his grandmother Melville—shot himself. He was eighteen, and instead of becoming an actor, he followed his parents' advice and got a dull job in an insurance firm. A scrivener and messenger boy, office temp of the nineteenth century, he was another son undone by his missing dad: Herman, locked in a room upstairs writing six giant books in five years.

The cracked and sunken asphalt path leads from the S and *M* markers to the family plot. Justin and I stroll with our bikes. Herman lies on the other side of a graveyard intersection, past headstones labeled Lulu and Stanley and beside a giant tree. There, with blue flowers behind them, the family members are assembled.

We drop our bikes in the path.

"Yo," Justin says reverently, searching for his whale, and I say, in the same tone, "Herman." He's under a headstone, beneath me. I'm kneeling on him, which feels unlikely. There's a scroll carved on the front of his stone, a sheaf of rolled writer's parchment that is oddly blank. I crouch in front of it and run my hand over the smooth surface, no epitaph, no last words.

"That's weird," I say, and Justin, whom I've nearly forgotten, is stretched out on his belly on Malcolm's grave, face-to-face with Malcolm's headstone, boy to boy, and he's running his fingers over the low stone's raised letters, only some of which are legible: "C-O-L-M," almost calm.

"Who's this?" he says.

"I thought you were the Melville freak. That's his son," I tell him.

"Malcolm?"

"He killed himself. He lived with his parents," I say, shifting into lecture mode, an occupational habit. "Mackie and his pals went out one night to something like an 1860s strip joint," I'm saying, "and when Mackie got home at three in the morning, his mom was waiting up for him. They had words. He was asleep in the morning when his dad left for work. Herman had given up writing by then. Instead, he had a job at the docks, at the foot of Gansevoort Street, counting tea cozies. European imports. He works late the day Mackie dies, gets home, and asks, 'Why is Mackie still in his bedroom?' Mackie's door is locked, and Herman breaks it down, and there's Mackie, on his left side, in the fetal position, holding his gun, a hole in his head. He lay there dead all day. No one heard the gunshot."

"That's intense," Justin says.

"He was eighteen and a half. His birthday is February sixteenth."

"Mine, too," Justin says. He lies on Malcolm, his fingers dreamily tracing the inscription on Malcolm's grave.

It's nearing dusk, and the sun through striated clouds is suddenly bright on Justin's back. In this light his T-shirt goes see-through, and his back is there, visible like a painted backdrop through a transparent scrim. His white skin is inscribed with a blue shark. A giant ineluctable tattoo. Crafted by Melville's islanders of Hivarhoo, who worked with shark teeth and mallets? It's a sleek fish, a lone shark rising out of waves across Justin's *latus dorsum*, his wide back, the shark's fins cocked and aimed at us.

Justin lies quite still on his belly, and I want to hold on to his shark's back, balancing on his sturdy frame as he moves through successive waves, his body out there, away from my heart. *He's not me,* I remind myself.

It's foolish to think you can be anyone else. I thought I was Zack, holding him from harm in some immortal chamber of my heart, and then he proved me wrong. I'm not saying his death was an act to show how distant we were. He would have died in any case, with or without me. Well, he might still be alive if someone had found the right drugs. I wasn't a chemist. I meant to save him with metaphysics instead, with literary conceits and unconditional love. But the last thing he wanted was love; it was drugs or nothing. "Get me a vaccination," he said. "Otherwise, leave me alone."

Still, he wouldn't let me go. He held me at arm's length, never closer than that, but never any further.

He has two days to live when I walk into his Chelsea apartment on a cool day after a rainstorm.

"Hey, Zack," I say, letting myself in. "What's up?"

"Isaac," I repeat, waiting for an answer, setting down my knapsack.

He's in the bathroom.

"Hey," I yell, and Maria, who practically lives with him now, comes out of the kitchen. She is wearing rubber gloves. She walks into the living room.

"Zachary," she calls lightly, "your company's here."

Zack is on the toilet and the bathroom door is open.

"Tom, oh, Tom," he says.

"Hey, handsome."

"Zachary, your things are laid out in the bedroom," Maria says.

"We're going to Macy's to buy a watch," Zack says, still on the toilet. He sounds like a kid. "We're buying a watch for Ava. And a gift for my cousin Myra, the beauty queen." He's unrolling toilet paper so loudly I hear the furl. "I've decided that I'm going to run all my credit cards over the limit. Isn't that smart? I'm learning to be more like you. I'm going to run my cards way past the limit and never, never pay." Then he flushes.

"I don't have any credit cards," I remind him.

"Because you ran them way over the limit and they got taken away."

"You always remember the worst thing about me."

"You speak as if there were only one thing." He comes out of the bathroom, wearing just a diaper. "The mistake you made," he tells me, "was that after you ran your cards over the limit, you were still alive. But I've found the solution to that."

Maria helps him into the bedroom so he can dress. I sit on the living room couch.

"Zack, how are we getting to Macy's?"

"We're walking," he yells.

"We're walking to Macy's? That's like ten blocks."

By now, he weighs so little that I have seen the wind blow him over.

"It's cold outside? I'll wear my coat. The ugly coat, the one you hate. The one that makes me look like an old Jewish woman. Is there anything that doesn't make me look like an old Jewish woman anymore?"

He comes into the living room, dressed in a shirt and sweater and his death-white jeans. "Maria's coming, too," he says. "Aren't you, Maria?"

"Maria," I say, "don't you get lunch?"

I'm trying to sound friendly but it comes out smug. I can't talk to Maria. She's witnessing the two most intimate weeks of my life, watching a couple of men lose each other, and she gets paid by the hour to do it. Underpaid. Gay men die of AIDS in New York City while island women do their housework. One of our economies of death.

I help gather medical supplies for our trip as Zack gets into his coat. It's a sight gag, not a garment. Floor length, flared at the hem, it has cuffs opening out like blue cowbells and a stiff blue collar halfway up the back of his head, like Dracula's cape. Zack wears it with an air of fallen grandeur, like Elizabeth Taylor shrouded in animal pelts in *Butterfield 8*.

"Zack, your coat offsets your creamy bosom," I say, but he ignores me. Maria opens the door and follows us downstairs. Outside, Zack moves slowly up Eighth Avenue, like a dancer in an opera staged by Robert Wilson, a figure in a flowing gown advancing incrementally across your field of vision. It's four o'clock in the afternoon, rush hour. The sidewalk is crowded. People bump into him and I want to kill them. Zack doesn't need my protection, however, because he screams whenever he likes. "You fucking asshole," he screams. "Zack," I say, "keep breathing," and he tells me to go fuck myself.

We're meeting his friend Darren at Macy's. Darren works in men's accessories, and he has a Macy's employee discount card. Zack is shopping on Darren's credit. "Never buy retail," Zack says. "Wholesale," he yells, moving up Eighth Avenue, nearing Macy's. We walk through the store's glass doors, past watchful guards, and Zack is concentrating on his growing audience. In the jewelry department he pokes his chin over the counter and says, "*Hi.* My name is Isaac, and I have *AIDS*. I just got out of the hospital, and the first thing I wanted to do was go shopping. This may be my last trip to Macy's, and if you're very nice, I'll put you in my will."

The woman behind the counter doesn't blink, smoothly asking Zack what she can get for him.

He says, "I'd very much enjoy a chair."

He turns to me as if it's my job to produce one. Maria holds my stuff, and I rush to find a security guard. I get halfway to the information booth at the Seventh Avenue entrance when Zack yells after me:

"Tom."

I can't make that sound loud enough.

"Tom."

I turn around and run back.

"What, Zack?" I say, out of breath.

He says:

"If we get separated, look for me here."

"Zack," I say, "I am here."

"Tom," he says. "Listen. If we get separated, I will meet you here."

"Okay. I'll come back. I'm finding a chair."

"This is where I will be. In case—"

"Okay, Zack."

"Oh. Kay."

I find a big, kind security guard whose name tag says he's Duke. He is gone as soon as I mention a chair, and he quickly comes back, holding one in his hand like he's taming a lion. The chair has a curved padded backrest and slender legs. I grab it, saying, "Thanks," hurrying away, surrendering him to peripheral vision the way I lose everyone lately in order to soothe or comfort Zack. Doctors, nurses, cab drivers, cashiers. I'm intimate for several seconds a day with dozens of people, drawing them into closeness with Zack, wondering what it's like for them, whether it affects their karma or their destiny or even their mood, whether we were picked for collision, why me, why them.

"Zack," I say, returning with the chair. He enthrones himself at the jewelry counter. He has been shopping, and there is a gold watch laid out before him.

"I'm getting this watch for Ava," he says proudly. "When she unwraps it I'm going to say, 'That's to remind you of all the times you checked your watch when you came to visit me at the hospital.' "

Then Darren arrives. He's a sweet, shy guy with a goatee. He hands his card to the saleswoman, and she rings up the bill, wraps the watch, and hands the package and the discount card back to Zack, who passes everything without comment to Darren.

"Now let's go upstairs," Zack says, beginning to enjoy himself. Before we can coax him out of the store, he's headed for the elevators. Darren, Maria, and I are rushing after him, Maria with the medical supplies, me with the chair, and Darren with the credit card and shopping bag.

We board the elevator with a group of stiff-haired white women, and Zack turns to one who looks like Nancy Reagan and says, in a stage whisper, "Hi, I'm *Isaac*. I'm a semifamous author. I just got out of St. Vincent's Hospital, and the first thing I wanted to do was go *shopping*. This is Tom, my best friend in the whole world. He's a semifamous author, too. That's Maria. She wipes my ass. Literally! Darren's the one clutching the plastic. I've got AIDS. When we reach the linen department we're buying towels for my cousin Myra, the beauty queen. She's a Jewish American Princess. I am, too, but I'm not anorexic, I'm dying. I don't have to stick my finger down my throat. Everything comes right out my *ass*. I weighed a hundred and fifty pounds until a month ago. This morning I weighed ninety-five. I've lost more than a third of my body weight. Do you know what happens to a person when he loses more than a third of his body weight? In six weeks?"

Before anyone has a chance to respond, the doors open again and we all squeeze out, headed for linens. Zack buys towels for Myra, the beauty queen. We stop at electronics and he gets an answering machine, another gift for Myra. We go back downstairs to men's accessories, where he repeats what he said in jewelry, in linens, in electronics: "My name's Isaac and I've got AIDS. If you're nice I'll put you in my will. Let's have some service."

Everyone is amazingly cool. Maybe the Macy's sales staff is used to really vicious customers. On the way out of the store Zack buys eight pairs of blue-and-green-striped Calvin Klein boxer shorts and four ribbed tank top T-shirts. I abandon his chair next to a display of a half-naked guy in a pair of boxer briefs. Zack has four bags, which Maria and I carry, and Darren has a huge credit card bill.

Three weeks later I get a package from Macy's. It's a pair of argyle socks. Zack's been dead nearly a month. I don't know when he bought them. No card. I was with him the whole time, except for getting his chair. I try to imagine what happened, whether he sent Darren or Maria on a mission, whether he left an order for socks at the jewelry counter while I was searching for help.

Justin is saying, "Professor? Professor? You okay, man?" He's beside me at the grave.

"Yo, man," he says. "Is everything okay?"

Zack shifts out of sight like a scene floating past in a Michael Bennett musical. *Dreamgirls,* I'm thinking. Zack would like the comparison. He glides by, still not dead, rotating away from me slowly. He isn't gone yet, but he's going.

I can feel Justin at my side, and I put my palm flat on the knob of his shoulder, touching whatever I'm not.

"What's goin' on?" he asks.

Then the trap door opens and Zack falls through it and so do I, dropped to the floor of the Bronx.

"Maybe we should eat again," Justin says. He's rummaging in his pack, searching for food. Nothing's there. "I guess we finished it off, biking up," he says. "Yo, but there's always McDonald's."

He's grinning.

"Sure," I say.

"You were agitating for a fish stick," he says.

"Yeah, okay," I tell him.

"I think I fell asleep. I mean, I sort of had a nap." He points to the ground in front of Malcolm's stone.

"You slept on a grave?"

He's grinning. "Cemeteries kind of weird you out, huh?"

"Not really."

"Come on," he says. "Let's get this done."

Visitors—religious Jews?—have laid rocks on top of the granite slab of Melville's grave, and Justin reaches in his pack for Moby Dink and insinuates the tiny whale into the gathering of stones. He shakes the plastic figure hard and sets it down, and we lean over and watch Jonah settle in the Dink's gut.

"You go next," Justin says.

"I didn't bring anything," I say.

"You gotta leave something."

So I give him my pen. It's a Sheaffer refillable cartridge pen, half empty. I don't have any extra cartridges to include, and I lay the pen on his grave and hope it's enough. It's standing among the rocks, but Justin laughs and says that's way too phallic. He makes me move it to the rolled-up bottom of the wordless scroll, and we leave it there, pad and pen.

Afterward, Justin sinks into one of his silent jags. I'm tired of cycling, and we take the train home. It's crowded, and we unload way ahead of my stop, carrying our bikes through Grand Central Station. The terminal is as white as cotton bedding and bright with giant brothel chandeliers and a golden horoscope across the vaulted blue dome ceiling. Outside, it's misty, not raining but gauzy with damp. Justin and I ride through the empty holiday streets to the East Village. Halfway home there is a sudden flood of spring rain, a ten-minute shower, drenching as a Super Soaker.

In the rain we come back to my apartment, dropping bikes and wet knapsacks on the living room floor. Justin takes off his shirt. He crosses his arms and peels his TEXAS IS THE REASON T-shirt inside out over his head, and for a second he's all wet chest, his torso bared, his face and arms lost in fabric. Then he pulls the shirt free and hands it shyly to me and I take it into the bathroom and drape it from the shower rod, tossing Justin a towel.

He dries himself in the living room while I look for something he can wear. Richie's Megadeth T-shirt is on top of my pile of clean clothes—fresh laundry, which I haven't put away. The shirt fits Justin fine. I change into jeans and a dry shirt. Justin's pants aren't wet, just damp, but he doesn't want to sit and wreck my furniture. He means the ratty green rattan couch.

"Sit, please," I say, adding, "it's just overpriced second-hand junk from a place on Houston Street." Justin lowers himself to the couch, trying not to look too uncomfortable. "Scott Fitzgerald's dad sold rattan furniture," I say, a nervous non sequitur. "That was one of his jobs." Justin shrugs, his knees together like a schoolgirl's. We are both silent for a while, staring at the room.

Like my school office, it's crowded with bookshelves. One shelf is lined with Zack's books, including the German version of his first novel, translated as *Abgestürzt*, which means, basically, "flung in a gut-scooping leap from terrifying heights to the desolate floor of the viperous world."

Justin is sitting on the couch. I search for a hammer to bang together the legs of my rickety armchair, which needs a good knock before it's sturdy enough to hold any weight. I clobber it a few times then carefully sit, setting the hammer back on the coffee table in front of Justin. Zack's literary award, an inscribed Lucite trophy that he won for his first book, stands on the coffee table. "This is your friend's?" Justin asks me, his first words in a while. He has heard about Zack. Mostly that he died.

I nod and Justin says, "Oh." Then he asks, "Were you, um . . . ," letting the thought trail off. I say, "Lovers?" and he says, "Yeah." "Kind of," I say. "Not really. He was my virtual boyfriend," I say, "which, you know, whatever," and Justin nods seriously like he gets it. So, I think, he knows I'm gay.

He presses his arms to his chest, gripping his biceps. With his solid body and his vague tone, he is a mix of density and vanishing that stops my thought. When I'm with Justin either I'm quieted and almost serene, or I'm hectic with desire. I wish I could deploy silence as strategically as he does. Instead, I bob and squeak like a noisy inflatable toy that bounces in your face each time you push it away.

Babbling, I tell him more about Malcolm, Herman's dead son. How Herman wrote silly bragging letters celebrating his birth, as he was considering names like Hercules, Samson, Bonaparte. Mackie joined the New York State Regiment just before his death, and he was buried in his blue uniform. His coffin was carried from his parents' East Twenty-sixth Street house on the backs of his regiment pals. They might have made that heartbreaking motion—lifting the casket and then, all at once, bouncing it high and resting it on their shoulders. They bore him to a special car on the New York Central and Harlem Railroad, and he was taken to the Bronx and buried in the family plot. He lay there alone until Herman joined him twenty-four years later.

That's my lecture. I'm thinking it will get Justin going. He'll say, "Yeah, my dad doesn't want me writing poetry; he says I should be an accountant." Or something. But when he finally speaks, it's as if he had just noticed I'm in the room. He tells me, "I made you a tape." Then he goes to his wet knapsack and finds a cassette, which he flips out of its case and loads into my stereo. "Okay?" he says. Sure, I tell him.

Most of the songs are about slacker boys with attitude, starting with Radiohead's "Creep." Then Beck's "Loser." Then, surprisingly, Stevie Wonder, yearning and religious: "Heaven Is 10 Zillion Light Years Away."

"Justin," I say, "you have a heart."

He laughs his three-tone "hee hee hee."

"We need him now," Stevie sings, meaning God the father.

Then Justin asks if I want to see another poem he wrote. He must have been waiting for this all day. Yeah, please, I tell him. He pulls white sheets from his wet pocket. I lean forward to reach his outstretched arm across the coffee table, taking the creased pages, which I carefully unfold.

"I'm trying something different with that," he says. "I know it sucks. Please don't tell me it's good."

While I flatten the poem against my chest, uncreasing the folds, he sits on my rattan couch, expectant, holding the hammer by its head and slapping the handle into his palm in time to the music. He puts the hammer down and swings his knees and bangs his hands against his flesh, and the noise of his arms against his chest is half his vocabulary, part of his word hoard. His percussive body.

"Are you planning to read it?" he says.

"I'm ironing it," I say.

He says, "Oh, man."

"I think it's presentable now," I say, holding it far from my face because my eyesight isn't as sharp as it once was. With my arms outstretched, I read:

AFTER HOURS

My dad worked a fireman's shifts, five days on,
three off. He came home, then slept. First, though,
jeans grimed with ash, he'd undress,
get down to his muscle tee and black briefs,
in the kitchen, with a beer.
His skin warm, hair on his back holding the heat
of fires in tenement buildings licking through doorways
and cracked windows, he scratched a belly no longer flat,
chest inked with fur, breasts going soft as a woman's with age.

I was ten, hugging his neck. He called me squirt,
then grabbed my arm, both hands twisting it sharp
at the wrist, an Indian burn.
"So tell me," he said, "all about your little girls,
and who's got a crush on you now?"

I'm reading it a second time when Justin, out of the blue, the poem no longer his major concern, says, "What was your friend like?"

"Friend?" I say, looking up, knowing of course that he means Zack. "Like?"

"You were in love with him," he says.

"Oh."

"You've got his pictures all over."

"Do I?"

"Was he a good writer?"

"Wow," I say. "I thought I was reading your poem."

"You never answer questions."

"I don't?"

"I keep asking questions all the time. You never answered a single one of them. Not if they were about you, I mean."

He is looking at me steadily.

"You mean I should trust you?" I ask.

"I was just wondering if your friend was a good writer."

"Okay," I say, cautiously.

I listen to my students talk about themselves for hours, and I never have to tell them what I'm thinking. It's a relief. Because I teach fiction writing I can say, "Have you figured out what your narrator wants?" Or, "Does she have anything at stake?" But I never have to say, "As for me, I sleep alone."

Now Justin is asking me to be present. I wasn't present when Zack was dying, though I was always there, almost until the end.

Well, I would like to be in the room for something that counts.

So I try to answer his question. "I don't know what his writing was like," I tell him honestly. "I mean, if, like, your girlfriend wrote a book, could you tell if it was good?"

"Nobody I know would ever write a book," Justin says.

He checks his watch, like he's closing out our moment of connection. Suddenly, I'm worried he'll leave. I am prepared to admit, even to him, that I don't want him to go. So I say, "Ask me something else. I'll answer it this time, I promise."

He looks at me a while, considering. Eventually, he says, "Do you have to be fucked-up to be a poet?"

"Well, I think being fucked-up qualifies you for every profession."

He's ignoring my joke. "I don't think I'm fucked-up enough," he says.

"Is that what you wanted to ask me?"

"Maybe," he says.

"Okay. What else?"

He asks me how I ended up a novelist—his phrase, "ended up." I tell him I have no idea. I don't think of myself as a novelist. "Come on, man," he says. "That's so transparent. You say you're not, and I'm supposed to tell you how great you really are."

"Anyway," I say, dismissing him. "Anyway," I repeat, "how would you know about my writing?"

"I read your book."

"Oh, you read it? So, fine. Good for you. I don't want to hear about it."

Which is a lie. Maybe he can tell I'm lying, because he's quiet for a while, waiting me out.

"Okay," I say, "I give up." I've never had a student asking about my writing before. "Did it suck?"

"I read, like, three chapters."

"There you go. Flatter me."

"I'm a slow reader. I like it, though. It's kind of sad."

" 'Sad' is code for 'gay.' That's what you mean."

"Oh, man," he says. "Shut the fuck up. You're insane."

"Justin, guys like you would normally be beating me up. I'm not wrong."

"Do you think I'm totally a jerk?" he says, like he's through with me.

But I still don't want him to give up. "Ask me something else," I say.

"Man, it's your call," he says, no longer willing to play. "Think of a question you *would* answer, and then answer it."

"I figured you were going to ask me how I knew I was gay," I say. "That's what straight guys usually wonder. Or they want to know if I'm the pitcher or the catcher."

Justin laughs. It starts out a giggle, but it gets louder. "Oh, man," he says. "Your *students* ask you?"

"The school should fire me."

"And you tell them?"

"I say, 'Gay guys don't play baseball.' Anyway, I can't."

We're both laughing like drunk pals in a sports bar. We're buddies. There's the plot twist: Finally, I'm safe with a man, and he's not my gay boyfriend, he's my heterosexual twenty-five-year-old student.

So what do I do now? And what does he do? Does he get up from the couch, as if to go? He does. We stand there a long time, his poem still in my hand. Did I stage this? What part of my life is not a Hollywood movie? I don't feel things, I portray them. I'm tired of being ironic. Zack died, and I wasn't with him. I don't know where I was. I rode my bicycle back and forth to his hospital, saying, over and over, "I can't believe this is happening." That was all I felt: disbelief. Not sorrow, not closeness. Terror and rage. Zack is with me, now. So is high school. So is Mark White, my first boyfriend. I'm thinking, "Did I love him?" Or any of them? I haven't had boyfriends; I've had trauma. "Tom," Zack says, "trauma isn't intimacy." When did Zack turn into Dr. Phil? "How do you feel?" Zack asks me, which is when I know for certain that he's gone. The real Zack, the living man, would never have asked about my feelings. Clearly, I've invented him, and the guy in my head is not Zack, and the man in my room is Justin. I'm in love with Justin. Is that true? Should I tell him?

I don't. Instead, I talk about high school. We're standing three feet apart. I have to say something. I tell him I was a fag in high school. It takes a while to get it all out. I start at the sixth grade, and I go forward through the years, talking too fast, giving him the rundown: Then I was circled by sixth graders and called a faggot. Then I was circled by the choir and called a faggot. Then I was circled in gym class. Then in the hallway. Then on the school bus. My entire childhood is a record that skips, playing the same scrap of lyric over and over. Every story is the same. Look, Justin: I was onstage. People were screaming at me. I'm worried he's bored. I'm thinking I have never told this to anyone else. Anyway, nobody straight. In a room made quiet by the distant noise of traffic six flights down, I confess to one of my attackers: a man.

He waits until I finish. Then he steps forward. He says, simply, "I wish I'd been there. I would've had your back."

"No way," I tell him, sounding adolescent.

"I would've," he says.

"Nobody did."

"Then you don't know me," he says.

Okay, am I supposed to not kiss him?

Stupid question. I'm not helpless. On the other hand, I'm literary. I mean, I invent stories for a living. I talk about narrative arcs, teaching my students. In the drama of my life, I'm vexed to climax by tortured and torturing boys. We're caught together in a web in which our dads are twisting our arms, offering love and abuse. Straight guys, gay guys, what's the difference? There always has to be a playground wimp, held close and outcast at the same time, the focus of desire and fear. I was that kid, the guy everyone prays not to be. I didn't want to be him, either.

If Justin loves me, I think, then I'm not that guy. It's a sentimental wish, but I make it, nonetheless. He takes another step closer. I have, right now, about a minute in which to withdraw. Reality check. I can pull back, shrug it off, turn the lights brighter, and send him home. I don't do that. It would look better for me if I told you I waited, and that he made the first move. We both move. I put my hands on his shoulders, and he holds my waist tentatively, and we kiss. I'm thinking, *Now I* really *have to help him get into grad school.* It isn't a screen kiss. He does it like a boy, like he's asking permission, offering the soft inside of his lower lip, with a vague sense of seeming resentful. Pulling away, I say, "Wow, I'm shaking," and he laughs. "I should go," I say, and he says, "You live here." "Oh, yeah," I say.

Do I love him? Yes, all at once and not at all. Not him, not just him, but the men who died, and my absent dad, and the guys in my creative writing classes, and the men who yelled at me while I watched. It's terrible to love them, and to be afraid of them. To want to be them, and to discover I'm no different from them. Freud says we're all born as boys, and here I am, kissing Justin and quoting Freud. "Can't you be present?" Zack says. I know Freud was wrong. I'm sure we started out as little girls, and the strain of having to become something else—a man, a scorched dad, burning his son's arm—drives everyone mad. I got caught in that transition, and I have spent my life with men who fired questions at me, maybe asking for help.

I'm a lab rat, Justin's experiment. I guess he's mine, too.

Whatever. We kiss again.

"Hey," I say, "your tongue's pierced," and he laughs his soft laugh.

It's no big deal. Not to him. I almost wish there were more of a fuss. What am I expecting? Border guards? Well, yes. After all, I'm making a treacherous crossing: jeopardizing my job, violating a sacred trust by getting too close to my student. People will call me a vile seducer, at best. There should be warning bells. Justin defuses drama, though. He seems to be saying, "Is this cool?" And then, "Let's give this a shot." He's an optimist, which means, I guess, that he counts on people to act in their own best interests, no matter who gets hurt, including him.

My legs are still shaking when he touches my shoulder, and says, "Let's go lay down."

Kevin Spacey Has a Secret

What one loses, one loses. Make no mistake about that.
—Henry James

We are Committee of 7," says the guitar player of the miasma band that is first up to Reign in Hell. The drummer knocks his sticks together, and the vocalist counts, "One, two, three, fuck!" Then the band kicks in with a droning moan called "Tenure Denied."

Ava's boyfriend Adam finally showed up, looking vaguely like J. D. Salinger, tall and thin with skinny legs and a long stretched face that ends in a pointed chin, and plenty of thick black hair. He's a preppie from the Upper East Side trying hard to be a regular guy. Of course, he is hanging with Richie. It was love at first sight. Richie mentioned liking *Evil Dead,* and they fell into ecstatic conversation about Grade Z horror films: *Hell Night, Prom Night, Rest in Pieces.* They're standing as far as they can from the bandstand, yelling into each other's ears, discussing Herschel Gordon Lewis and the *Psychotronic Review.*

Justin is sitting mute and anxious near the bandstand with

Tammy, waiting for his turn to play. I'm with Ava, side by side at the bar, alone together in the crowd. We're buying each other shots of tequila. She wants to do the whole ritual, salt, limes, beer chasers. We're sticky, and there are lime wedges littering the salty bar top where we rest our salted palms. It's impossible to hear each other speak without screaming, which is actually a relief. We both have too much to say—about dead men and unexpected sex—and we don't mind putting it off. Silently drinking, we're communing through Cuervo.

After five more lame bands perform—Dildo Lady, Hegemony, The Heuristics, My Gorgeous Come Receptacle, and Jane Horatio Gansevoort and The Little West 12ths—it's finally time for Justin's group, Kevin Spacey Has a Secret, to do their two numbers. Their first song is "Fuck Spot." It goes: "Fuck! Spot! Fuck! Spot! Fuck! Spot!" The second is a cover of a Jane's Addiction song, "Face It, Ted," from *Nothing's Shocking.*

Around the room kids bliss out, nodding to music I hear but don't get. Where's the melody? I'm feeling old and unhip. Hell is full of people who were born during the Carter administration. Punk rock was their lullaby. By the time they were learning to walk, Ronald Reagan was Big Daddy. Junk bonds were their cash flow, global warming their promise of spring. Their first vocabulary words were "anal receptive sex." What is the definition of innocence or innocence lost when your favorite record in the eighth grade is called *Ready to Die*? "Sex is violent, sex is violent," yells the vocalist of Justin's band, and the kids in the bar nod like they take this information for granted.

Maybe all Americans under age thirty were abused as children, and now they don't know the difference between violation and attention. Straight people don't like their children. That's the great secret of heterosexuality. I know, because I read their kids' confessional stories in my creative writing classes. Of course, my students are hopeful: Their optimism is a quick burst of hot air through pursed lips. "Can't complain," they tell me. "Pretty much." "I guess." "History is a nightmare from which I am trying to awake," says James Joyce's hero Stephen Dedalus, proto-slacker of the early 1900s. Unlike my students, however, he at least wants to wake up. My students are afraid to sleep. They're insomniacs pacing hardwood floors, watching DVDs, *Night of the Living Dead* to get them through to four in the morning, *City of the Living Dead* to last until dawn.

I'm not saying Justin is hurt. In fact, the opposite. Nothing seems to bother him. Sex with his teacher? Sleeping with a guy? Actually, all we did was kiss. Even in bed, he never undressed. He slept in his shoes. I pressed against his back, my arm around his chest. It was like catching a cat nap with a construction worker. "Listen," I told him, "I'm a gay guy. Which means, whatever, I kind of want—"

"What?" he said. He didn't seem tense. Maybe he spends a lot of time cuddling with men. Maybe he grew up in a log cabin like Abe Lincoln and learned to share beds.

How do you ask a guy if you can hold his dick? Anyway, that's what I did. We were both laughing. He said, "Sure." It was as if I had asked to borrow his car. A big favor, but not an unmanageable one. He knew he was being generous. On the other hand, whatever. That was his tone.

So I put my hand down his pants, like a guy in the sixth grade harassing a girl. Actually, he unbuttoned his fly. "Knock yourself out," he said. I held his penis. He didn't get hard. "It comes and goes," he said, "even with girls." What did I think would happen when I touched him? Would he slug me? Would my high school gym class show up in the doorway carrying bats? Would he turn to me, put his hands around me, and say, "I would give everything up just for you?"

Nothing happened. I was in bed with a man, grasping his dick. What's new about that? I mean, to me. Justin's right, it was no big deal. The thrill of the forbidden faded in about five minutes. Now I had a guy taking up half my bed, and he liked the spot near the wall, my place. I didn't sleep very well. That's the punch line: I got a bad night's sleep. I finally dozed off at dawn, and when I woke up a few hours later, I crept out to get caffeine, and never came back. Though I left him a note that said—his words—"Later, man."

Now we're together in hell. Is he weirded out? He doesn't let on. I can't tell what he feels. Nothing affects him. Like getting his tongue pierced. "It was cool," he told me. I want what Justin seems to have, the ability to separate object from desire, pain from self, a talent for watching. I'm a romantic; I need to be inside things.

If only my students swung between extremes, from squashed to zany. Or if they took drugs to get them up high before they landed. But they use drugs the way cars have bumpers, as padding and protection, defense against contact, avoiding collision.

Justin's band is done. Suddenly, the crowd is voting for its favorite. Of course, the worst band wins, and Committee of 7 is chosen to come back next week to Reign in Hell. The crowd breaks up quickly, and Ava and Tammy are consoling the losers.

"Don't worry," Ava says, touching Justin's arm. "I'll find a way to mention your band in my next column."

"Anyway, this crowd is a bunch of Jersey assholes," Tammy says.

Richie bangs Justin on the shoulder. Then he studies Justin's chest, and says, "That's my shirt." He's laughing, not accusing. In any case, he is entirely distracted by his burgeoning friendship with Adam. They are so into each other. Richie is holding Adam in a neck-circling buddy crunch, tipping him, testing his balance. I'm with Ava, Justin is with Tammy. These are our couples, going out on the town. Tomorrow is Memorial Day, no one has to work. Justin sends his drum kit home with his guitarist. It's still an early night, and we are standing near the door deciding what to do.

Does Justin know about Tammy's blind date? Did Justin tell her about me? There are too many unanswered questions. Are Justin and Tammy dating? How come he never told me? Have I already lost him, or did I never have him, at all?

Am I watching him fall in love with a girl? That won't be fun.

Whatever, I act like I'm Justin. I'm all, "No big deal." I'm not really in a position to make a claim on a straight guy. Shrugging, I ask, "Are we set, then? Has everyone stopped pretending they're somebody else?"

"I was never anyone to begin with," Tammy says.

"You are all going to read about this in *Yo*," Ava says, "and then you'll wish you *were* someone else."

Ava is responding coolly to every insinuation. If she cares that she has lost both her dates to, well, each other, she's not letting on. "You know they're cute together," she says, maybe meaning Justin and Tammy, maybe Richie and Adam.

Then Richie announces that we have a plan. We're going to the beach. It'll be empty, he says. The beach is great when it's empty. Motherfucker, and he's got a car! We'll take a trip to Rockaway, Jacob Riis Beach. Naturally, I drive. We pile into Richie's car, and I head back the way we came, to Brooklyn, over the Brooklyn Bridge, on the BQE, around Red Hook, past Sunset Park, circling Bay Ridge. Ava is in front with me, sitting on Adam's lap. Richie is in back with the kids. I'm trying not to think about Justin and Tammy together. Driving helps. It's a sports car, and we're all smooshed. Adam's head brushes the ceiling. When I shift gears I brush Ava's thigh. Tammy, squeezed between Justin and Richie, complains. "Get your elbow out of my fucking ribs," she tells Justin.

On the Shore Parkway we cruise by Coney Island, Brighton Beach, and Sheepshead Bay. If Long Island were a big fish, we'd be in the lower jaw, where hooks lodge, dangling snapped threads of fishing line. While I aim for Rockaway, Richie and Adam get involved in a very boylike conversation about slasher/splatter/horror films. It's a competition, which goes like this:

"Did you see *Slumber Party Massacre?*" Adam says.

"Awesome," Richie says. "Did you see *Meat Cleaver Massacre?*"

"No shit. Did you see *Texas Chain Saw Massacre?*"

"You have to ask?"

"Sorry I asked."

"I can't believe you asked."

"I liked *Pretty in Pink*," I say.

"Did you see *I Spit on Your Grave*?" Adam asks.

"The girl gets raped and goes on a vengeful rampage?" Richie says.

"It's a feminist film."

"Word."

"Oh, yeah, that sounds feminist," Ava says.

"It's very feminist," Richie insists, scoring no points with Ava. "She gets back at all of them. Castrates one guy. Come on." He realizes he shouldn't argue with girls about what's feminist, but he can't turn away from the facts. "Back me up, here, Adam."

Adam, holding Ava, knows enough to keep his mouth shut. He shrugs.

"In *Pretty in Pink* Molly Ringwald sews her own prom outfit," I say.

"Dude," Richie says, disappointed in Adam but wanting to continue the action. "Did you see *Three on a Meathook*?"

"*My Bloody Valentine*?"

"*I Dismember Mama*?"

"*The Last House on the Left*?" Adam says. "It's a splatter remake of Ingmar Bergman's *Virgin Spring*."

"Just what Bergman has always been lacking," Richie says. "Chain saws."

We have crossed Robert Moses Bridge and reached the Rockaway peninsula. I slow the car as we reach the causeway, and we listen to the hushed sound of rubber tire on concrete road top. There are nine thousand empty parking spaces at Jacob Riis Park. High weeds and dusty pines line the causeway. Sand drifts against tree trunks and hurricane fencing. We shoot beams into the brush, our headlights brighter than the park's nineteenth-century street lamps, their white bulbs dim through smoky glass. The road curves past the esplanade, where a giant Moorish bathhouse is ringed by silver chain-link fence and lit like a film set at a night shoot. It's being renovated, but it looks far gone, spotlit ruins of lost New York.

I drive to the esplanade, jump the curb, kill the engine and the headlights, and let Richie's car roll over the plaza past the bathhouse to the beach. Tires crunch and the car whooshes against air as it loses momentum and stops on its own. We come to rest a foot from the sand. The beach is just below us. Behind us a green light burns midway across the front of the tiered bathhouse.

"What an eerie building," Ava says softly.

"The facing is Ohio sandstone," I say, "and Barbizon brick."

"Are you never not on the job?"

"I read a book about it."

"That should be on your tombstone."

"You are constantly killing the moment," Richie agrees. For some reason, we are all whispering. Then Tammy speaks up. "Let me out," she says, loudly, and we open our doors and leave them open, taking two steps from the esplanade down to the beach.

Adam sparks a joint, which puts him forever in Richie's good graces. The two guys stand together with their hands cupped around their mouths, gulping smoke. Tammy jumps on Justin's shoulders. "Giddyap," she says, and he runs down to the water, as if he means to throw her in. "You asshole," she laughs.

I'm still talking about the bathhouse. "The guy who designed it did the old Central Park Zoo," I'm telling Ava. "I have to say his name. Please? You'll like it. It's Aymar Embury. Doesn't it sound like a cookie?"

Ava has taken off her sandals, to get the feel of sand between her toes. It's a cool night, and there's a breeze.

"Your pal Adam has a new soul mate," I say. We turn to watch Richie and Adam walk down the beach, talking and passing their jay.

"And what's with you and that straight boy?" Ava asks.

Our voices, damped by the sound of waves on sand, are muted, almost apologetic.

I turn and watch Justin carry Tammy down the beach. "That's a drama of my own creating," I think. I don't know how I got to be so manipulative. I want to tell Ava that I'm a good teacher. I was a good teacher. I know I've helped students see themselves. Is that a terrible gift? Justin was writing jokey baseball poems when we met. Now he's digging up what he buried: his dad, I guess. For starters. No doubt there's more for him to reach, and he'll get into graduate school, and read a lot, and learn how to make something: a poem. His parents want him to go to business school! How many days could Justin sit behind a desk from nine to five before he got up and walked out?

I want him to have a chance. So what if poetry is elitist? And impractical. He'll never make a dime. Still, rich kids have access to privilege. Why shouldn't Justin? Nobody gives a shit about a white guy from Queens. Of course, Justin is luckier than most: He's handsome and he can always find a cab willing to take him uptown after dark. There are certain indignities he will not have to face and punishments he won't be forced to endure.

Teaching in Queens, however, I've learned that some people, not the expected ones, get overlooked. The media-friendly version of Queens is that it's "multicultural," filled with glamorous "postmodern" arrivals. Yet the kids with the lowest expectations, and the shakiest grasp of standard English grammar, are not from India or the Caribbean. My neediest students are often fourth-generation Greeks and Italians and Irish and Russian Jews, products of New York City's public school system, where angry civil employees abuse future generations of cops and schoolteachers and postal workers, offered only celebrity worship and faith in God to console themselves. The girls are sometimes allowed to be creative or smart, but the boys are supposed to be stupid and mean, with sensible jobs. If they are not mobsters, if they can't rap, if they're not openly gay and attractive to slick Manhattanites, if they don't have terrible ambition, or amazing technological skills, if, like me, they get out of college not quite knowing what to do with themselves, they're lost.

Well, they have already given up. How I yearn for them to want something! I got hassled all my life by guys like Justin. Here's how I survived: I learned to defend my attackers. Keep your enemies close? They're not my enemies, though. They're sensitive boy poets, at least some of them are. Am I trying to rescue myself from the sixth grade by osmosis? If I can teach twenty-two-year-old boys not to be afraid of their desire, then, perhaps, retroactively, I'm saved. So I want something for both of us. I want Justin to know he has a self with which to receive impressions of the world. Why shouldn't he be Henry James gathering "impressions," turning them into art? I hope I have filled him with the desire for words. What do I wish for myself?

Well, I want Justin, of course.

I'm lying if I say that I think of him only as a chance to get over my past. Sure, buddy, back me up. Help me out if you can. That would be swell. It would almost be enough. On the other hand.

"I'm in love with him, Ava," I say.

Ava looks at me from across twenty-five years, and says ruefully, "You haven't changed."

"Don't be mean to me."

She sighs. "How am I supposed to help?" she says. "You won't return calls."

"I guess I don't like help."

"Does it always have to be that? 'Help me, Ava'? Don't you ever have a stupid, dull, ordinary day? Which you'd like to share?"

"I'm a drama queen."

"You must get some downtime."

"That's when I go to the movies."

"All men are exactly alike. You're Captain Mute from the Planet Shut Down."

"I mean, I miss you."

"I miss you, too. That's what I'm saying."

"It's not like you're ever not *there*. I think about you all the time. Anyway, I think about Zack all the time."

"I'm not Zack."

"It's just, it seems like we've already talked. Because of Zack, I mean. What else do we have to say? I kind of ran out of words."

"You?" She laughs. "That's the last thing you'll ever lose."

"I'm such a fuckup."

"That's an excuse? Who's not a fuckup? If you're feeling guilty, well, don't bother making excuses. Guilt isn't love. It's an excuse not to love."

"Now you sound like you're writing your magazine column."

"All I'm asking for is a phone call."

"You don't want to hear about my life. You just said I haven't changed. It's true. If I called you, it'd just be, 'Oh, I met this boy, and he's so *cute*.' How much of that can you take? I'm sick of it myself."

"God, you have only two modes," she says. "Tragic and smart. Don't you ever stop thinking?"

"Stop thinking? Have you met me?"

She laughs. "Tell me about this boy," she says, giving in.

"He's my student."

"I figured that out."

"Wow. I've been dying to talk about this all day. I've been rehearsing my monologue. It was a really good speech! Kind of funny, kind of sad, and it cast me in the best possible light. Now I can't think what to say."

She grabs my hand. "Come on," she says. "Tell Daddy what you did."

We're holding hands on the beach. If I could send a grainy videotape of this scene back to 1978—a handheld shot, cinema verité, Tom and Ava face-to-face in the sand—and screen it for the two of us in college, we might have smirked, we might have thought we understood, we might have tried to come up with a backstory that explained our situation. Could we dream up AIDS? A deadly virus that kills homosexuals and black people? We would have laughed ourselves silly. "Don't be so immature," we would say. We were older then, it seems: a Bob Dylan song.

Anyway, we didn't have VCRs in 1978. How I yearn for a world in which we didn't get information so fast. Viruses moved slower, too. The past is not a foreign country. It makes perfect sense. What I can't grasp is the present. Nothing happens to me until it's over. What is the present moment anyway, except something made entirely of its own passing? Now I'm a Joni Mitchell song.

I have waited six years to know how it feels to hold Ava, how it felt to hold her, six years ago, after Zack died.

I wasn't sorry he died; I was sorry he died without me. I'm mad I wasn't there. I was at school instead, lecturing about Ernest Hemingway, near as I can tell. After class I went with my students to a bar on Kissena Boulevard, a few blocks from campus. I called Zack from the pay phone in the back of the bar. There was no answer, which was impossible. He had round-the-clock care. So I phoned Ava. I knew what she was going to say.

"He died this afternoon," she told me, "in the emergency room. We took him there. Maria and me. He wasn't conscious. He lay there, and then he—what is the word? Seized? He seized up."

I didn't say anything. I was thinking, There's no way to talk about death without repeating words you've already heard on TV. In death everybody sounds like dialogue from *E.R.*

"Then he voided," she continued, still being official. "Pissed himself, shit on himself. His body kind of arched. And there was the smell. Then he flattened out, and lay down, and that was it."

So this is how I was going to find out, I thought. I was in a Queens bar, on a public phone. At the other end of the room six of my students were standing together drinking Irish car bombs: a shot glass of Jameson's dropped in a pint of Guinness, and then a burst of foam.

After he died we had all the formalities of death to arrange. We called his parents. Ava got him a box made of pine. He died on Wednesday and was buried on Friday. We had to wait for his parents, who drove in from Florida. They left their house Thursday morning, in a rental car. A flight would have been too expensive on such short notice, they said. It was chilling to be in contact suddenly with the source of Zack's anxiety about spending money on himself. "I'm so cheap I drove three days in a borrowed car to see my son die!" I could hear him making that joke. Of course, his parents were two hours late for the service. It had to be finished by sundown, because he was Jewish, it was Friday afternoon, and his parents had insisted on religious last rites.

We waited for them in the chapel. Riverside Memorial Chapel, on the Upper West Side of Manhattan. It was the fifth time I had been there for a dead friend. And we went through two rabbis. Each of them stayed an hour and then had to leave. The place was rented; it was full. Zack was naked in a pine box loaded with ice to keep the body "fresh." The coffin was sweating as the ice was slowly dissolving. We had a bucket under the corner to catch the drips. I thought of Zack floating inside this cocktail like a lemon wedge. All the mourners were sitting quietly in the pews listening to the *drip, drop, drip* into the bucket.

The stage was set, in other words, and the effects were starting to melt, and we had no parents, and now suddenly no rabbi.

Try finding a rabbi free on Friday night in Manhattan. I made an announcement in the chapel, really a plea. "Does anybody know—?" It turned out that somebody had a cousin. I made the call. The sun was setting. Thank God some Jews are not so observant. He answered the phone. Ava was standing beside me. "Don't mention AIDS," she said, though I wouldn't have. I wasn't sure he'd do it. I said, "Dead guy on ice," which sounded like a hard-core band. The rabbi understood, and he came to the chapel. Why wasn't he busy on a Friday night?

Whatever, it was a blessing. He showed up five minutes ahead of Zack's parents. Their rental car had broken down in Philadelphia—never mind that the quickest route is not through Philadelphia. That's why God gave us the New Jersey Turnpike. It's a straight shot from Jacksonville to Bayonne on I-95.

Just before the parents appeared the rabbi took Ava and me into a small room and said, "Quick, tell me about your friend. Say three things. I don't need more than three."

Ava and I stared at each other. Suddenly, we were drawing a blank. I said, "Well, he spent a lot of time at the gym." It was an awful thing to say, that he was a gym-going muscle queen, a gay cliché. It was true, though: he went to the gym the way Baptists go down to the river. Still, he had published three books. What kept me from mentioning this? Grief is sneaky, not sobering; it refuses to suppress your worst impulse.

Then the parents appear.

So there is the sudden attention to the parents. Who, I guess, have precedence. Though they had not visited Zack, had not in fact seen him in more than a year, hadn't called except when the rates were low on Sundays, and had sent, as a token of their concern, only a package of home-baked chocolate chip cookies, and that for someone who could not digest so much as a piece of dry toast without soiling his shorts. Zack made me eat the cookies in his hospital room while he swore at his nurses. Then he swore at me.

The rabbi ripped cloth from the parents' garb in honor of some tradition that did not include Zack, who had wanted to have his wrist tattooed at the last minute so he couldn't be buried in a Jewish cemetery. Kaddish was said. It was endless. I don't know when I've hated God so much. Or parents. I had tracked down the last photograph of Zack taken before he went into the hospital, and we had gotten it blown up, and it was standing on an easel next to the rabbi.

An awful picture, though it was how I would always remember him now: a huddle of bones under sacked skin, which happened to be my dying, now dead, friend.

His body had nothing to do with him. His funeral service had nothing to do with anyone who cared for him. I had to be polite to his parents. They knew he was dying. Why didn't they visit? If he were my son, I would have moved into his hospital room. I would have postponed my life to be with him, which is basically what I did. They were his parents. They sent cookies. I despised them. I wished they had died instead. I hoped they would die soon, lost and alone and uncared for by their own flesh and blood.

Afterward, Ava and I talked to them as if we thought they were human. They barely registered our own humanity or our closeness to Zack. They had us down as "good friends," official funeral parlor role. I had exactly a minute to cry. It happened in a closet. I was not going to cry in front of someone's parents. I left Ava with the parents and found a coat closet, oddly empty for November. I thought, *Well, as well here as anywhere else.* I don't believe in God, but I do believe in the fated emptiness of coat closets and private moments of sequestered grief. I leaned in a corner, folding myself into the crease of a papered wall as if the angle of the building could hold me.

In a minute I was going to have to walk out into the reception room and answer questions, give directions, to the cemetery in Queens, to the ice-skating rink at Rockefeller Center. That's what the parents wanted to know. They had driven all the way from Florida and they were not leaving without seeing the sights, buying souvenirs.

For now I was crouched under coat hooks. Ava discovered me there. She leaned down and put her arms around me. We didn't speak. I couldn't tell her the truth, which was not that I was sad but, in fact, grateful. I'm not proud of this. He was so mean for the last three months of his life that I had stopped liking him. Not just at the time, but for all time, both in the season of his death and retroactively, forever. His dying erased our five years of friendship, and I lost him in retrospect. I don't remember what I ever liked about him. People say they can't believe their beloved husband, mother, son is gone, but I had another feeling. I couldn't convince myself that I had ever known and loved someone named Zack.

Now, years later, Zack's still gone, and Ava is still holding my hand. We're on the beach. We hear waves above the distant voices of our friends, all four of our dates, who wander even farther up the sand. The sky is black and flat, tilted open like a coffin lid lined with bunched silk and pricked with paste gems.

Ava lets me go and heads for the car. She leans across the front seat, finds a cassette, and pushes it into the tape deck. Then she turns the keys to spark the battery, and pumps the stereo high. Suddenly, Richie's car is a giant red music box. She comes back to the beach, her sandals still in her hand.

She holds her arms out. "Come on," she says. "Dance with me."

"I can't dance."

"Neither can I."

"You'll have to lead."

"Okay," she says, simply. Her arms are raised, and she's waiting. I put my arm around her shoulders and hold her right hand.

"Like this?" I say.

The music coming from Richie's car is Billie Holiday singing "I Can't Get Started With You." Not the kind of thing Richie likes. Where did Ava find it? "Baby, but what good would it do?" Holiday sings. Then Lester Young does his sax solo, yearning and slow.

We keep sinking into the sand. I lift her, and she stands on my toes, and that seems to work. Even hoisted on my feet, she knows how to lead.

"You haven't told me about your date," I say. "This Adam guy."

"Oh," she says. "What's to say? He's not gay. And," she says, as we spin, "he's not a girl. You think men are trouble, you should try dating girls."

"Girls are nice."

"That's what I'm saying."

"Girls are always checking in, you know. Asking what's up."

"Which is exactly what you can't stand."

"Does Adam do that? Ask you what's up?"

"All the time. It's terrible," she laughs. "He's very, very, very attentive."

"Except when Richie's around."

"He knew you and I had to talk. He's giving us 'room.' "

"Are we talking?"

"About you."

"Wow. My only topic. Adam sounds nice."

"We can share him," she says.

"I'd rather share you," I say.

I'm only half kidding. Ava would make a great boyfriend. Actually, I'm not sure what she's like, because I have always kept my distance from her body, even when we were having sex in a doorway. It occurs to me that I have never held her except in the abstract. We haven't touched without theorizing the gesture. Okay, maybe there's no such thing as touch without an explanation. Maybe bodies are ideas, as well as objects. Still, we watched Zack's body dissolve, and I think we both know better than to imagine that flesh is just a concept.

Bodies are so overwhelming. Here is Ava's. The top of her head brushes my chin, and I feel her spiky black hair at my nostrils and lips. Her breasts press against my rib cage, and I wrap my arm around her slender waist and feel its flatness and softness. I hold her small hand in my palm. What if I desired Ava? Would I feel the ache of loss that twists in my gut when I look at Justin or Richie? Sometimes I think my desire has to do not with what happens when I hold people, but when I lose them.

Ava's sandals are dangling against my back. Her hand is in my palm, tiny in my grasp.

"Ava," I say, sentimentally, "let's fall in love. I mean, not aching-I-hate-you *in love*, but, buddy-I'm-backing-your-play. That kind of *in love*."

"Like teammates?"

"Chuck Knoblauch and Derek Jeter!"

"Then we'd both have to be men."

"You'd be the perfect man."

"You're such a dope," she says. "You'd hate me if I were a guy. If I were a guy, you'd be watching me run off down the beach with somebody else and feeling terribly pained and pleased with yourself. And what if you were a girl? Instead of always pretending you think you're a girl? This is what it would be like: You'd stand in a roomful of straight guys watching football, and you'd stand in a roomful of gay guys watching the Oscars, and you'd have exactly the same experience. You'd be invisible. Nobody would notice you. Could you stand that? Tom, you're not invisible. Zack was obsessed with you. Do you think he would have gotten so angry at anyone else? That kid down there with his girlfriend, he's in love with you, too. Just because he wants a girl doesn't mean he wouldn't rather be with you. What's your problem? People love you however they can. Why don't you learn to want what you have?"

She holds me tighter and we spin on the beach, my heels sinking hard. I lift her, turn twice, and set her down. Now I'm out of breath.

"I can't love someone unless I'm ignored," I say.

"Oh, you have no idea what it's like to be ignored. Or watched. Always ignored, always watched, except never in the right order."

"You just described me. Watched and ignored, in the wrong order."

"You're not a girl," she says, "so just give that up. I've been in love with plenty of guys, gay and straight, and do you know what? In each case, it turned out the woman was me."

Then Richie comes running up the beach, waving his arms. He gets closer and closer, and I can hear him yelling, "Buddy, my house is on fire."

The Destiny of Me

I stop somewhere waiting for you.

—Walt Whitman

We're in Todt Hill, in Richie's parked car. It turns out that Tammy does live in Staten Island, and Richie and I are in front of her house, having a cigarette, though neither of us smokes. We both smoked in high school, of course. Richie's brand, Winstons. Then Richie went occult and got into Old Golds. The last time we had a cigarette together, in 1982, before we both quit, we had been reduced to Merits. Tonight, we're puffing Newports. Tammy had a pack in her dainty knapsack. She just left us, and she is inside her stepdad's house with Justin, sleeping or hanging out or whatever.

It's 4:00 A.M. Before we left Rockaway Ava called a car service from Riis Beach and had herself delivered home to Manhattan—with Adam. They were both packing cab vouchers issued to them by their magazine editors, in case they needed to be snatched back to the real world from the edges of whatever story they might be reporting. Adam, being a gentleman, used his voucher. He handed Ava, in her bare feet, into a black sedan paid for by *Rolling Stone*. She settled into the red velvet upholstery of the backseat and waved good-bye. It was like watching Marilyn escape adoring fans in the protective custody of Joltin' Joe. Then Adam nestled in beside her, and the car circled the esplanade, gliding smoothly away under blue pines and the gold glow of the predawn lamplight.

Richie and I drove Tammy home with Justin, her beau. We paid the seven-dollar toll and crossed the Verazanno Bridge, while Richie rattled off dialogue from the appropriate scene in *Saturday Night Fever*. The Slosson Avenue Exit of the Staten Island Expressway took us to Todt Hill Road, which climbs straight up, past exclusive housing projects to a neighborhood of rich Italians and old Dutch folks living in frame houses and big mansions. Tammy's mom, whose maiden name is Taurino, is remarried to a man named Van Sielen. They have a neat white frame house past St. Francis Seminary, where Francis Ford Coppola shot the wedding scene in *The Godfather*. Near Tammy's house is the former mansion of Paul Castellano, who was murdered in a restaurant in Little Italy by one of John Gotti's guys.

The car windows are unrolled and the engine is off. Richie and I are taking a break, smoking idly like hit men who have finished a job. For the length of a cigarette, we don't speak. Instead, we admire the view. We're at the highest point on the eastern seaboard from Maine to Miami. That's what Tammy told us, in a surprising burst of local pride. Well, it's the highest *natural* point, she said. The Fresh Kills dump is slightly higher. It's rising to the southwest, along the Arthur Kill. We're facing east, overlooking the ocean. In the distance we can see a green light at the furthest point of Sandy Hook. Behind us, below us, the curved steel arch of the Bayonne Bridge is brightly lit and bending to Jersey over the Kill Van Kull. Manhattan is just out of sight. On the clearest morning we could probably glimpse the lit tips of downtown transmitter towers.

Finally, Richie speaks. Flicking his cigarette butt out the window, he says, "Blech, menthol. It's like smoking underarm deodorant."

I finish my cigarette and toss it on the pavement. I'd snuff it in the ashtray, but that's where Richie keeps gum and scraps of paper scrawled with notes to himself. We sit a few more seconds in silence.

Then a question I've been postponing all day floats into my awareness.

"How come you never learned to drive a stick?" I say.

"Oh, buddy."

"I'm sorry. Did I just ask 'Who's Rosebud?' "

"Nothing like that," Richie says. "Nothing like that."

"You know, I never used to drive before. You always did, unless you were passed out. I remember once, we went to a party in Glen Gardner, and I drove home, all the way down 513, on the wrong side of the road."

"Who did we know in Glen Gardner?"

"Some guy. We dropped acid on his sunporch."

"They don't have sunporches in Glen Gardner. They have beat Fords on cinder blocks."

"We drank tequila. Wow, I was high. I didn't even have my learner's permit."

"I don't remember any of that." He sounds depressed.

"Richie?" I say, worried.

"I'm in trouble, man," he says. "Big fucking trouble."

I have never seen Richie cry, except almost, for a minute, after Cleveland beat the Yankees in the '97 ACLS playoffs. He's not crying now, but he's close.

"What's up?" I say.

Despite what he yelled on the beach, his house was not on fire. The girlfriend had rung his cell phone to say she had walked into their apartment to find the living room rug in flames. It was no big deal. Richie had left a candle burning, and that got something started. She easily put it out. She was not pleased, though.

Now it seems likely that he *is* going to cry. "I'm not in love with her," he says. "I'm not at all in love with her. Not one bit. I'm not a bit in love with her, and we're getting married."

I watch the light at Sandy Hook.

"Okay," I say. "I missed a transition."

He doesn't speak.

"Richie," I say. "Are you getting married?"

"I told you this," he says.

"You sure didn't."

"Just now I did."

"You're getting *married*?"

"I need you to come be our witness. Don't mention that I never loved her."

"Richie, we're over forty. Both of us. You know? People over forty don't not get married because they 'aren't in love.'"

"We don't come at the same time."

He says it quickly, not from shame.

"You what?"

"It takes me much longer," he says.

"How drunk are you right now?"

"She's done really fast. Girls are supposed to take forever. Aren't they?"

"Am I a sex manual? What do I know? Some women probably take a long time, and some women probably don't."

"Even when I jerk off," he says, not listening to me. He is confessing to the night air, to the spring sky. "I just can't be fast. She's done, and then I'm not done, and I can feel she's just tolerating it. You know? I'm not saying I can't get there. Buddy, I get there just fine. I need time, that's all. What am I supposed to do? Ask her to hold me, you know, let her flick through the TV talk shows, holding on to me while I finish? Plus, I used to shoot, like, a kilo. I'm saying it landed on the headboard. Not anymore. Which, whatever, I'm getting old."

He lights another cigarette, sinks lower in his seat.

"I'm grateful I don't need Viagra," he says, exhaling. "Anyway, it isn't just sex. She's hot, she keeps her figure, she's smart, she balances the checkbook. It's just, I can't get married. I'm nobody. Nobodies never get married."

He smokes almost luxuriously, relieved to be finally having it out.

"That's me, a nobody," he says. "Okay, I've got personality to spare. So what? I've got *several* personalities. You gotta be able to refer to yourself when, for instance, you're in the hardware store. 'I wonder where you keep extension cords?' Right? Except, who's asking that question? Me, a nobody. You're a writer, man. What happens when your characters don't show up on the page? I'm not on the page, man. The words don't stick to me."

We are both quiet for a long time after that.

"I'm sorry, Richie," I say.

He ratchets his seat as low as possible, leans back, and closes his eyes.

"I've never come at the same time as anyone else," I tell him, feeling slightly foolish. "It's no big deal. You know, 'simultaneous orgasms,' Hugh Hefner made it up. That kind of stuff only happens in *Playboy*."

His arms are folded on his chest. He seems to be already sleeping.

He's not, though.

I'm leaning over to grab his burning cigarette out of his fingers, when he says, out of the blue, "I can't have sex with you, man." I'll never know if he was talking in his sleep. He repeats, "I can't. If I had sex with you, I would never want to see you again. And I don't want to never see you again. Who would come to my wedding?"

Then he is asleep.

When I think about my friendship with Richie it seems that most of it has taken place in his car. We stopped hanging out when I moved to the city and there was no more reason for cars. That's one explanation of how we drifted apart.

Here's another:

It's 1976. I have just walked off the stage of my high school auditorium, to the sound of my classmates screaming, "Faggot." Our play, *Impromptu*, is over. Richie has killed the lights, and my fellow actors and I are standing backstage in the dark. Thank God our director decided ahead of time to be groovy and avant-garde and cancel the curtain call. We are just supposed to disappear, and when the lights come back up the stage is empty. Anyway, that's how we rehearsed it. There are always surprises in performances, though, and, in our case, we find our way to the wings to the sound of fourteen- and fifteen-year-olds screaming, "Kill yourself now, faggot, and spare me the hassle."

I step into the light booth. "Richie," I say. He doesn't have to be told. "This way," he says, and we climb a metal ladder up to the catwalks over the stage. Then we go out on the roof. It's like a James Bond film, Richie and me emerging into daylight from a danger zone. He already has a lit joint in his hand. "Smoke up," he says, giving it to me. I follow him across the roof to the back of the building. He shows me where we can easily scale the wall to the ground.

Then we head for his car. Speeding away from school, Richie has a plan. "What we need now," he says, "is to get laid."

" 'Eat shit and die, faggot,' they said."

"Are you listening?" Richie says. "We need to get laid. Both of us," he says. "I ain't kidding. You know any girls? We'll have an orgy. Get some chicks up to your house. You've got a pool. Chicks dig that."

"Oh," I say, putting my face in my palms. My cheeks are smeary. I can smell the makeup on my fingers. "I'd like to wash," I say.

"No shit. Or, you know, whatever, tell them you're Bowie. You know any girls? I know some in Pittstown. We'll call them up. Have a meeting of the, uh—"

"I'm not calling girls to invite them to an *orgy*. Richie?"

"Why not?" he says. "You're rich, I'm sexy. That's a good combination. We'll need supplies." Letting go of the wheel, he claps his hands. "Rubbers," he says. "Come on," he cajoles, inspired.

We drive to a drugstore in Hackettstown, where nobody knows us. Richie gets a twelve-pack of Trojans and a carton of Winstons. After that he stops at a deli for two six-packs of Michelob.

The dogs are howling when we reach my house. No one's around. My dad is in the city, working late. My mom went straight from my play to a dog show in Connecticut. Richie uses my parents' phone to call available babes. I go to the bathroom and wipe most of the makeup off my face with my mom's cold cream. When I get back to Richie, he's wound up, rubbing his hands together and saying, "We got a response. We got a response. One girl only, but she said she maybe had friends. Her name's Cheryl. She's cool. She'll be on her way," he says, happy.

We're hanging in my bedroom, which is not a room at all but a transition from house to yard. The back wall is nearly all glass, louvered windows and sliding glass doors leading to the pool. Wall-to-wall carpeting drifts through the doors to the poolside and its surrounding woods. To add to the illusion of being half outdoors, there is a red-brick fireplace built at an angle like a patio grill in a corner of the room, connecting two walls. Its hearth is the height of your hips. You could stand in front of it and flip burgers. In the middle of the room, there's a picnic table with a laminated top, with benches scarred with burn marks and carved initials.

"Cheryl is cool," Richie's assuring me, putting George Harrison on the stereo. *All Things Must Pass*. George is having his stripped-down blues moment. Over and over, he's singing, "I dig love."

Richie sits at the picnic table and cleans a bag of pot. I'm across the room on a built-in window seat, not talking. I'm pretty high. There are things I mean to do, but I can't keep them straight. That goes on for a long time, my sitting there trying to tell stuff apart.

Richie's in the room, too. Then, kind of to everyone's surprise, Cheryl shows up.

She's a pretty Polish girl with long hair ironed flat and hanging straight down her back. I can tell she's sorry I'm here. She's not going to have Richie alone. She has to cope with the fairy friend. She's decent enough to realize, however, that it's my house; so she decides to be nice. She'll treat me the same way she treats one of her ugly or overweight girlfriends.

"Check out my handiwork," she says, turning around in the middle of my bedroom. She's wearing a Deadhead outfit, blue jeans ripped apart and made into a skirt with panels of red and black velvet, and a tie-dyed T-shirt that she did herself. "I tied it up in rubber bands and threw it in dye for like an hour," she tells me. "It was easy."

I'm horrified that Cheryl thinks I care about designing clothes. Fortunately, Richie isn't paying attention. He's flipping through my record collection. Cheryl is between us, spinning. She tips her head back and stares at the ceiling, which is covered with a photo collage. Decorator touches—I guess I am gay. I cut up issues of *Life* magazine and Scotch-taped pictures together: college kids smoking bright green marijuana cigarettes; astronauts landing on the moon; the Beatles posing in their psychedelia; hippies enjoying a love-in; ducks smeared with oil spill; frames of the Zapruder tape showing Kennedy's death; a young man putting a flower in the barrel of a National Guardsman's gun; and Richard Nixon campaigning with his hands held up in matching vees.

"That's trippy," Cheryl says.

"You like Pink Floyd?" Richie says. He's crouching on the balls of his feet in front of the wooden milk crate where I keep my records.

Cheryl doesn't respond. She's got a beer, and she lights a cigarette, walking slowly around my room. "Who cleans your windows?" she asks. "God, all that glass."

"Dogboy has housemaids," Richie says, which is both a lie and the first time he has used our private name in public.

"Richie," I say, trying to sound edgy.

"Procol Harum?" he says.

Cheryl says, "Whatever."

So he goes for Emerson, Lake and Palmer. I can tell he's planning to make it with Cheryl, because he picks the double album, the live recording, *Welcome Back My Friends To The Show That Never Ends*. Richie stacks both LPs on the stereo. The first side is "Karn Evil 9," the far-out satanic suite from *Brain Salad Surgery*. Richie and I listen to it for hours when we're lying stoned on the floor of my room.

"Gonna whip some skull on yer," Richie says, an in-joke: *Whip Some Skull on Yer* was the original name for *Brain Salad Surgery*. It's also slang for oral sex.

"Gonna what?" Cheryl says.

"Never mind," Richie says, laughing.

Cheryl looks from Richie to me and back, worried she's being mocked.

"Tell me," she says.

Richie says, "I can't."

"Why not?"

"It's too foul."

Now they're standing together by the mattress, which is on the floor. "Whisper it," she says, and Richie leans close, his nose to her ear. He's talking really low. I'm still on the window seat. The room's dark, and moonlight shines across the floor in strips cut by louvered windowpanes. Richie whispers, and Cheryl laughs, and they spark a jay and sit on the mattress.

I go outside and lean on the hood of Richie's car, carrying Richie's pack of Winstons. I'm in front of the house, listening to the music cranked loud and coming from my stereo. The dogs are barking. When people ask if I have brothers and sisters I say my siblings are dogs. Richie is also my brother. While he gets laid I sit on his car smoking his cigarettes and staring into the woods behind the house.

The Jersey wilderness is dense and empty, moonlight shining down the pine trees and lighting the underbrush.

I'm not sure how much time has passed when Cheryl comes outside, though Emerson, Lake and Palmer have just begun their acoustic set. You can hear the boys in the rock arena yelling as Greg Lake, alone with his guitar, sings, "Do you want to be the lover of another undercover?"

Cheryl doesn't see me, or she pretends she doesn't, which is a feat, because her car is parked behind Richie's. But she's in a hurry. She gets in, revs up, backs out of the driveway, and she's gone.

Inside, Richie's in my room in the dark, striped by moonlight. Still in his pants and T-shirt, but with his boots off, he's crashed on the mattress.

Casually, I say, "She was here awhile."

"Yeah," he says. "Didn't need these," he says, and he throws me the unopened box of condoms.

"She didn't . . . ?"

"No, man. *I* didn't."

"Oh," I say, all low-key. Then I'm worried. "Oh! You mean you—?"

"Listen, there wasn't no problem with Mr. Happy, if that's what you're implying." He adds, "She's skanky, that's all."

"She liked you."

"Well, it ain't all up to her. I should've let you have her."

I say sheepishly, "She wasn't into me."

"Yeah, well," he says. "It's played out." He gets up and goes to the picnic table. There are two beers on the table and he opens them and pushes one to me.

"Big plans I had for Mr. Happy," he says sorrowfully, swigging Michelob. "The night is now officially fucked. Here I am with Dogboy."

He's being snide, and for the first time all day, I feel good.

"We should do something outrageous," I say.

"Yeah, what's your plan?"

"I'm not saying I have one."

"Can't rob a bank," he says. "Banks are closed. Can't go to the track. Same problem. If we were Visigoths, we could rape and pillage."

"We could get stoned," I say. "Except we already are."

"Dogboy's a genius," he says. "Here's to you." He hits my bottle with his, and we both take long gulps. "Think of something you've never done that you always wanted to," he says. "Some crazy thing."

"I've never streaked," I say.

Richie swallows more beer.

"Run around naked?" he says.

I'm not sure I have said it until he repeats it. "Sure," I say, "like, through the Clinton golf course."

"Streak the links," Richie says, liking the idea.

"Anyway," I say, "I guess I'd do it if nobody saw. Like, if a tree falls?"

"If a naked guy runs by and no one sees him, do his nuts swing in the breeze?"

"Sort of."

We drink more beer.

"Tell you what," Richie says. "You run naked down your road, and I'll drive along behind you in case somebody comes."

"Wow," I say. "That's a stupid idea."

"You suggested it."

"You'd *follow* me? To make sure nobody sees? But wouldn't their seeing me be, like, the point?"

"No, because then you'd have the pleasure of knowing that you pissed them off without their finding out. You can look them in the face and think, 'I streaked you, motherfucker, and you didn't even see.' "

"What fun is that?"

"Oh, come on," he says. "Take a risk. I mean, otherwise, we could knock down mailboxes. Are we small-time, or what?"

He wants to drive behind me while I'm running naked down the road? It's a setup. He's like everybody else; he means to humiliate me. *No way,* I'm thinking, when I hear myself saying, astonishingly, "Okay."

I guess I'm really stoned. Maybe Richie is, too. He jumps up and bangs me happily on the arm. "Oh, you're the shit," he says.

Considering that we're high, we plan it out pretty well. Richie goes to his car. I stay in my room and strip off my shirt and trousers and white jockey shorts, until I'm finally out of my stage costume. Because I figure the road might be rough on bare feet, I slide back into my powdered white bucks. Then I go through the pool door and out the side gate to Richie's car, where I get in beside him. He's barefoot. I'm sitting there naked. It's totally weird. Even weirder is that I'm wearing shoes. I'd feel less naked without them.

Richie drives out to the road, a narrow country road that used to be dirt. Neither of us speaks, though we both light cigarettes off his car lighter, which Richie uses first and passes to me. Half a mile up the road he stops the car, spins a broken U, and kills his headlights. He'll follow me with parking lights. I smash my cigarette in the ashtray and open my door.

"Anything happens," he says, "I'll honk."

So I step outside and run down the road.

My shoes whack on packed gravel. There's noise in my ears from the air as I slice through it, and I feel my arms and legs moving and hear Richie's car. I'm thinking, *He's seeing my ass.* I'm thinking, *God, my hips.* Then I'm thinking I don't care what anyone thinks of my hips, because in the darkness I suddenly know the difference between the world and my skin. I will never like my body. I'll always wish it weren't me. But if I have ever been able to allow myself to take shape, I feel it now, the hollow I fill.

Richie's tires hiss on the pavement, rubber on tar, and the rubbery soles of my shoes crack surprisingly loudly against the surface of the road. We reach my house. The driveway banks uphill from the road and turns a circle, past the pool gate. It's open, and I sprint toward it. Leaving Richie to crunch his wheels over pebbles, I run through the gate. The pool lights aren't lit, and I leave my shoes on the diving board and jump in the water, pushing myself down and touching bottom and hanging there, motionless, submerged.

I don't know how long I'm underwater when Richie jumps in the pool. He's naked, diving, then both our heads are above the surface, and Richie is tossing his hair, spraying water, and saying, "Fuck." He says it again, and he dives back underwater. After he swims two laps he pulls himself up over the side of the pool onto the patio and says, "Getting out."

He goes through the door to my room. His car is parked with the driver door open and the parking lights on. His clothes are on the ground in a trail from the car to the pool, T-shirt, trousers, shorts. I follow him to my bedroom, and he's sitting at the picnic table naked, lighting a cigarette.

I sit across from him. We're both dripping, and he shakes his head again like a dog, getting water on the table, on his cigarette, on me. I can't see most of his body because the table's between us. But he's there. His head and neck and chest and arms are there. I'm ashamed of my chest, and I cross my arms, tucking them into my armpits, saying I'm cold, which is not true. Richie smokes, and nobody speaks.

Then Richie says, "Why don't you hit somebody?"

I don't breathe, and he says it again.

"Why don't you fucking hit somebody?"

We sit in the quiet in the dark for what seems a long time.

Of course I know exactly what he means.

How come you let those assholes call you faggot?

I'm sixteen years old. For the past five years, since I turned eleven, or, in other words, for nearly half the time that I have been aware I exist, people have been calling me a faggot. I know they're right. What I don't know is why, for the past five years, no one has ever asked me how it feels to be followed around by my classmates and my teachers and warned about my body. The choir director comes up behind me in the hall and says, "Watch those hips."

Now I'm naked in my bedroom with Richie. It's not sexy; it's scary. Richie is the most beautiful person I have ever seen. It's awful. Did you think I could touch him? It never crosses my mind. What I want instead is to be asked—and not to be asked—what no one has ever asked me. Thank God nobody does. Though not being asked is also amazingly painful.

Now Richie is basically asking.

His hair's wet and flat and smeared on his head and his arms are shining with droplets of water. The moonlight has shifted and I see his reflection in the louvered window. His head and arms and chest appear to hang above the pool. The two of us seem to be treading water in my glassy room, launched by moonlight into the dark, simultaneously facing each other across pool water and the scarred table.

"I'm sorry, Richie," I say.

"You're what?"

"I'm sorry. I said I was sorry."

"No, man. Fuck," he says. "Don't be fucking . . . *Sorry*? You're fucking sorry? No. Man. Why do you *take* that? Why don't you bash somebody's skull? I wanted to fucking rip their fucking heads off their fucking shoulders. Why didn't you . . . Christ." Then he says, "Get up."

"What?"

"Get up and hit me," he says.

"I can't—"

"Shut the fuck up," he says. Then he stands and walks over to me with his fists clenched. I see his naked body, his flat belly, his pubic hair, his hands closed in tight fists, his kneecaps, which are scarred. He hits me on the shoulder. Not hard.

"On your feet."

"Fuck you."

"I'm not kidding," he says, and he grabs me by the shoulders and hauls me up. Then he slugs me in the arm.

"Hit me back," he says.

"I don't—"

"Like this," he says, and he slugs me again. We're both standing, and he starts to dance around me, his fists near his cheeks. "Swing at my face."

I push him on the shoulder.

"Harder," he says. "Hit me."

"This is stupid."

He hits me really hard. So I hit him. He hits me back. I don't like hitting him; it's worse than getting hit. He's prancing with his fists around his face. "Come on," he says, over and over.

I don't want to be hit. Still, it's sort of a relief. It's like we're both admitting to each other that I have a body, that I am a body, this body. My body has always been a secret that everyone tells. Secrets have to be shared—in my case, shouted—in order for people to know there are secrets to be kept. So I'm constantly named to remain unmentionable. I'm the secret itself, and I'm the giving away of the secret.

Richie and I keep sparring, for twenty-five years.

"Come on," Richie says. "Fight back."

He's talking in his sleep. It's 6:00 A.M., Memorial Day, the turn of the twenty-first century, and Richie is sleeping beside me in his car. I'm at the wheel, dragging us home from Staten Island, driving my drunk friend through the early dawn. We take the Staten Island Ferry, and I get out and sit on the car's hood, watching Manhattan approach. Rich snoozes in the car in his low seat, curled up with his suit jacket rolled and pressed against the passenger door to cushion his head. Even the ferry ride doesn't wake him.

Lower Manhattan gets gigantically bigger as we glide toward it. After the ferry docks Richie wakes on the island of Manhattan. He's a heavy sleeper, but a quick, frenetic waker. Right away he wants coffee and Aretha Franklin on the radio. He's got a tape, he pops it in. Aretha's singing "Maybe I'm a Fool."

"If Aretha exists," I say, "maybe God does."

"Buddy," Richie says.

I'm going to drive him as far as the Queens side of the Midtown Tunnel. Then he's taking over the wheel, and I'll get out and walk to the 7 train at Hunter's Point, headed home. He doesn't think he can handle the clutch well enough to get from the mouth of the tunnel to the toll plaza. Just that stretch, he says, where you slow down and ready your change and hand it through the window to some poor bastard stuck with a job like that, breathing noxious fumes, collecting bills from drunk fucks on their way home to the island after a night not getting laid in the city. Richie's contempt for Long Island is one of the notes of our holiday morning, a bracing dose of bitter invective as reviving as the rotgut coffee we pick up at a deli on Third Avenue.

The city is an empty crypt. We duck down into the Midtown Tunnel. There's so little traffic we could change lanes without getting busted.

Peeling back the plastic tops of paper deli cups, careful not to cut our lips on the jagged lids, we drink coffee and listen to music, saying nothing. Richie doesn't mention his wedding plans. He'll get married, of course. It'll happen in his girlfriend's mom's house in Wantagh, not next week but a year from now in August, with a reception in the backyard under a hired tent. Justin'll be there with Tammy, Ava with Adam. Afterward, I'll drive Justin to graduate school in Iowa, while Tammy, who can't sit in a car for more than an hour, flies out a few days later.

For now, I focus on getting Richie over the border, into Queens. There will never be any discussion of anything anyone said when they were drunk in Staten Island. Or drunk in New Jersey in 1976.

We go through the tunnel. Richie keeps his eyes closed. "If taking you back would be foolish," Aretha sings. We come out in the light of day. I downshift, ease up, and reach the toll plaza. Richie hands me change. A hundred yards past the plaza I pull up, and we get out. I go around to Richie's door and give him a guy hug, one arm around your buddy's shoulders, the other arm hanging down, just in case he's packing heat. Always leave a hand free when you're in your buddy's arms. We thump each other on the back. He swings around to the driver's side. "Just go easy," I tell him. He waves me off. "Whatever," he says, but I don't wait to see him drive away. I go down the entrance ramp to the LIE and walk through Long Island City, past new high-rise apartment buildings to the end of a long pier of varnished wood that juts into the East River.

I don't want to get the subway home. I walk to the waterfront.

Down the middle of the pier is a long wooden butcher block fitted with a steel trough for gutting fish. The trough metal is shiny in the morning sun. Nobody's on the pier but me.

"Me," a loaded word. What if *this* is me, I wonder, this standing-in-the-morning-light in Long Island City? I'm staring across the river at Manhattan and the green and silver-gray facade of the United Nations building. Upriver I see the Queensboro Bridge, which is strung across the water so delicately you can taste it like marzipan, the sugary silver span of it dissolving inside of you, as if whatever you beheld you could also consume, the air and the mist and the salt stench of the river current. And it could also devour you, the *you* you don't believe exists—the nobody you say you are. Except that there's this pain like a fishhook in your lower lip that draws you into someone's capturing palms, and maybe he wants to gut you and clean you on a long sleek table with a handy trough to catch your blood, or maybe he wants to hold your mouth to his as if to bite you free of the line and then release you, the hook still stuck in your jaw.

Either way, there's one thing for sure: He may not know that he's there, but you do. You're the ache that proves him, and—in a kind of existential circularity—you. "Refute that," you say, rubbing your mouth, spilling your guts, certain at least that if it hurts you enough you'll have to admit that somebody caused it, whether or not you want to call that someone "me."

Abgestürzt

Jesus, what a morning!

—John Cheever

It's Ausgust 1995. Zack's been dead nine months, and I'm in Santa Fe, seven thousand feet above sea level and four feet off the floor, flat on my back and clutching crystals. I'm stretched on a healer's table. My healer's name is Bishop Ann Street. She lives in a white house trailer with a cat named Angelique and a collection of hanging Indian artifacts on a dirt road way off the highway in the foothills of the Sangre de Cristo Mountains. Blood of Christ. Her healing room is a cube-shaped plywood yurt to the side of the trailer. It's got four picture windows gathered around a wooden table upholstered in padded red Naugahyde. I'm at the center, and I'm supposed to be focusing on nothing. Bishop Ann is circling me, burning sage and waving feathers.

"Grandmothers and grandfathers of the East," she says, invoking the Anasazi elders, the ones our ancestors slaughtered. It's imperialist nostalgia: We're longing for cultures we ruined. For instance, I've got a silver Navajo bracelet on my left wrist. I bought it in Taos on a field trip to find D. H. Lawrence's house. Bishop Ann reminds me of Lawrence. She's mystical and wan and energetic, and she has turquoise on all her fingers and dangling from her ears.

"Grandmothers and grandfathers of the West," she says, making a counterclockwise turn to face another window, still waving her stick of burning sage in the air over my head and flourishing two different kinds of feathers: a turkey buzzard feather to clear away the energy that collects in dust balls around the edges of my aura, and an eagle feather to slice to my core.

"Grandmothers and grandfathers of the North," she says, turning again. The room is full of incense and I'm coughing. I want to cover my mouth with my palm, but Ann has filled my hands with amethystine shards that she mined in Oklahoma. "Grandmothers and grandfathers of the South." She finishes her circle and lays her hands on my chest. Then she moves to my stomach, my hips, my thighs, my knees, my toes. She comes back to my head and touches my brow, my neck, my shoulder blades, my heart.

My heart's why I'm here. It beats too fast or it hardly seems to be beating at all, jolting me awake at three in the morning or slurring like a sloppy drunk. Either I'm frantic with knocking or I'm lulled by the murmur. I won't see a doctor. Instead, I'm paying Ann $150 an hour. So when she takes a sharp breath and whispers, "Your guardian angel is here," I think, "There damned well better be an angel."

"Do you want to give him a name?" Ann says.

Him? What's the point of heaven if they still have genders? I'll be a faggot there, too. But Ann is so earnest. I want to please her.

So I say, "Buster." A dog, my childhood pal. "We'll call him Buster."

"All right," she says. "Buster's here. Do you want to ask him something?"

"Was it a lone gunman?" Ann's not laughing. I feel guilty. I say, "My heart."

"Go past the physical. Your angel knows what you mean by your *heart.*"

And because I do kind of want to believe, I say, very softly, "Well, this friend of mine died."

"A lover?"

"Not exactly not a lover."

"What was her name?"

"Zack."

"Well," she says, not missing a beat, "Zack is here, too. He came with your angel, crowned in glory and trailing sapphire highlights."

With an angel? Crowned? And sapphire highlights? Zack?

"Zack would like to talk to you," she says. "He thinks you have something to say. What do you want to tell him?"

"Sorry I left your laundry in the cab?"

"Try and relax," Ann says.

"Too bad we never got to Carrie Fisher's party?"

"Talk to Zack," she says, maybe impatient with me. "He's ready to listen."

"Ready to listen? Have you *met* Zack?"

"I think so."

"This will never work," I say. I'm halfway off the table when Ann spreads her hands, palms flat, on my chest.

"Tom," she says, so sternly she sounds like my father. Then, more gently, she says, "You don't have to believe it. Just try. That's all you can do."

I'm always mesmerized by people with total conviction. Reluctantly, I lie back down.

"When did you see him last?" she says. "Go there," she tells me. Then she says, "Go inside."

Inside what? The last time I saw Zack, he was dead.

The day after his death was crisp and dry, the sky a naked dome except for shocks of blue curling out of the gray like a punk rock haircut. It was just past Halloween, and the streets of the West Village outside St. Vincent's Hospital were still lined with wooden police barricades and littered with debris from the parade: papier-mâché, crumpled streamers.

He spent the night in a refrigerator at St. Vincent's Hospital. Then his body was sent to Redden's Funeral Parlor on West Fourteenth Street. I saw him at Redden's. He was out of the refrigerator but not yet in his pine box.

It's morning. Eight A.M. Harsh wind of early November. I'm on the corner of Ninth Avenue and West Fourteenth Street, wearing a suit and tie because I'm going to see my dead friend. What do you wear to visit the dead? A copper-colored sharkskin suit, the jacket double vented, the pants too tight. I'm fat. My gut hangs out. My shirt collar pinches my neck. My wide green polyester necktie is ugly. Turning, I walk toward Redden's Funeral Parlor. There are concrete steps down to the door. I don't have an overcoat. The fabric of my suit is slippery and cold, and my shoes are new, shiny black police officer's shoes I bought months ago at the PBA store on First Avenue, picturing today. My shirt is white, my hair's short. I should have cut my fingernails, I think, opening the door to Redden's, where I walk into a carpeted room.

What do you say to the attendant in the funeral parlor? He's aggressively quiet. Why is silence the best response to losing people? I don't want to be quiet. On the other hand, I'd like to be polite. So I whisper Zack's name.

"Is he here?" I say, and the man says, "Would you like to see the body?" For a second I'm not sure what he means, it sounds so weird to call Zack "the body."

Finally, I nod. The man nods back. Then, not speaking, he lets me know I should follow him through a door in the back of the room. He is like a bad actor indicating "being quiet." I go where he says, and I'm dropped through a trapdoor to a level the audience doesn't see, where the room is carpeted and hung with muffling drapes. And there on a gurney wrapped in a white shroud like a pharaoh is my friend Zack.

The funeral attendant does what you picture when you read the words "He withdrew."

I am alone with Zack.

Nothing shows but his head and neck. Even his arms are inside the sheet. I guess he's naked. He probably weighs eighty-five pounds. Though I remember reading somewhere that your body gains weight when you die. Eighty-six pounds. If I touch his body it will crumble like parchment in my fingers, he looks so brittle and creased. I don't think I want to hold him. His face is razor sharp, all the roundness leeched out of it, the color drained. He is pale, wrapped, dead. His mouth and eyes are shut and there is the slightest line of white on his lower lip, as if he had been dusted with brine. His face is clean shaven. His unfamiliar clean-shaven face. I know it from weeks of caring for him at home and in his hospital room, but it is not Zack's face. He lost his face last July when his body surrendered to parasites, and though I recognize him, though I had wanted to save him, I don't know him.

I'm carrying his book, his novel. Not the new one but the first one, his favorite. I've brought my copy, which he gave me at our first lunch. I wanted to have my book to give him before he died. Instead, he's dead, and it's his book I've got in my hands.

I say, "Here, Zack."

I don't know what else to say.

"Zack. I brought your book."

I put it on his chest. He is so skinny, there is hardly room.

I say, "Zack. Isaac. Yitzy."

There must be a German word for what I'm feeling, a long compound noun with *schmerz* in it. I don't have a word. I don't have feelings, what the hell are feelings? They are what you leave out,

Hemingway says. If you stick to what happens, the emotion will always be there. Give the sequence of motion and fact, what people say and do, and remember the weather and the time of day, and keep track of what you're holding and what you let go . . .

Literature doesn't help. Nothing helps. That's the feeling I'm having. I can't find anything in the room to express it. Zack. Me. Zack's book. The funeral attendant waiting in the other room. It's fall outside; it's cold. My breath. My gut, my fingernails. Zack's pale skin. My heat, my palm on his forehead when I touch his brow and feel it cold as if he were dead.

"I'm sorry, Zack," I say, which doesn't work either.

Oh, I told myself over and over that when he died it would feel like a woman tearfully waving good-bye to her soldier boyfriend as he takes the train back to camp in a women's film from World War II.

Jesus, I was wrong.

It was nothing like that.

He was a corpse.

I wasn't.

That's how it felt.

I took my hand off his forehead. Then I turned out of the room, through the door, and I was gone.

And Bishop Ann says, "You've got wings."

I'm in Santa Fe. My heart's still beating. Down my body, past my feet, through the window and across the landscape to the foothills are the mountains, blue in the distance, under the sky, which is rose. There is the sun in the center like a hammered thumb swollen fat and held high as if to give the go-ahead, no matter what.

"Your wings are silver blue," Ann says.

"Will that cost extra?"

I watch her upside down as she untangles my wings.

"This one is hanging by a slender thread," she says, moving her hands in the air over my left shoulder. "I'll just make an adjustment. There," she says. "This one is still hooked up," she says, moving to my right shoulder. "But it's gotten all twisted around." I see more gestures and a suggestion of stroking, and she fluffs my two blue wings and says, "I think we're done."

She's taking back my crystals and putting away the feathers.

"What about the angels?" I say.

"Their work is done," she laughs. She touches my head. "You can get up now."

I stand slowly in her small room, feeling dizzy. While the earth rights itself through her windows I reach into my pocket and hand her a wad of cash. We embrace. I walk outside and say good-bye to her cat, Angelique. Then I get in my rented white Buick Skylark and drive an hour south to Albuquerque. It's the end of summer vacation, I'm headed back to school. Back to Queens. I'm just in time for my flight, and I strap myself into my airplane seat with my headphones on, ignoring the order to shut off anything electronic. What are orders? I've got wings. On my mix tape Louis Armstrong is singing Hoagy Carmichael's "Star Dust"—"That was long ago"—and I'm sitting back and closing my eyes and waiting for takeoff, for the reassuring swoop in my stomach that means I've left earth again without dying.

It's Monday morning, Memorial Day, the year 2000. I'm in the East Village, on Avenue A, sitting in a beat armchair in a hip dive, the Alt.Coffee Café, trying to finish Saul Bellow's *Ravelstein*. Instead of taking a train back from Queens after Richie dropped me off at the side of the LIE, I walked across Newtown Creek on the Pulaski Bridge to Brooklyn, through Greenpoint and Williamsburg, to the Williamsburg Bridge. I took the pedestrian walkway over the East River, and rather than going to my apartment, I headed for Avenue A.

Now I'm drinking tea and listening to mopey white boy music. Pavement whines, "Career, career, career," or maybe they're singing "Korea." Who can tell? The point of privilege in America is to raise children who mumble their complaints. I go to the john. It's crowded with defunct computer equipment: Wang and Xerox and Kaypro monitors and keyboards and hard-drive consoles are piled in a bathtub. I'm sick of technology. Instead, I'm nostalgic for industrial waste, its oiled iron parts dug from the earth and shaped into something in which the human body could fit, fat cars as big as boats and scraping the dirt. Let me die inside a '57 Chevrolet, all that steel molded hot and hammered tight to the frame by men and women in Detroit sweating and waiting for their cigarette break.

I go back to my chair to get my book and I see him, Justin, walking through the door. I can tell right away that he is never going to mention what happened between us Saturday night. Not because he's ashamed, or guilty, but just because he doesn't talk about things. I guess I'm relieved. Whatever, now he's with Tammy. He comes toward me, moving carefully, hardly willing to be on the planet but manifestly, despite himself, present. Skin pulled around a blur of random urges. But also Justin, his shoulders and arms, his head and chest, his legs, wearing jeans and Richie's Megadeth T-shirt. He's headed for me.

"Man," he says, looking sleepless and slow, though he's in his excited mode, his voice high and his words rapid and soft, "I been looking all over for you. I had this amazing night with Tammy," he tells me, avoiding my glance. "She's awesome. We sat in her mom's kitchen and talked. It was awesome. Then I got the ferry back to the city. I wrote a new poem. I don't know if it's any good. Are you okay, man?"

Justin's hair is curled from moisture. He rode his bicycle here, he tells me. It's chained outside. His bike? He didn't have a bike when I left him at Tammy's. Did he go all the way home to Queens to get it? I can't keep track of people's things.

Whatever. Justin looks at me and says, "I think you need to sleep."

"I'm fine."

"You ran out on me yesterday morning," he says. "What was that about? I had to leave your door unlocked. You oughta go home."

He's going to ask me to click my heels, or something.

"There is no Justin," Zack tells me. "You made him up. He's you. Ninety percent of what you like about him is you."

Yeah, well. He's taking me home.

First, of course, he wants to show me his poem.

He finds it in his bag and hands it to me, unfolded.

"Be honest," he tells me, like a warning.

"When am I not honest?"

"Do you want an answer?" he says, but I wave him off.

He stands beside me and we read together.

AHAB'S OTHER LEG

The good one, not
the busted one the whale bit,
symbolizing loss, which is way too easy to picture:
show what's missing.
Everyone can pretty much see the gone leg.
And its ivory prosthesis.
What about the one that didn't come off?
How come it don't make waves?
After all, he sleeps with it,
stands on it to track his, like,
obsessive, you know, whatever.
And I mean it's not like Ahab had no legs.
Man, he got three. Oh, yeah. *One lost, one faked, one*
real one still jointed to his hip.
A good sturdy leg overlooked because it worked,
didn't ache, and wanted nothing.
Okay, it leads them to death and disaster. What doesn't?

Are we gonna sweat his good leg for what it
withstood? Ahab and his shady intentions,
his deadly passion, his wandering rage,
balanced on the left leg,
the leg left,
on which he slung
himself, his body and the ivory peg
that stabbed him in the balls the day it got loose.
Bum leg. So I sing what's left.
Not "sinister." Remaining.
This is the song of things that don't come back
because they never went away, the poem of the act
of the uneaten leg. Stand on it. See
how it holds you up.

"Gosh," I say. "You wrote this?"

"You're saying it sucks."

"Tammy wrote this?"

"I showed it to her. She's really smart. She's mean, too. That's cool. I like mean girls. It's better when they're mean to me!"

"Tammy's your editor, now."

"Does it suck?"

"No, it doesn't suck."

"Really, man, don't lie. You're nice to everybody. Tell me the truth."

"So you *are* going to leave me, in other words," I say.

"Oh, man," he laughs. "I'll tell you what. I can't promise I won't leave. But you'll always know where to get ahold of me."

Then he says he'll pedal me home on his bike. It's a ten-minute walk, I tell him. "Whatever," he says. "Come on." His bike's across the street, along Tompkins Square Park. His silver GT Pro Performer. "How are you going to ride me on that?" I say. He points at the back wheel, where steel posts jut from the hub. I'm gonna balance there while he takes the seat and handlebars and pumps down the street.

"Everyone on Avenue A will think we're in love," I tell him.

He laughs his three-note laugh and unchains the bike. I say, "I haven't done this since I was ten."

"Hold on," he tells me, getting in place. I'm on breakaway bars. "They'll carry me?" I say. He tells me just to grab on.

He means his shoulders, I guess. Is that it? He's standing on the pedals, starting off. I put my hands on his shoulders and try not to think.

I'm beached across his back like a shipwrecked harpooneer riding a fin whale to shore as it leaps through the waves. Can I put my head to his neck, scared and saved, in and out of the deep, on his back, heading home?

I rest my palms lightly, getting my balance.

"You're not holding on," Justin says. "Can you hold on?"

It's the fall of 2000, months past Memorial Day. School's in session. Queens College. I've been staying late in Klapper Hall, hidden in my cave of spleen, a quote from Alexander Pope. In this case it refers to the third-floor student computer room, where I write. Of course, the room's mislabeled. I teach at a public school in New York City, which means that there will never be working computers in anyone's classroom or office, and that a space set aside to benefit students will be filled, not with them, but me: a teacher writing a novel late at night, while the campus is locked down like a prison. Queens College is a drive-up window. Register, graduate, and go, your degree passed by a withdrawing hand.

To get out of the building after ten o'clock at night, I have to kick open a fire door and escape like a flaming faggot up a narrow concrete passage onto wet grass in a corner of the campus quad. It's late. There's no point waiting for the bus to Forest Hills. At this hour, the Q65A never comes. It's faster to walk.

I go across the quad, past Spanish-style buildings that used to be a boys' reformatory. It might be 1912, the campus feels so insular and Edwardian at night. Ghosts of truant boys and starlings in the eaves of Jefferson Hall make their eerie chatter. I cross the green quickly, before I turn into an Alfred Hitchcock film. After dark the school gates are closed, but there's a hole in the fence on Melbourne Avenue, and I sneak out like a runaway. I load my diskman with Radiohead's *Kid A*, Justin's music, and make a break for it, to Main Street, through the empty walks of Hyde Park Gardens, where I creep down back stairs to the service road for the Van Wyck Expressway.

Then I'm on Jewel Avenue. Across Flushing Meadows Park the Mets are playing the Yankees in Shea Stadium, the last night of the Subway Series. There's a balloon loaded with cameras hanging over the game. Radiohead sings, "Release me," but I'm not sure what I need to escape. Zack died and I got used to being without him. That's the worst thing that happened. Otherwise, what's holding me in place? Not the fear of epidemic loss or the dream of collective unrest, everyone rising or burning at once. My body is here and I'm in it, stuck with being myself.

The Q65A finally arrives, gliding past, empty and without me on it. The bus carries all that bright emptiness as delicately and importantly as a child holding nothing in her arms except the hope of reaching out. It's October, and the breeze is as sharp as bubble wrap when it makes that satisfying snap between your fingers. The air pops, percussive. In Shea Stadium Mike Piazza is standing against Mariano Rivera, waiting, anticipatory, to take the game's last swing. The Goodyear blimp hovers like a reminder that we once floated great balloons above the horizon, before the twentieth century got more sophisticated and planned its own demise.

"Hold on," Justin tells me.

I haven't said how I left Justin.

Labor Day 2001, I drive Justin to graduate school in Iowa. We leave Richie's wedding reception in Wantagh, Long Island, and load into my car, which I bought with the money Zack left me—just enough for an '86 Honda Accord the color of a can of Starfish Tuna with its label peeled. Justin is still wearing his one suit and my tie, the ugly wide polyester tie I wore to see Zack's dead body. I lent it to Justin for Richie's wedding. We were ushers.

Now Richie is married, and we're in a dead man's car in borrowed clothes. Justin stares vaguely at a map, trying to find his new address, the apartment in the Midwest that he's sharing with Tammy. He shrugs, gives up on the map, and reads poetry out loud from a new anthology. "Then the air was a brutal architecture of sugar!" he barks, in his Jack D. Ripper voice, and we both laugh.

I stay the night at Justin's new place, sleeping on his bare floor. There's no furniture yet. That'll be Tammy's job, to buy things. "She's the one with the taste," Justin says. In the morning I leave Justin and get in Zack's car, and I drive home, back the way I came. As soon as I cross the border into Indiana, it starts to rain, to hail, hard. I have driven Justin away and now I'm racing through the rain to Ohio, as if that were a refuge. The passenger seat beside me is ratcheted low to Justin's grade, the seat imprinted, empty, with his shape. I'm playing the same Bob Dylan songs over and over, bootlegged cuts scrapped from an early recording of *Blood on the Tracks*. Bob is singing, "I never knew the spring to turn so quickly to autumn."

In Ohio I pull off the road for gas in Holiday City: a grocery store, two motels, a restaurant, and a Quick Stop with gas tanks and a Subway counter in back. I get a turkey sub with pepper jack cheese. Afterward, I go outside and watch the rain.

It's falling straight and hard into the flat earth with the sound of rain hitting dirt. Beside me is a neon sign for the Rainbow Motel. A pole supports two sticks backing the word VACANCY. The letters are thin and red, joined and glowing, the ANCY crackling, unstable. I stand there watching the sign blink. Then I get in my car and drive home. The rain stops in Pennsylvania, it's dark, and I keep going. I reach New York at dawn, sleepless and stupid, which is how I end up accidentally taking the George Washington Bridge bang into the Bronx. A long way out of the way, I get the Whitestone Bridge across the East River to the LIE, like a novel swinging back to the plot, riding the straight line of highway to its ending in Manhattan.

"The city seen from the Queensboro Bridge is always the city seen for the first time," Scott Fitzgerald says, but he died fifteen years before they built the LIE. He never felt the rise and fall in your stomach as you swoop along the expressway. From Kissena Boulevard you swoop four times. There's the swell when you first see Manhattan. It's true, you think, the skyline is not a mirage, and you can be inside of it, naked in that gold light. The highway sinks, as carnival rides from the sixties rise around you. Then it climbs past the Elmhurst tanks, which are missing or present, depending on the year you are imagining or in. "That was long ago," Louis Armstrong is still singing, as you come back to earth, and the highway widens and flattens like a python's head pointed to strike. In a flash forward you are lifted over the BQE. That's the third jump, another swell. There's one more, over the Dutch Kills, where you pass between a red-brick church and a cemetery. A neon sign says "Shenanigans" in a shamrock, and there it is, "the great and final city of America," Jack Kerouac says, "rising before us in the snowy distance."

Well, it's not snowing, it's September. And it isn't final or cloudy or—if only!—distant. It's here. It's clear, the skyline shines and you're inside of it, like being caught in the skin of a grape, the globe of a bell. It's on me and in me. Balanced on the last swell of highway with my headphones blasting Mahalia Jackson—"I dreamed I saw a city called glory," she sings, stunned—there's a pause for breath. You get one breath before the East River pulls you under, your stomach falling like a counterweight. I wish I smoked. I want an addiction. Otherwise, explain my surrender. I'm home, a terrible word. I close my eyes and think of more delays. I haven't mentioned that I owe money to everyone in this story. I haven't named all the places I left my car, or lost my car, or someone else's car. The subway platforms where I waited, safe between extremes, leaving here, not yet there. The heartbreaking curve of the N train into Queens.

So many entrances and exits. So many highways leading home. I was in the rain, now I'm out of the rain, years passed, people died, I can't remember why I miss them. Tunnels carry me under, bridges across. To Manhattan. I open my eyes. Home is what you don't deserve, says Robert Frost. I'm forty-two years old. "Want what you can have," Ava says, and there it is. Manhattan. The skyline of Manhattan. The missing and the dead. I gather change for the toll. Last breath. Wheee. Here we go.

New York City:
Flushing and the East Village, 1997–2005

CPSIA information can be obtained
at www.ICGtesting.com
Printed in the USA
JSHW020029040522
25492JS00014B/50

9 780823 299454